AFTER THE STORM

JUDITH RICHARDS

PEACHTREE PUBLISHERS, LTD.

Published by
PEACHTREE PUBLISHERS, LTD.
494 Armour Circle, N.E.
Atlanta, GA 30324

Manufactured in the United States of America

Design by Paulette Lambert

1st printing

Library of Congress Catalog Card Number 86-63533

ISBN 0-934601-17-8

To my dragon slayer:

Terry Cline

Books by Judith Richards

Sounds of Silence

Summer Lightning

Triple Indemnity

After the Storm

AFTER
THE
STORM

One

A WARM WESTERLY BREEZE brought the tropical smells of South Florida to Terry and he breathed deeply through his nose. The sweet scent of oleander mixed with the muskiness of rotting vegetation.

"I hate the stink," Mama said.

He liked it. The odors were a mix of swamp vegetation, abundant flowers, decaying humus and rain-swept air. Beyond a limestone and shell dike, Lake Okeechobee stretched as far as the eye could see. The aromas of the area were accented by the sounds — the whirr of insects, the croak of amphibians, a distant cry of waterfowl —

Mama tore rationing stamps from a book, counting. The man putting gas in their car stood with a foot on the running board, watching amber fluids whirl a propellor inside a glass bubble. Each gallon made musical "tings" as audible proof of delivery.

"That'll be two dollars, ma'am."

Mama gave him her stamps, then paid him.

"You folks with the government?" he asked.

"No."

"Don't see much traveling these days unless it's government people. Where you headed?"

"Belle Glade. Camp Osceola."

The attendant examined a dipstick. "Oil's okay." He slammed the hood and squinted toward the horizon. "Looks like rain, don't it? Rains here every day come June."

"I know," Mama said. "Belle Glade is home."

Home. It had a comforting ring of finality. Terry considered asking if he could go up the dike, but he also wanted to hurry along. *Go home.*

A gentle breeze set saw grass in motion, serrated leaves rasping. An iridescent blue dragonfly rode cattail fronds. Everything was green here. Not like Birmingham, Alabama, where smelting smoke smelled of sulphur. Airborne iron ore turned white clouds gray and a red silt powdered everything. He'd never smelled a single flower there.

"I'm thirsty, Mama," Ann said. The four-year-old sat in the rear seat of the '41 Chevy amid boxes, blankets, items they'd need immediately when they got to Camp Osceola.

Mama bought three Coca-Colas with change from her snap purse. She stood under the service station parapet next to a container marked "kerosene."

"How much longer, Mama?" Terry asked.

"Drink your cola and we'll go."

Soda seared Terry's throat, bubbles up his nose. Ann made sucking sounds, pulling the cold drink between compressed lips.

"How much deposit for two bottles?" Mama inquired.

"Four cents."

Mama paid, got in. Terry wished he hadn't hurried his own drink. Ann sipped with agonizing slowness. She always made good things last longest. Terry secretly suspected it was a way to torment him for bolting his own.

"Smell the lake, Mama?" he asked.

"Stagnant," she said.

"I have to go to the bathroom, Mama," Ann announced.

"You should have asked at the station, Ann."

"Maybe you shouldn't drink any more cola," Terry suggested.

Mama laughed.

"If she drinks more cola," Terry reasoned, "she'll have to go all the worse."

"It's a good ploy, but I don't think it'll work."

A long row of Australian pines curved along the highway. A hyacinth-choked canal ran like a ribbon beside the road, black waters cloaked in blue flowers.

"Do you think Mr. McCree will still be there, Mama?" Terry asked.

Mama brushed away red hair with the back of her hand. Her face was a fiery blush.

"I can't wait to see if he's still there," Terry said.

"He was old, Terry. Four years ago, he was old."

"He could climb trees."

"That didn't make him any younger."

He caught a hint of impatience as Mama looked across a sugarcane field. The chant of workmen brought Ann to a window. A long line of shirtless men labored in unison, sweaty bodies glistening, keeping cadence with a singsong melody. The Gullah ballad was a lyrical refrain, men moving in concert, machetes falling on thick juicy stalks.

The sound fell away as they passed.

"Will we live in the same house as before?" Terry asked.

"No. Your daddy isn't manager anymore. But we'll be somewhere in Camp Osceola."

Mama glanced at him, her hair wet from humidity and perspiration. She manufactured a smile, asking, "Happy?"

"Yes, ma'am."

After a moment, she said softly, "It can't be any worse than Birmingham."

Terry watched her lapse into thought, a now common thing: thinking about Daddy overseas, maybe. Or the war.

"An alligator!" Terry shrieked, pointing. It was past. But then, another. And another — basking on the banks of the canal like prehistoric logs. Mama's expression told him it *could* be worse than Birmingham.

But he loved it. The flowing fields of tilled cane, the rich black muck drained by canals, the thumping of pumping stations drawing water from some lower level on an apparently flat land. He enjoyed the heat and the sticky night air, the hum of insects. Yes, there were mosquitos, and gnats could envelope the face in a maddening horde, but these were prices small enough to pay for the truly good things. With Mr. McCree he would eat wild bananas, small and pungent. They would cook fish basted with tiny limes that sweetened the meat. Even the ever present fetid stench of decaying matter was heady perfume.

"Mama, I have to go to the bathroom," Ann warned.

"Stand on your head," Mama commanded.

Ann dutifully assumed an upside-down position on the rear seat, her skirt covering her face.

"Look," Terry remarked, "the airfield."

Bi-wing craft with open cockpits stood outside a small hangar. On the metal roof, there was a painted circle with an arrow designating "north." The planes were used to dust crops with insecticides.

They drove by Belle Glade Elementary School. He hated it before and didn't anticipate it now. But this was summer and fall was eons away.

They passed between packing houses and the rumble of conveyor belts was wonderfully familiar to Terry. He saw women in rubber boots and aprons, culling vegetables. The hiss of the washing machines sent a misty spray over the platforms. Terry smelled tomatoes.

"May I come back, Mama?"

"Not today."

The icehouse loomed and Terry leaned out the window looking for Bucky, his cross-eyed friend of four years ago.

"Tomorrow, maybe?" he asked.

"Maybe."

He saw no child. Only men feeding three-hundred-pound blocks of ice into a shredder, the flume of crystals blown up a chute and into one end of a railroad fruit car.

"Lettuce, I think," Terry said, as if answering a question.

"Celery, perhaps," Mama added.

They cleared the packing houses, bumped over railroad tracks and crossed a bridge, the auto tires sucking hot asphalt and viscid creosote. There it was: Camp Osceola.

The administration building was whitewashed and blinding in bright sunshine. Tractor-drawn mowers were cutting grass. Oleander blossomed in pinks and red and filled the air with their sweetness. Guava trees and date palms had been planted as ornamentals. Terry had never been happier than there, when Daddy managed the

migratory labor camp before the war started. The flux of
workers was constant — leathery-skinned men and their
wives with carloads of children to assist in harvesting
crops — Camp Osceola gave them refuge. The free clinic
inoculated their children. There were movies every Thursday night at the camp auditorium.

"It's the same," Terry exulted.

"Yes." Mama didn't sound relieved.

"Mickey!" A scream. "Mickey!"

Mama parked at the administration building and even
before she opened the door, the car window was filled
with Velma Mason. Her broad shoulders pushed through,
her arms around Mama's neck. Velma was crying, saying
again and again, "Mickey. Mickey."

On the back seat, Ann pushed aside her skirt for an
upturned view of the woman.

"What in the world?" Velma demanded, seeing Ann.

"She had to go to the bathroom," Mama explained.

"Does that work?"

"Up to now."

"Come on, child," Velma said, taking Ann. "We'll find
you a potty somewhere."

"Mickey Calder," a man with a round face and dimpled
chin approached, his arms outspread. "You get younger
and more beautiful every year, Mickey."

"Edward, you liar. But I love you for it."

"Which is our house?" Terry questioned.

"There," the man pointed down "C" Street to an
asbestos slate-sided dwelling not two blocks distant.
"First house on the right."

Then, to Mama, "It's the best we could do, Mickey.
There's nothing for rent in town, as you know. We had to
pull strings to get this."

"It's fine, Edward."

"We've aired it, cleaned it. Thanks to Velma, mostly."
The man cast a blue-eyed glance toward the office, as if
wary for Velma. "Burrell lost the newspaper. Alcohol.
The thing with his boy. They live across the street from
where you'll be. Well! The moving men got here
yesterday."

"Before us?"

"The mysterious ways of war, Mickey. Some things are
late, some never come and others stun you with early
arrival. Say thanks to the Almighty and be glad they came
at all."

"I'm glad, believe me."

"May I send some of the workmen to help?"

"No. It's a one-person task, I think. I don't know
where to begin, Edward."

"How is Gerald?"

"He's in Poland investigating some sort of atrocity."

"What are his chances of coming home?"

"I don't know. He doesn't let me forget that there is
also a war in the Pacific —"

"Surely to God he'll not be going there."

"I pray not, Edward."

Terry was standing in the shade of the administration
building, listening.

". . . *man's inhumanity to man* . . ."

That was something from Daddy's last letter. A part
Mama skipped in the reading of it to him and Ann. Terry
always went back later to read what Mama's impromptu
censoring had omitted.

". . . *unbelievable, deliberate and systematic murder of*
. . ."

Velma Mason was returning, holding Ann's hand. The

woman moved with heavy-footed strides, planting her thick legs firmly, her shoes bent over at the heels and sides. She swung her free arm with each step, and a roll of fat above the elbow jiggled in syncopation.

Alone with Mama for a moment, Terry asked, "Who was that man?"

"That was Edward Rollins, Terry. You remember Mr. Rollins. He became manager after Daddy left here."

"I don't remember him."

"I should have introduced you. Come on — let's go see the house."

There was a small screened porch. Two bedrooms. Not as spacious as the manager's house. But still —

"I'll go get my boy, Lamar," Velma volunteered. "He can help unload your car."

"Velma, not now. We can —" But Velma was moving with astonishing speed toward her own home across the street. All of the houses were the same on "C" Street. Farther back in the camp, more houses, one-bedroom only, set side by side as were these. Then there were the "shelters" made of metal with a single large room for bunk beds and a kitchenette to feed the most transient of the camp's inhabitants.

"Our house is full of boxes and things," Ann reported.

"We'll get it straightened out in a day or two," Mama responded.

"Where can we sleep with all the boxes?"

"I could go stay with Mr. McCree," Terry said.

Mama ignored him. She gave Terry two packages to carry. Toothpaste, soap, things for the bathroom.

"All the beds are broke," Ann cried.

"They aren't broken, Ann. They come apart for moving."

"Get out of the way, Ann," Terry ordered.

"Hey, Terry!"

Terry knew Lamar. But it had been nearly four years since December, 1941. He was unprepared for the size of the sixteen-year-old. Lamar's head seemed too small for such girth, his neck thick, flowing into rounded shoulders. His biceps rippled when he walked, but the impression of athletic prowess was lost in a rolling gait that reminded Terry of Lamar's mother.

"I can help," he said. "I'm strong."

"Okay. Ask Mama which —"

But Lamar didn't wait. He stacked several heavy cartons one atop the other and lifted them.

"Move out of the way, Ann!" Terry yelled. Lamar brushed past, through the door, and Terry heard mama exclaim, "Oh! Lamar. You startled me. My, how you've grown."

"I'm strong now, Miss Mickey. Want to see my muscle?"

"I see your muscle, Lamar. Put those boxes over there."

Terry eased the screened door closed, using his fanny as a buttress, and walked toward the bathroom.

"Feel my muscle." Lamar extended an arm, fist clenched.

Pressing with a single finger, Mama said, "That's something, all right."

"My ma said for me to help you, Miss Mickey."

"Lamar, I don't think there's that much to do."

"I'll get the big stuff, Miss Mickey."

"Lamar, wait a minute —"

Lamar lunged across the room, going for the door. "I can get it, Miss Mickey!"

He threw open the screened door, slamming Ann backward off the steps. Her scream brought him up short, his brown eyes wild as he wheeled to look at Mama. "I didn't mean to," he squealed.

"It's all right, Lamar." Mama moved around him, going to Ann sprawled in a clump of hydrangea.

"I didn't mean to hurt her."

"It's all right. Come on, Ann," Mama lifted the girl to her feet.

"I skinned my elbow, Mama!"

"We'll doctor it."

"I'm bleeding blood."

"We'll take care of it. Come inside."

Mama turned to reassure Lamar, but he was gone.

"He ran," Terry noted. "I think he got scared, Mama."

"Finish unloading, Terry. You can do that while I tend to Ann."

A rumble of thunder made Terry hurry. Up the street, toward the rear of the migratory labor camp, a steady pelting downpour marched evenly toward him. He heard children yelling. A man laughed in a house nearby. A radio blared. He was aware of eyes at the next-door house, peering through windows as he carried items inside.

"Rain coming, Mama!"

Ann was whimpering now, more to milk kindness than from any pain.

Terry dashed out, rolled up the car windows, slammed the door and before he could return to the porch a deluge fell.

Steady, straight, heavy drops in tandem, the pavement sizzled and steam rose. The roar of rain on the roof drowned all other sounds. Terry stood at the porch door watching a silvery torrent cascade from the eaves. Beyond it all, a clear, blue sky.

It was over as suddenly as it had begun.

"It doesn't rain anywhere else like it does here," he said when Mama came to join him. She put an arm around his wet shoulder and pulled him to her.

"Watch how the grass gets greener, Mama."

Hibiscus blooms drooped, each petal hung with a liquid jewel of water that reflected the world around it. The scent of guava came stronger and Terry's mouth watered in anticipation of that nearly forgotten flavor. Clusters of dates hung in golden racemes from the dripping fronds of palms. Crimson blossoms deepened in hue, the wet lawn responding as if to a painter's brush. Pools of water made mirrors that captured the now white clouds passing overhead.

"I love it here, Mama."

"I know you do."

"I'm glad we came back."

"We didn't have much choice after I lost my job," she said. "But I'm glad you're glad." She squeezed his shoulder gently.

"May I go out to Chosen, Mama?" *To find Mr. McCree.*

"Tomorrow, perhaps."

"I won't be gone long."

"Tomorrow would be a better day."

He trembled, a physical reaction much like that of an animal caged too long, waiting, waiting, waiting for the moment to jump and flee.

"Terry, you mustn't expect too much. Remember how old he was? Things change."

"So far, nothing is different."

"But things — some things — have changed."

"Please, Mama — tomorrow?"

She tried to smile, then gave a quick nod. "Tomorrow," she said.

Two

TERRY WOKE WITH ANTICIPATION, like Christmas or the morning of a birthday. He knew immediately where he was. In Birmingham, he'd often come out of a sound sleep disoriented, the aroma of industrial fumes caustic. He'd never felt at home living with Grandmama. Her house was dark and somber. Mama had said she felt like a child there — a child, with children. Grandmama was "too set" to have children underfoot again, Mama said.

The bed sheets felt moist from night miasma. Through the window he saw a far row of arching palms, Brazilian oaks, thick stands of bamboo. The blossoms of hibiscus were only now opening after a night tightly closed.

He remembered to shake his trousers vigorously — a precaution against scorpions. He reached for his shoes. A city requirement. Then, with a sense of joy, he shoved the brown oxfords beneath his bed.

"Awake?" Mama called softly.

"Yes, ma'am."

She stood in the hall, her worn blue robe tied at the waist, a cup of tea in hand. Her face still bore "bed scars" from sleep.

"Mama, today is tomorrow. May I go?"

She watched him, her unwavering brown eyes filled with a sadness which had become fixed in the months since Daddy left.

"I hope you won't be disappointed, Terry."

"No ma'am, I won't be."

"People change very quickly when they're separated. Or they may no longer be here."

He anticipated her next remark. "I'll be careful."

"Be home before dark."

"I will."

"You're going to Chosen?"

"Nowhere else, unless I come tell you so."

He grinned, kissed her quickly, and bounded out, whirling to return and grab the flung door before it could slam. Nose pressed to the screen, "Bye," he said.

"Bye."

Dew blanketed the grass. Every step was cool to bare feet. Looking back, he could see where he'd been as surely as though he'd walked through snow. There'd be no snow here. No bone-chilling mornings shivering on the way to school.

School. He had all summer before he had to think about that.

He detoured through guava bushes near the manager's house. Skirting a thick symmetrical web of a black and yellow "dancing" spider, he picked enough fruit to fill his pockets, eating as he harvested — this would be breakfast aplenty.

His feet were tender, too long shod, and he had to stay off the pavement as he walked toward Chosen, two miles distant. When he'd skipped school in the first grade, this is where he always came. His goal then, as now, was Mr. McCree's house out near the settlement of Chosen. With Mr. McCree he could count on a day of hunting snakes or gathering wildflowers which were sold to biologists and botanists somewhere afar.

He almost didn't want to go, for fear Mr. McCree would be gone — they hadn't met since the day in court when the truant officers threatened to put Terry in a state school and Mr. McCree in a place for irresponsible old men. Only war had saved them, Mama said. Terry had felt kindly toward Japan ever since, but he couldn't admit that to anyone. Pearl Harbor had made them enemies.

So he was fearful this morning, but go he must. He wouldn't hurry. Savoring the return of familiar images, he paused at a sweet acacia covered with movable yellow blossoms. Not flowers. Vivid sulphur butterflies at rest, clusters of them clinging to the tree, to one another. He ate guavas, watching them.

Maybe Mr. McCree would be angry because he nearly went to jail. Maybe he would be afraid of fresh troubles if Terry came around. But this time, Terry wouldn't claim to be an orphan. This time, he'd say, "Mama let me come," and it would be true.

His hands were sticky. Gingerly, he eased through tri-angular-bladed saw grass that could rip clothing and flesh at a touch. He parted cattails, wary for reptiles, the sod beneath his feet oozing black water between his toes. In the ebony canal, whirligig beetles zipped in circles, their frenetic ripples crisscrossing. A spider-like waterstrider rode the surface on feet like tiny pontoons. Terry brushed aside algae and washed his hands of guava juice.

He paused to touch a knot in a hollow reed — the home of a gall wasp. Inside, sleeping, a tiny future wasp was developing from the egg injected by its mother. Down the stem of the reed Terry found snail eggs glued like barnacles. In the roadside grass again, he stooped to look at the opal heap of a foam created by spittlebugs.

Everything here was perfect! Birmingham had been awful. The boys shot songbirds with BB pellets and left the fluttering bodies for ants to devour. They didn't know the names of the birds they shot. They killed for no purpose — harmless ring snakes and blind lizards — acts that horrified Terry and won him no friends when he protested.

The first rays of sun burned away remnants of ground fog, lifting swampy vapors to form massive heaps of white clouds which, later in the day, would return as purified rainwater.

He approached the path leading to a single board crossing a canal, and stopped. Suppose nobody were there? Suppose his friends, LuBelle and Eunice, were gone?

White people in Birmingham didn't have friends like LuBelle and Eunice. Like snakes, dark-skinned people suffered abuse for a reason never apparent to Terry.

He'd tried to tell his classmates about LuBelle and Eunice. How Eunice could carry a huge basket on her head without using her hands. How they sometimes cooked rattlesnake steaks and a pot of beans outdoors. How LuBelle and he helped stir the lye water in a simmering cauldron when Eunice washed clothes for white folks in town. The stories brought ridicule, so he quit talking about it — but he never stopped thinking about them.

Somewhere afar, a rustle of weeds: muskrat, rabbit, raccoon, maybe. A joree called. A musical warbler replied. The bamboo, as thick as Terry's legs, whispered as a breeze passed.

He walked the plank slowly, careful not to make the slightest noise. Would they remember him? Eunice would. Maybe not LuBelle.

Mr. McCree might be here. Trading "meat for squeezings."

Terry heard a low voice and crouched, peering toward an unpainted shack on stilts. The moist coolness of the glade was the same he knew from long ago. The house was Eunice's with board shutters which were pushed out at the bottom and propped open with a stick. The black cauldron was gone, but dark ashy residue of many washing days remained. Mushrooms grew where the pot had been.

The voice again. A man. But too low for Terry to judge whether spoken by black man or white. He circled the house. A car. Would Eunice have a car? She'd never had before, always walking to Belle Glade to return the laundry.

"You got to go now." A woman's voice. There was no delicious melody to that sound — she was white.

"One more time."

The woman protested, but not strongly. Terry heard her giggle.

"Come on," the man wheedled, "one more quick one."

"I got to think of my boy."

"Hell, he ain't here."

"He's someplace. Get up now and be gone."

Terry backed into dense foliage, waiting. He heard the

clump of a shoe on flooring. This drew Terry's eye to the
dark underside of the dwelling and there — squatting in
the shadows — a boy looked up through cracks in the
floor overhead.

"Where's my belt?"

"You didn't have one."

"How'd I keep my pants up?"

She laughed. "You didn't."

The boy beneath the house moved like a giant spider,
on the tips of his toes and hands, arms outstretched, his
rump high — going toward the far side of the shack.

"Ossie!"

He was on his feet now, running toward an outhouse.

The woman appeared at a window, "Ossie, where are
you?"

"Out back."

Silence.

"You need me, Mom?"

"No," she said. "Just wondering where you were."

The man made his exit through the front, went to his
car as if sneaking away, shutting the door behind him
softly. Any effort to go undetected was destroyed with the
growl of the motor, revved a few times before noisily
shifting into gear and backing down a crooked lane
toward the paved road.

Terry watched the boy come lazily back to the house.

"Hey, Sweetie," the woman said. "Where you been?"

"Out."

"I got to get ready for work," she said. "Take care of
yourself this morning."

"Mom — there's somebody outside. I saw him."

Terry's blood ran cold.

"Who is it?"

"Looked like a town boy."

The woman appeared at the unscreened, open front door. "Who's there, please?"

Hands clammy, Terry stepped forth.

"May I help you?" she asked.

"I was looking for Eunice and LuBelle."

"Who?"

"They used to live here."

She said something to the boy and he shrugged. Terry saw they were both dark-skinned, but not black. They didn't speak with the same inflections of blacks.

"We don't know anybody by that name, Son," she said. "Won't you come in?"

Feet leadened, Terry swallowed hard. Surely they heard the sound of air going down his esophagus.

"What's your name, Son?" She spoke to him with that peculiar tone used by nurses tending patients. Maybe she was a nurse.

"Terry Calder. I live at Camp Osceola. We just moved back from Birmingham, Alabama. I was looking for my friends, Eunice and LuBelle."

"We live here now. This is my boy, Ossie. I'm Mrs. Knight."

Ossie's gaze held no warmth.

"I'm sorry to bother you," Terry said.

"Wait a minute," Mrs. Knight questioned. "Didn't your father used to manage the camp?"

"Yes ma'am."

"Where is he now?"

"Poland. Investigating a trocity."

"Doing what?"

Terry lifted one thin shoulder, dropped it. "With the Red Cross," he said.

"Well. It won't be long now. He'll be home soon."

"Unless he has to fight the Japanese."

"Surely not," she said sincerely. "Surely." She adjusted a strap to her brassiere with one finger. "I got to go to work. You two boys go have a good time together."

Together? Ossie Knight didn't look like someone about to have a good time. He glared at Terry with dark eyes.

"Run along, Ossie — go play with your friend."

Ossie stepped out into the diffused light of morning and for the first time Terry could assess his potential adversary. Taller, stronger, older by at least two years.

Afraid to run, too uncomfortable to stay, Terry said, "I was going to look for the snake man, Mr. McCree."

"He ain't around anymore."

Terry's distress must have seemed acute even to this stranger. Ossie said, "You knew him?"

"Yes."

"Probably dead by now," Ossie suggested.

"Not Mr. McCree."

"Hell, he was ninety some years old I think."

Not far wrong. Still —

"People don't live forever," Ossie stated. "Unless they're coddling up to the conjure woman."

"The conjure woman?"

"She tends my grandfather. I go with him sometimes. She could be a thousand for all anybody knows for sure."

"I've got to go," Terry said.

"Looking for the snake man? He's bound to be dead. Handling poisonous snakes, tramping through swamps. Like a Indian or something."

Without invitation, Ossie was following Terry.

"Folks that live in swamps don't live long," Ossie

observed. "They're like animals. Animals in the swamp don't live long."

Ossie spit between his teeth, stared ahead. Terry felt no less observed.

"Don't you like Indians?" Terry said. "You look like an Indian."

"How many you know?"

"I used to go to the Seminole reservation with Mr. McCree. He knew lots of Indians. He taught a young chief to catch catfish with his bare hands."

"Oh piss," Ossie snorted.

"He did."

"If you really knew Indians," Ossie said, "you'd know they can't do those crazy things white men say. They don't see better or smell things better or walk any quieter than you. They're half black and dirt poor and that's the only difference."

"The Seminoles are poor because of white people."

"Who told you that?"

"Mr. McCree. And my daddy."

Ossie assessed him with chocolate eyes. "Well, that's true."

"What do you know about Seminoles?" Terry challenged.

"More than you, Red."

"Don't call me Red. So, what do you know?"

Ossie spit between his teeth again. It went an awfully long way. "If you want to see the snake man's place — there it is."

Terry stared at the shack. The building had shifted and leaned precariously. Vines grew through cracks in the walls, curled under the eaves. Pieces of sheet metal roofing had torn loose, peeling back from the rafters.

Heart hammering, he went inside. Gone was the holi-
day aroma of drying cones which Mr. McCree sold to
nurseries for seeds. The walls were denuded of dried
snake skins. Jars of multicolored ingredients were missing,
or broken.

"You really thought he'd be here," Ossie said.

He followed Terry through, past discarded hampers and
a few burlap bags left behind. Out back, the rusting hulk
of an old washing machine stood where Terry remembered
it. In this, Mr. McCree had kept the awesome rattlesnake,
Crotalus adamanteus. From him, Terry had learned the
"true" names of things — Latin that described the creature: *Crotalus* meaning "rattler" and *adamanteus* meaning
"unyielding."

"You really knew him?" Ossie stood so close, Terry
could smell onions on his breath.

"Hey, Red —"

"Don't call me Red."

"Terry Calder, right? Yeah; I heard of you. Long time
ago. We met once down at the reservation."

Reservation? "The Seminole reservation?"

Ossie lifted his chin, back straightening. "My name is
Osceola," he said. "My grandfather is the grandson of the
chief, Arpeika."

"You're the son of a chief?"

"My grandfather said the snake man could catch fish
with his bare hands. I didn't believe it. You ever see him
do that?"

"Yes."

"My grandfather knew him. Grandfather said the snake
man had been blessed by the conjure woman. If she kissed
him on the lips, nothing could hurt him."

"He hurt. Like everybody else."

"If the conjure woman kissed him on the lips, he might live forever."

Terry fought an overwhelming urge to weep. He took quickening strides toward the road.

"Red — Terry — where you headed?"

"Home."

"Want to go swimming? I'll show you how to dive off the bridge at Chosen."

"No."

"We could get some catalpa worms and go fishing."

"No."

They were trotting now, their approach making grasshoppers leap around them. Gnats swarmed and Terry ran through.

"You live at the camp?" Ossie confirmed.

"Yes."

Ossie stopped. "Hey, Red!"

Terry halted, turning.

"Listen," Ossie said, "don't tell anybody, okay?"

"About what?"

"You know."

"What?"

"This morning."

"What about it?"

"What you saw and all."

"I don't tell anybody anything," Terry said.

"Then we be friends, you and me."

Terry began again, picking up the pace until he was loping easily. When he looked back, Ossie stood there yet, watching.

McCree dead? The thought brought back an unpleasant memory of a dog he'd seen die. The final quiver, the limp body that mysteriously stiffened. They'd buried it. A few days later, Terry dug it up again.

"Why did you do that?" Mama had questioned.

"To see him again, I guess."

Despite what preachers said about dying, it couldn't be good.

He couldn't imagine Mr. McCree stiff and lifeless. His memory was of a creased, unshaven face and gentle blue-gray eyes that never wavered when he listened. Mr. McCree had smelled of "flora and fauna" and chewing tobacco.

The dog didn't smell good.

Dead.

No. It wasn't good.

Three

MICKEY SAT AT THE white enamel kitchen table, hot tea going cold, staring at a sheet of stationery. The paper was tissue thin, designed for airmail. She had written: "Dear Gerald —"

What?

Nearly nine o'clock and Terry was at the packing houses looking for another friend. Ten years old, too young to be out there — but she reminded herself he was doing this at age six.

She heard the rumble of a train, a clacking of boxcars being shuttled from one spur to another. In the dark, small for his age, fleet of foot — but, Terry knew about trains. He *would* be careful.

She sat with pen poised over paper.

. . . Terry went looking for Mr. McCree, Eunice and LuBelle today. He didn't find them.

. . . I begin work for Okeelanta Sugar refinery next Monday. I'll be earning twenty-eight dollars a week.

. . . Ann is enrolled at the camp day-care center. She'll be assured of a good lunch and adequate supervision. She took her shots at the clinic without crying. Such a brave little blue-eyed baby.

All so dreary.

Beyond the kitchen window, insects bumped the screen trying to come in. She could see the glow of lights from the Blue Goose packing house beyond the railroad incline. The sounds of machinery denoted activity, vegetables going north to feed a nation at war.

She crumpled her letter, began again: "Dear Gerald —"

She thought of Velma. Once lithe and sophisticated, now overweight with shoes rundown at the heels. This was not the Velma that Gerald remembered.

"Velma and Burrell are living here at the camp," she wrote. "I'm afraid Burrell has become an alcoholic. He lost his newspaper and they've fallen on hard times."

Burrell Mason — once robust, aggressive, his newspaper a Pulitzer prize-winner. That was the Burrell they knew in 1941.

Mickey threw away the letter.

Describe something good.

Yes. Well. To do this, she had to think like Terry, not herself. The aroma of rancid canal water and decaying vegetation was an elixir to Terry. He'd developed blisters on his feet from walking barefoot all day but refused to wear shoes tonight. He came home from Chosen, disappointed but didn't admit it. Mickey knew he'd failed to find his friends by what Terry didn't say. He had been enraptured with scents and sights, following her as Mickey prepared dinner. He spoke of a flock of egrets —

he was sure they were "snowy" and rare — he described alligators and other reptiles, his eyes wide.

"He's like a caged bird set free," Mickey wrote. "The change is astonishing. The pernicious anemia he suffered in Birmingham seems forgotten — he has more energy than he can burn now that we're here."

A sound from the back bedroom made Mickey pause. Ann was mumbling in her sleep. After a moment, Mickey continued her letter:

"Velma and Burrell's son, Lamar, is as large as a grown man now. He and Velma helped us move in and here I sit now with boxes unpacked and things in disarray. The one thing that has not changed is Lamar, as you might suppose. He is still the same mental age as when Burrell ran over him with the car twelve years ago. Lamar, so handsome, so physically powerful and yet so childlike — he towers over Terry and seems to adore him immensely. Something about our son attracts the lonely and disenfranchised. Terry reminds me of you, always allied with the underdog. Your blood runs in his veins. My only contribution seems to be flaming red hair."

She read the lines again. Mundane. Trivial. Mickey arose, poured another cup of tea. She spooned sugar from a ten-pound sack given to her at Okeelanta Sugar Mill when she'd gone out to be interviewed this afternoon. Would Gerald approve of the gift? It was a violation of rationing laws. Mickey decided not to mention it.

"A little plus to help compensate for the labor we do around here," the mill manager had explained. "We give away all broken bags."

With that, he'd stabbed a sack with a pocketknife. "Like this one," he'd said, and stabbed another. "Twenty pounds will hold you until you come to work next week, won't it?"

"Are you kidding?" Mickey had laughed nervously. "I've been doling out sugar with tweezers for three years!"

She would be doing bookkeeping, harking back to her late teens and early twenties during the depression. Mickey sipped hot tea, leaning against the kitchen counter, watching the dark hulk of moving fruit cars on the rails behind the house. She could hear the high whine of insects "singing" in the night. Frogs peeped and croaked along the banks of the canals that kept the camp drained. The grumble of mechanical things droned afar.

So lonely.

She wondered where Gerald was, how he was. In Europe, it would be daylight now.

The clatter of conveyor belts was music. The women looked stout in their rubber aprons and boots, their heads tied in bandanas. The platform trembled under Terry's bare feet as he walked through. At the concession stand, where workers could buy snacks, a thick-chested proprietor laved mustard on wieners and ladled onions over that — the smell intoxicating.

"You remember me?" Terry yelled at the cook.

"I remember."

He hadn't looked.

"My daddy managed Camp Osceola," Terry said.

"What you want?"

"I'm looking for Bucky Dallas."

"Don't know him."

"He worked at the icehouse," Terry said.

"Get out of the way, boy. You're blocking my window."

"Bucky had a crossed eye," Terry persisted.

"Boy — move!"

The zing of crates in a chute passed overhead, spiraling down from a loft where the boxes were constructed, going to the conveying lines to be loaded with vegetables. They were working on celery tonight.

He didn't see anyone he knew, except the surly cook. He'd been to the icehouse and they'd chased him away twice. He'd finally grabbed a chunk of crystal clear ice, sucking it as he strolled the familiar area, wary for guards put here to intercept trespassers.

Loaded crates moved the length of the building, passing into washing machines that gave the vegetables a final rinse before emerging on the far side. Two men were there, tacks in their mouths, hammering lids on the crates and shoving them onto another belt for transport to the loading dock.

Finally, the parcels went into the yawning door of a boxcar — these laborers had no humor, working in silence and poor light to pack the wares from floor to ceiling. Terry watched them for a few moments, then darted between dollies, over a mound of burlap sacks, and out the other side.

At the end of the packing platform the icehouse served the boxcars, blowing man-made snow into a fruitcar to keep the contents chilled. The scream of the shredder was deafening, huge blocks of ice chewed to shards and expelled into cars as the engine of the train idled, waiting to position the loaded carriers for dispatch later tonight.

Frustrated, Terry left the brightly lighted arena, walking toward the Silver Dollar Café where he and Bucky used to go, four years back. He could hear a jukebox, the laughter of men and women. Terry slipped inside, his bare feet sliding in sawdust thrown on the hardwood floor.

He stood at the bar, his eyes just above the counter, watching the waitresses put together their orders on little metal trays that advertised Coca-Cola.

The jukebox was a beautiful thing to behold. The pulsing lights beckoned the eyes, colors changing constantly. In tiny tubes that stretched from floor to top, bubbles arose hypnotically as if the music were boiling within. The volume was so high, Terry could feel the throb of the instruments. People talked to one another in shouts. Cigarette smoke hung in a veil under dim light bulbs positioned over each booth along a wall.

Terry saw the woman he sought and called, "Miss Renée!"

A man touched her rear end as she passed, carrying a foaming pitcher of beer to a table.

"Miss Renée!"

He'd drawn the attention of the owner, sitting on a high stool behind the bar. The man shifted a cigar over yellow teeth and blue lips, disturbed, but still indolent.

Terry waited for the waitress to come his way again. Men in a booth said something to her and her reply made them erupt in laughter. She stopped at the jukebox and put in a coin, punched a button to make a selection.

"Miss Renée, do you remember me? I'm Terry Calder."

She glanced at him, spoke to the owner, "Another round for table four. Two burgers all the way."

"Miss Renée, I'm looking for Bucky Dallas. You know Bucky."

Now she looked at him.

"He had crossed eyes," Terry said.

"Ain't you the red-on-the-head that always played hookey?"

"Yes ma'am. Do you know where Bucky is?"

She tossed her head slightly, saying to the owner, "Wisconsin, I'd guess." The man's belly jiggled up and down in mute laughter.

"Where you been, Redhead?" Renée inquired. She put beer bottles under the counter as she spoke.

"We moved to Birmingham, but we're back now. Can you tell me where Bucky is?"

She was squatting behind the bar. Terry could see up her skirt. She looked at him with such a strange expression he felt a tingle of alarm.

"Bucky ain't here anymore," she said hoarsely.

"He moved away?"

Renée shot a glance at the owner. He lifted shaggy eyebrows, turned away.

"Bucky had a accident," the woman said.

"Accident?"

"He fell in the ice shredder. You know what the ice shredder is?"

Terry stepped back a pace.

Renée grabbed him with one hand, her chin dimpling as if she might cry. "He was your friend, wasn't he?"

"Did he die?"

"A cuter little bastard never was," Renée said softly. "I thought I'd never get over it."

"He's dead?"

"Yes," she said tenderly. "He's dead."

The man on the stool pulled the cap off a large orange drink and handed it down to Terry. He took it, but stood there staring at Renée. A tear rolled out of her eye and carried mascara down her cheek.

"This ain't no way to learn something like this," she said. "I'm awful sorry, Red."

He imagined Bucky, reduced to icy particles, being shipped to Wisconsin in a boxcar.

"I don't have a nickel," Terry whispered. He gave her the drink, turned and ran.

Before daybreak, Mickey was up, struggling to complete her letter to Gerald. Boiling water on the stove made the lid of a kettle hop softly, sputtering steam.

"Terry came home last night distraught because another of his friends is no longer here. A child who worked at the icehouse, apparently. We forget that this is a region of migratory laborers who come and go."

"Mama?" Terry stood in the hallway, dressed.

"Good morning," she said.

"Morning, Mama. Ann is waking up."

Mickey hastily concluded the letter. "Gerald, the children are arising. We love you with all our hearts and souls. Be careful. Today I'll complete the unpacking and try to put this house in order. We have too much junk for these confines. But it will be done. I love you. I love you. Love, Mickey."

The children ate cereal while Mickey washed dishes. The cloy scent of oleander wafted through the window. It was this fragrance which Mickey most associated with Camp Osceola. The plants had been established as hardy ornamentals before anyone knew how poisonous they were to livestock and people. But then, in an effort to eradicate the noxious growth, they'd discovered that even the sooty smoke of burning oleander could be toxic. So now, all newcomers were simply warned, "Don't taste it; don't burn it."

"Ann spilled cereal, Mama," Terry said from the table.

"Be careful, Ann."

"She needs a napkin."

"See if you can find one, Terry."

Terry searched boxes marked "kitchen." Mickey turned to look at Ann and the child returned her gaze, huge blue eyes set in a round face, puffed by too much food behind tightly clamped lips.

"Take smaller bites, Ann."

A single round Cheerio clung to Ann's chin. She dared munch and her freckles moved in unison.

From the radio, Don McNeil's Breakfast Club chorus sang, *Good morning, everybody, and howdy-do-ya . . . Good morning everybody, and welcome-to-ya* ——

"I found a dishtowel," Terry announced. He wiped Ann's mouth, then cleaned up sticky circles of cereal which formed cheery "O's" Ann ate.

Mickey looked out the window. Beneath Australian pines this side of the railroad, in dark shadows, a boy stood so motionless she'd been lucky to notice him. It was his immobility that held her — like a deer at the edge of a glade.

"Terry, who is that child?"

He peered past her. "His name is Ossie."

"Ossie?"

"He's the son of an Indian chief," Terry said. "His real name is Osceola."

"What is he doing?" Mickey questioned.

"Waiting for me, I guess."

Taller, older than Terry. But Terry had always preferred older companions. "You could ask Ossie to come in," Mickey suggested.

"He doesn't want to."

"Call him."

A moment of hesitation. Terry went to the screened back porch and yelled, "Hey, Ossie! Want to come in?"

No response.

"Ossie! Want to come in?"

Terry reappeared, "He doesn't want to, Mama."

"Terry, I would feel better about your friends if they came to the house."

"He doesn't like white people."

"What does he think you are, redhead?"

"He's afraid, maybe."

"Of me?"

"Grown-ups," Terry conceded.

"Nevertheless," Mickey said gently, "I want you to tell Ossie he's welcome to come in, hereafter. He doesn't have to stand out there waiting for you to appear."

"Yes ma'am."

From the front door came a rattle of the latched screen. "Yoo-hoo, Mickey!"

Velma Mason stood on the second step, legs apart, feet firmly placed as if expecting a bodily assault. Behind her, the boy, Lamar.

"I brought my own coffee," Velma lifted a pot she carried. "And the muscle of my boy. Lamar can help you move things around today."

Lamar's blond eyebrows bobbed up and down, "I'm going to — uh help you, Miss Mickey — if you want me to."

"Come in, Velma."

"I'm strong, Miss Mickey."

"Yes, you are, Lamar."

Velma placed her coffee pot on an eye of the stove and held up a finger on which were hooked the handles of two cups.

"Then again," Velma grinned, "we could send Ann to the day-care center and let Lamar and Terry go play while you and I tackle this mess in a slothful fashion conducive to adult conversation."

"That idea I like."

"Mama —" Terry jerked his head toward the back, where Ossie waited. "May I go play?"

"Couldn't Lamar go with you and Ossie?"

"I guess so."

"Take Ann to the day-care center for me."

"I'll go tell Ossie." Terry went out the rear door. Velma came to the window and stood beside Mickey. "Do you know that child, Velma?"

"Yes. The Seminole boy, Ossie Knight."

"He won't come to the house."

"Would you," Velma responded, "if you were accepted by neither white or red or black? Terry will probably be the only friend the kid has."

The two boys were standing close to one another, Terry shorter and more slight than the Knight child. Then Terry raced again for the house.

"All that energy wasted on kids who don't need it," Velma sighed.

They turned to find Lamar finishing Ann's cereal.

"Lamar," Velma said, "you just ate!"

Mickey laughed, "It's all right, Velma."

"No wonder that boy weighs as much as he does." Velma retrieved her coffee pot and poured two cups.

"Okay, Mama!" Terry yelled.

"Get Ann ready," Mickey instructed.

Terry hurried Ann into the bathroom and Mickey could hear animated debate between the siblings as Terry washed his sister's face and hands.

"I want to go with you," Ann demanded.

"You can't this time. We're going swimming."

"No you aren't!" Mickey called. "No swimming in these canals. You'll have eye and ear infections."

"Not if we swim out at Chosen." Terry was at the hall door now, a soapy washcloth in hand. "The water at Chosen comes fresh from Lake Okeechobee."

Mickey looked at Velma and received an almost imperceptible nod.

"All right, then. Chosen. But no canals."

"No ma'am."

"I'm going — uh, going swimming too, Ma?" asked Lamar.

"If you stay with Terry."

"I will, Ma. I will."

Resigned, Mickey waved the back of one hand in a pushing motion and Lamar scooped up Ann in an easy swing, placing the child on his shoulders, her legs locking around his thick neck as Ann issued a delighted shriek.

Watching them join Ossie out front, Mickey said, "I'd feel better about that Knight boy if he'd only come into the house."

"Far as I know," Velma replied, "he has never been trouble to anybody, if that's what's worrying you."

"Terry picks such strange friends," Mickey said. Then, blushing, "I'm sorry, Velma. I didn't mean —"

"Forget it. You're right. I have to tell you though, Lamar is overjoyed to have Terry across the street. It's been a long time since I heard my boy jabber so happily, Mickey. That's good for me and mine. I hope for you and yours."

"Of course it is."

"Lamar is such a —" Velma's gaze fell and she stirred

her coffee. "Such a child," she concluded. "By God, Mickey, I've missed you these past years."

"I've missed you."

"Sit down, Mickey. Relax. You give me the jitters staying tense all the time like you do."

Mickey sank to a chair and the two women gazed at one another fondly. Velma put a rough hand on Mickey's wrist and squeezed. "The world is the old world yet. Now that you're back, I feel that all's right despite the war and no gas, no tires, no nylons."

Mickey submitted to the lingering pressure of Velma's hand. Suddenly both of them laughed. For the first time in a long while, Mickey felt at ease.

Terry sat on a limestone outcropping beneath the Chosen bridge. Nude, Lamar squatted with elbows on his knees, hands clasped. Ossie chewed the stem of a long grass shoot. They were watching a dragonfly which Terry held by the wings. Everything Terry fed into the mandibles of the insect, the dragonfly devoured.

"Looks like it'd get so full it would pop," Terry remarked.

"Never does though," Ossie said.

"They'll eat anything," Terry noted.

"Even their own tails if you feed it to to them," Ossie said.

"How come, hu-how come they eat like that?" Lamar asked.

"That's all they do is eat," Ossie said. "If it wasn't for dragonflies we'd be up to our asses in mosquitos. Some folks call them mosquito hawks."

Terry released iridescent wings and the insect remained

on the tip of his finger, legs postured so the "knees" stuck out sharply.

"They'll eat warts if you've got one," Ossie said.

"Do the warts come back?" Lamar questioned.

"Nothing cures warts but jimson weed juice or the conjure woman," Ossie said.

The dragonfly was nibbling Terry's finger and he shook his hand gently. Instantly, the insect was gone.

"Last time I went to the conjure woman," Ossie said, "she said she could make all kinds of things happen if a person could pay enough. She made my grandfather the stud he was when he was young."

"Is that true?" Terry asked.

"He didn't say she lied," Ossie said.

"Is the conjure woman as old as your grandfather?"

"No telling how old she is really. She could be over a hundred. She could conjure herself younger, couldn't she?"

That made sense.

"I'm cold," Lamar said.

"Put your clothes on, Lamar," Terry suggested.

"Are we going to swim anymore?"

"Not today. Put your clothes on."

Ossie watched the older boy dress. "He does mighty near everything you tell him, don't he?"

Terry shrugged a shoulder.

"Tell him to do something."

"Like what?"

"Wait until he's dressed. Then tell him to take off his clothes."

"Why?"

"To see if he'll do it."

"I don't like to tease Lamar."

"It ain't teasing. Just tell him and see what happens."

"No."

Ossie spit weed pulp dryly. "No skin off my nose," he said. "But if I was leading a bear around on a string, I'd want to know what he will and what he won't do."

"I can't uh button my pants, Terry!"

"Suck in your stomach, Lamar. Breathe out and do it."

Lamar did that.

"I broke it."

"Broke what?"

"Broke my pants. The button came off."

"Put it in your pocket. Your ma will sew it on when you get home."

"Tell him to take off his clothes and see —"

"No."

Ossie rose lazily and stretched. Every sinew of arm, back and thigh drew taut. The movement made Terry think of a cat rising from a long nap.

"One more dip?"

"I don't think so."

Ossie ran toward the water and dove, leaving scarcely a ripple.

"Terry," Lamar cried, "you said we wasn't going swimming!"

"We aren't, Lamar. Just Ossie."

"I broke my button, Terry."

"It's all right. Your ma can fix it."

"You think she'll be mad?"

"Everybody breaks buttons now and then."

Ossie surfaced midstream, pushing away a floating hyacinth and backstroking with ease.

"Hey, Ossie," Terry called, "we're getting ready to go."

"Another minute," Ossie said.

Terry dressed, having waited for his body to dry so his buttocks wouldn't itch in wet clothing. Ossie emerged from the water, gave a quick shake to ebony hair and walked smoothly to his own clothes.

"Hey, Lamar," Ossie said, softly, "take off your clothes."

"Why?"

"Cause I said do it. I'm going to throw you in the river. You don't want to get your clothes wet, do you?"

"No, uh no, I can't go back in the water. I'm cold."

"Cut it out, Ossie."

"Take them off, Lamar," Ossie said.

"I can't get my clothes wet, now. Ma will be mad if I get my clothes wet and break my pants, too."

"You aren't going to get wet," Terry said.

"He is, if he doesn't take off his clothes."

"Cut it out, Ossie."

"Tell him to take off his clothes then."

"Let's go, Lamar," Terry said.

Ossie moved so quickly it caught Terry by surprise, even though he was warily expecting it. Ossie threw himself at Lamar as if sliding into home plate. His legs locked around Lamar's ankles and with a twist, Ossie had thrown the larger boy face forward.

"Quit it, Ossie!" Lamar squealed.

"I'm going to chunk you in, Lamar."

"Ossie, leave him alone."

Terry grabbed Ossie, pulling him backward and they rolled toward the water.

"Hey!" Ossie yelled as Lamar lifted him bodily and threw him headlong and fully clothed into the river.

"Jesus!" Ossie came up screaming.

Terry doubled over, laughing. "Run, Terry!" Lamar

hollered. "Run!" Lamar was clawing his way up the dike at top speed.

"I'm going to get you, Lamar!" Ossie shrilled.

Terry sat on the bank, laughing as Ossie floundered ashore.

"Run, Terry!" Lamar yelled once more — and then disappeared over the embankment.

Ossie collapsed beside Terry and the two of them laughed together.

"Did you see how he picked me up and threw me?"

"Like a sack of salt."

"I sailed through the air."

They laughed again and Terry looked up, but Lamar was gone.

"Like I said," Ossie wheezed, "if I was leading a bear around on a string, I'd want to know what he's going to do when I say do it."

"He isn't going to hurt me."

"Not today," Ossie said soberly.

Four

TERRY SAT WITH Ann on the back porch steps. She drew nearer to better see his book. Purple shadows of evening stretched long across the camp. In the living room, Mama huddled beside the Bendix radio console, listening for news. The commentator's voice was emotional, broken by static of overseas transmission.

". . . bodies stacked like cordwood . . . gas chambers in which thousands, perhaps tens of thousands went to their deaths . . . men, women, children . . . atrocities unbelievable in magnitude . . ."

Almost what Daddy's last letter had said.

Ann poked a photograph with one pink forefinger. "It looked like that," she said to Terry.

"That's a squash bug. Stink bug."

"It had horns like that one," Ann said. "Turn the page."

Usually, Mama insisted that Terry and Ann listen to the evening news, claiming, "This is history in the making, children." But not tonight. Not since Germany surrendered. Now, Mama sent them outside while she listened, alone, her face starkly pale.

Once, when an announcer began talking about "atrocities" Mama had cried aloud, frightening Terry. Perhaps Germany had not surrendered. Maybe the war was lost! But no, Mama said the Germans were beaten. It was "atrocities" that made her cry.

That night, Velma Mason had said, "They ought to gas every last German."

"Should they, Mama?" Terry later questioned.

"No."

"But they tortured people."

"Who?" Mama had said sharply. "Who tortured people?"

"The Germans."

"Not the Germans. The *Nazis*. Not all Germans are Nazis, Terry."

Stung, Terry blinked, uncertain.

More softly, Mama asked, "Remember Mr. Schmidt who owned the jewelry store in Birmingham? He was a good man, wasn't he? You liked his children, Alex and Maria, remember?"

Somebody threw rocks through their store window one night. Students taunted Alex and Maria and they didn't even talk like their father who said *ve* for "we." A few days later, the Schmidts were gone — who knew where?

"The Schmidts once lived in Germany," Mama had said. "Most Germans are like you and me. Most Japanese, too. Mothers keeping house, children going to school. People are not always responsible for things their governments do. Remember that, Terry."

Terry remembered. Everytime he went to the movies and the audience cheered fallen Zero planes, or clapped their hands as German soldiers died, Terry wondered, What about their children, those fallen enemies? Where did they go to school? Did they see such films and weep?

Ann brought him back to the present with a jabbing finger, "It was green, like that one."

"That's a squash bug, Ann. A different kind, but still a squash bug."

"Can it hurt you?"

"Not that one. But it smells bad if you squeeze it."

He heard Mama adjusting the radio. Fireflies blinked in yellow semaphore, rising from pools of darkness along the canals. Toward the rear of camp, farther down "C" Street, somebody was listening to the *Lucky Strike Hit Parade*. More cheerful than atrocities. Terry heard a man singing, "Don't fence me in . . . let me wander over yonder . . ."

"Can this one hurt you?" Ann indicated a blister beetle.

"Yes. It stings."

Mama had tuned in the rapid-fire voice of Walter Winchell: "Good evening Mr. and Mrs. North America and all the ships at sea . . . ."

"It's getting too dark to see, Terry. Let's go in."

Mama was irritable during the news. To hold Ann, Terry said, "Look at the fireflies. They're winking at us."

Ann pressed against his thigh and he put an arm around her to still a primitive quiver as she responded to the coming night.

"I wish my tail would light," Ann said. "We could see in the dark."

"The dark is good," Terry comforted. "A lot of things come out at night that are afraid of the day. We'd miss all of them."

"What things?"

"Fireflies. Moths. See the bats swooping up there? They sleep in the rafters of packing houses all day. At night we can hear the crickets and tree frogs."

"Tell me —"

He knew without prompting. Terry pitched his voice high, mimicking, "The baby frog says, 'Mama, Mama, Mama.' The mama frog says, 'Hush child, hush child.'" He dropped his voice as low as he could make it. "The papa frog says, 'Spank him, spank him!'"

He thought of Mr. McCree who taught Terry the parody of talking frogs.

Terry had looked everywhere he knew to look for Mr. McCree. Eunice and LuBelle gone — Bucky Dallas in Wisconsin —

He hadn't told Mama any of this. She might restrict him to the camp area, or set limits on his time away. Besides, Mama said people shouldn't talk about sad things to people who were sad. That's why she didn't tell Daddy about some things. He was sad, overseas and lonely.

Terry glanced through the screened door, watching Mama's face, seeking an indication of her assessment of the news. She looked tired in the ocherous light of a single naked overhead bulb. Lamar had accidentally broken the globe by lifting a chair.

Mama turned off the radio. "Children. Supper! Come in now."

Terry took his insect book, trying not to appear protective of the prized publication, and held the door open for Ann.

"It was a stink bug, Mama," Ann reported.

"Um-hm."

Sitting at the table, Ann covered her plate as beets were spooned. "I don't want any of that."

"Move your hand, Ann." Mama put a single beet on the plate, cut it in half, then gave the balance to Terry. He despised beets.

"Did we get a letter from Daddy today?" he asked.

"No. Maybe tomorrow."

Terry watched Ann quarantine beet juice from other, more palatable vegetables.

"No meat, Mama?"

"No, Ann. Eat what's there."

"People are hungry all over the world," Ann mimed.

"So eat your beets too," Mama commanded.

In silence, they sat still as Mama walked past, out onto the front porch. Terry heard a squeak of wicker furniture as Mama sat, alone in the dark.

"I'll trade you a beet for some beans," Ann whispered.

"No, thanks."

"Free then."

"No."

"I'll give you some beans if you take the beet," Ann bargained.

"No, Ann."

"I don't like beets," Ann said unnecessarily.

"Eat the beets," Mama called.

Ann lifted a particle of the awful vegetable, touched it with her tongue and recoiled.

Terry elected to take his like medicine, all at once and in a gulp.

"Tastes like a stink bug," Ann cried.

"Stop the nonsense, Ann," Mama said sharply.

Terry poured salt into the rut of a stalk of celery and took a bite. He refused to acknowledge Ann's ordeal as she spooned tiny pieces of the beet chased by huge swallows of milk. From the porch came the sound of Mama rocking, woven rattan creaking like a ship at anchor.

He thought about Daddy — now a vague form without face. To remind himself, Terry looked at a tinted photograph on an end table. Daddy smiling, wearing an officer's hat with the familiar Red Cross emblem. Red Cross people didn't carry guns and nobody was supposed to shoot at them. The Nazis who killed women and children — what would the Red Cross mean to them?

"Mama, do I have to eat all my supper?" Ann asked.

"You do."

"I'm not hungry any more."

"Eat it anyway."

"Ugh, ugh, ugh," Ann said. "My beet is bleeding!"

"Ann —" ominous tone from the porch.

"My stomach is beginning to hurt."

"Eat it!"

Terry heard Lamar's voice at the front door. "Miss Mickey, can I come in?"

"Yes, Lamar."

"Is Terry here?"

"He's eating. Have you had supper?"

"Beets!" Ann warned.

"I uh ate supper," Lamar said, entering. He sat beside Ann, his pale eyebrows rising and falling. Ann spooned her last piece of beet and extended it to Lamar. Mama appeared in the door just as the older boy took the dreaded gift.

"Good," Lamar said.

"All right, child," Mama grabbed Ann, "go take a bath and go to bed."

"He was hungry, Mama!"

"A bath. Then bed."

"I had to go away," Lamar reported at large. "My ma and pa are having a fight. Ma said Pa wouldn't've fought the war even if he had good legs."

"Lamar," Mama attempted, "you shouldn't repeat what is said in your home."

"My pa wears braces," Lamar told Terry. "He can't walk good. He had polio like President Roosevelt."

Seeing Mama's distress, Terry seized the moment. "May we go out and play?"

"Rinse the dishes," Mama said, "and go."

"Ma says Pa is a crybaby." Lamar helped Terry clear the table. "She says Pa is sorry for hisself."

He looked at Terry and withheld Ann's plate. "Can I have this?"

"Sure."

Lamar wolfed the remnants. "Ma made Pa cry."

Uneasy, mostly because Mama seemed distressed, Terry said, "Want some iced tea, Lamar?"

"Yeah — uh, is it sour?"

"No."

"I don't like it sour. Ma hit Pa with a broomstick."

Mama's face flushed and to Terry's surprise, she went to Lamar and hugged him. The young man threw his arms around her and sobbed.

"Everybody has arguments, Lamar," Mama said. "Sometimes we say things that hurt those we love. But we still love one another. Velma and your father are going to be all right."

"But Ma made Pa cry!"

"We all cry now and then. Look at you."

She wiped Lamar's runny nose. Then, using her apron, wiped her own. She laughed abruptly. "See?" she said.

"We all cry."

With Lamar waiting in the living room, Terry gave his teeth an obligatory brushing before leaving. He heard Mama in the bedroom with Ann.

"Hey there, Annie."

"I hate beets, Mama."

"I won't give you any more, then."

"Promise?"

"I promise."

"They bleed blood on my plate."

"That's juice. Not blood."

"Tastes like blood."

"No it doesn't. Someday you will grow up and eat beets and wonder why you ever felt this way."

"No I won't. Beets and okra. I won't eat them and if I have a little girl I won't make her eat them either."

"I'll remind you of that, someday."

When Terry returned to the living room, Lamar stood there shifting from one foot to the other, rubbing the tips of his fingers with the thumbs. "Ma said Pa is just a drunk old cripple."

"Mama, we're gone!"

"Ma said he threw away the newspaper business, too. She said he drank up the profit. What's profit, Terry?"

They walked to the packing house, but a guard drove them off. They returned to Camp Osceola the long way, through the main entrance, because Lamar was afraid to cross the canal on the one shaky board that formed a span. At the administration building they paused to watch insects whirling in an undulating cyclone beneath the security light. Sometimes Terry collected interesting specimens here.

"I hope Ma don't beat up Pa any more, Terry."

"That'll be over by now, Lamar."

"I don't want to go home if Ma's still mad."

"They're probably kissing and making up. You go on home and I'll stand here until you get inside."

He waited in the street as Lamar approached the house. Lamar peeked inside, then entered cautiously.

A truck with a faulty muffler puttered through camp. Near the auditorium, children screeched, playing hide and seek in the dark.

Terry wished he could find Mr. McCree. He wished he could go far into the Everglades like they used to, where there were no sounds except from creatures that belonged there. He felt a tinge of what he'd always felt in Birmingham — loneliness, and a yearning to be out there where everything was natural.

The living room light was on and Terry eased through a hedge to peer in the window before entering. Mama was reading old letters from Daddy. She pushed them away and sat back, a cup of tea between her hands. Terry heard her sigh. She stared — at nothing. Finally, she stood up wearily, went to the calendar and wrote a new number: 674. The days Daddy had been gone.

When he entered, Mama sat on the couch. "Is Lamar all right, Terry?"

"Yes, ma'am. He went home."

"Velma came over. Everything's okay now."

"Why were they fighting, Mama?"

She studied him a moment then patted the space beside her on the couch. "Burrell suffers demons of his own making," she said. "He makes life harder on himself. I think Velma tries to shake him out of it now and then."

He didn't understand, but Terry said, "Yes ma'am."

"Some bad things have happened to Burrell and he can't

seem to get past it. He ran over Lamar — you knew that."

"Lamar was playing in the driveway," Terry provided.

"Then Burrell got polio right after the war started. And he drinks too much."

"Yes ma'am."

"He was different four short years ago." Mama stroked his back. "We all were."

"Mama, will Lamar ever be different?"

"No."

"He's not dumb all the time."

"Not dumb at all," Mama said. "But he'll always be a child. Like Ann is now."

"What made him that way?"

"When the car hit him, it hurt his brain. His body keeps growing, but his mind doesn't."

He lingered under her caress until she turned and kissed him, asking, "Aren't you ready for bed?"

He stopped at the hall door. "Do you think Lamar would ever hurt anybody, Mama?"

Her quick inhalation of breath surprised Terry.

"Ossie said he might," he explained. "I don't think he would, do you?"

"Lamar should not be encouraged to fight, Terry. He's stronger than he realizes."

"He won't fight," Terry said confidently. "He'd just hit and run."

When her expression did not ease, Terry said, "Lamar is all right, Mama. Really." He blew her a kiss. "Good night."

Undressed and in bed, Terry listened to Ann's easy breathing across the room. He heard Mama making more hot tea, her spoon tinkling against the cup when she stirred it.

He had no friends in Birmingham. They called him "Florida cracker" and "nigger lover." They shot marbles, a game he had never mastered. Nobody up there ever put their salty nuts into their soda pop. Their fathers came home still wearing masks of coal dust — maybe *that's* why they didn't like colored people!

Mama warned him that things had changed in Belle Glade.

His chest ached with the thought. This was the only place he'd ever been where he felt really free.

The birds and the flowers and the wonderful creatures were still here — but things *had* changed.

Quietly, so mama wouldn't hear, Terry wept into his pillow. For Mr. McCree. For Bucky, melting in Wisconsin. . . .

Five

"WELL?" MAMA turned slightly.

"You look good."

Nonetheless, she twisted first one way, then the other, trying to see her legs. "At least the seam stays straight." She had colored her legs from a bottle, drawing a seam with an eyebrow pencil. Terry wondered what would happen if she perspired.

"How about my slip, Terry?"

"I can't see it."

"I'll pick up Ann from the day-care center when I get back from Okeelanta. Stay out of trouble."

"I will."

"There's food in the refrigerator. Be sure to put the cap back on anything you open."

Terry waited beside the car. Nervously, Mama re-checked the contents of her handbag, put a towel on the torn front seat of the vehicle and got in.

"Be good, Terry."

"If I can't be good, I'll be careful." It was something he heard a man say at the packing house.

"Lord help," Mama sighed. She cast a glance at the rear view mirror. A few hairs had pulled loose. Her face was moist. Terry wondered if her "stockings" were getting runny.

"Well," Mama said. She started to pull away and a truck came by slowly. "New," Mama marveled. "Where do you suppose he got a *new* vehicle?"

"You'll be late, mama."

"I'm going. Kiss me."

He did. Then Terry watched Mama drive through the camp entrance and turn toward town.

Alone. All day with nothing he had to do.

Lamar was working today, pulling weeds from endless rows of tomatoes. Terry thought about Ossie, but he wasn't in the mood for Ossie.

The man in the new truck had parked close to an unoccupied house down the way. On the lawn! Driving on the grass was forbidden.

Terry strolled toward the truck. Morning heat came steadily; no clouds to cut tropical warmth this day. The new truck gleamed dark green. No chrome on it. The war had taken all chrome. But it was new. The tires were etched with deep treads and tiny latex needles still protruded from the sides of the rubber.

Terry considered telling the driver about parking on the grass. Grown-ups didn't like children telling them the rules, but that was better than having Mr. Rollins storming, "Get that vehicle off the lawn!"

The truck door opened, a harness thing fell out. Terry

watched two hands hooking clasps and snaps — and with a push the driver swung out suspended on the contraption. He had thick, muscled arms, unruly black hair that curled around his ears. His chest was huge —

No legs!

Dangling in his harness, the man pulled a folded wheelchair from the van, adjusted it. This done, he slipped into the chair. But where could he go? The house had four front steps rising to the porch door. The grass was lush, not suitable for riding a bicycle, much less a chair.

The man tried to move, but the wheels slipped. He alternately pushed and pulled on the wheels, seeking traction.

"May I help?" Terry called.

He peered at Terry from eyes the same color green as his truck. "Tell you what," he said. "I can make the steps if you will bring my chair. Think you could do that?"

"I think so."

With a lurch, the man threw himself forward, striking the ground, rolling. Then, using his arms as crutches, he swung his torso, landing on his buttocks, and crossed to the steps.

"Are you going to live here?" Terry questioned.

"Maybe."

He turned his back to the steps, placed his hands flat on each landing, and lifted himself one level at a time to the door.

"I can open it," Terry volunteered.

"I got it." He awaited his chair. "I'd hate to do this in a pouring rain."

Terry dragged the chair inside the screened porch, but the man ignored it. Using the same locomotion as before, he moved inside, looked around, then bumped toward the hall.

"The bedrooms are back there," Terry advised.

"You've been in here before?"

"The houses are all alike."

The man pivoted, extended a hand while balancing himself with his other arm. "Name's Deke."

"I'm Terry Calder, Mr. Deke."

"No 'mister.' Just Deke."

"Call me Terry."

"Done, Terry. Will you do me a favor?"

"Sure."

"While I unload my truck, will you run down to the administration office and tell the manager I'm staying?"

"Yessir."

"Damn it, kid. No *sir*. Ever. I've had all the military jargon I can stand. Where're your parents?"

"Mama's at work, Okeelanta Sugar, and Daddy's investigating atrocities in Poland."

"Tough duty."

"Yessir."

"Can't you help it?"

"What?"

"Saying sir."

"No sir."

"Okay. Scoot. Tell the office T. R. Dekle is staying. They're waiting to hear my decision."

Terry raced down "C" Street and into the camp office. "Mr. T. R. Dekle is staying!" he reported.

The lady at the admissions desk made a clucking sound. "Bless his heart."

"All right, Terry," Mr. Rollins said. "Thanks."

"Was he in the war, Mr. Rollins?"

"Yes. Tarawa."

"Where's that?"

"It's an island in the Pacific."

"Is that how he lost his legs?"

"Yes. Run along now."

"Bless his heart," the lady said again.

Terry ran back to Deke's, offering to help unload the truck.

"How do you drive it?" he asked.

"Everything is on the steering wheel. Take a look."

Strange levers. A strap to hold him in place. On the seat, a magazine, *Southern Horticulture*. Deke said, "Grab a box, will you?"

"Brakes and everything on the steering wheel," Terry observed. "Pretty smart."

"Necessity is the mother," Deke noted, handing down boxes from the enclosed rear of the vehicle. "Put them anywhere."

The house was sweltering. Terry opened windows and the rear door. He heard water gurgling in the commode. "They'll come fix that, if you ask them."

"I can get it. Bad alignment of the plunger, maybe."

"when will they bring your furniture?" Terry asked.

"This is it."

Boxes of books. A sleeping bag rolled tightly. A serviceman's footlocker. Large cushions. Not one table or bed.

"What's this?" Terry asked. It was a metal frame with wheels.

"I'll show you. Watch."

Deke mounted the device, pumped a handle and elevated himself to the height of the kitchen sink.

"Hey, that's great."

"Built it myself."

"You did?"

"It's fine on even floors," Deke said. "The trick is finesse. Getting hurried invites a fall. Well, that's it. What do I owe you?"

"Sir?"

"You want to be friends?"

"Yessir."

"You don't say 'sir' to your friends, do you?"

"No sir."

Deke shook his head. "What the heck. Sir it is then. I say, Terry, what do I owe you?"

"For what?"

"For helping me move in."

"Nothing."

"How about a quarter?"

"You don't owe me anything."

"I took your labor, took two hours of your time."

"I didn't have anything to do."

"Your mom must need your help at home."

"Today's her first day at work. I didn't have anything to do."

"So be it then. I accept your generosity. But at least allow me to buy your lunch."

"Okay."

"Fine. Now then. Where's the nearest restaurant?"

"The Silver Dollar Café at the packing houses. That's where the truck drivers eat. There's a restaurant in Belle Glade."

"Which is your favorite place?"

"The hot dog stand at the Blue Goose packing house, behind Wedgeworth's Supply. They make super hot dogs and they sell cold drinks."

"Sounds good. Let's go."

Terry opened his mouth to speak of the irascible guard

who drove away strangers and children. But Deke was already outside, bumping down the steps calling, "Better bring the chair. Who knows where this trail will lead?"

Fascinated, Terry hopped up to the front seat, watched Deke hoist himself into the truck, strap his body, start the motor, shifting levers, and then smoothly back onto the pavement.

"Did you win any medals?" Terry said.

"In the war you mean?"

"Yes."

"The usual stuff. A purple heart because I cut my hand on a can of rations —"

Terry burst into laughter.

"Your pappy is in Poland?"

"Yessir. Investigating atrocities. Deke?"

"Left here?"

"Left. Deke — what is a *trocity*?"

"When helpless victims are brutalized. The Nazis annihilated anybody that didn't meet their Aryan standards."

Confused, Terry said, "Mama said it's crimes like murder and torture."

"Sometimes that's the least of an atrocity."

Terry pointed, "There it is. They have tables at the hot dog stand." Terry leaped out. But Deke sat, muscular hands on the steering wheel, looking through the windshield. Men with hand trucks passed on the platform overhead, canvas aprons whisking; women at the conveyor line cast glances at the deep green *new* truck and the stranger sitting there.

"Deke?"

He jolted slightly. Then he grabbed his harness. The first attempt to snap a clasp failed and Terry heard him swear softly. Then, throwing wide the door, Deke pushed himself out of the cab.

For an instant, it was as if the cacophony of the entire packing house paused. A breathless moment of awareness as Deke wrestled with his wheelchair. Two men leaped down from the platform and came toward them.

"Need a hand?"

"I can make it, thanks."

Tomatoes passed unnoticed on conveyor belts. The helpful laborers shifted awkwardly as Deke secured himself and squinted at Terry. "Which way?"

The steps to the open platform were half a block away. Terry had always jumped up, grabbing a rail to hoist himself onto the decking.

"Long way," Terry admitted.

"Hey, buddy," one of the workers said. "If you'll let us. Our pleasure."

Deke swallowed. "We're headed for the hot dog stand."

Immediately, several other men were there, lifting Deke high, over the rail, placing his chair on the platform. Women in faded cotton shirts and slacks stepped aside to let them pass. With a galloping heart, Terry saw the fearsome guard appear, hesitate, then yield.

"Lead the way," Deke directed.

Then they were there. The tables, with benches attached, were not crowded at this hour. Deke rolled up to the window to order. He had to lift himself with his fingertips to be seen. Terry realized now that when Deke was seated in his chair they were the same height.

"What'll it be, Terry?"

"Hot dog. Lots of onions. And salt. Tastes better with salt."

"Make it four then."

People were gawking, but Deke sat with his hands

clasped and stared straight ahead. He saw. "Peripheral vision," Mama called it. She said all mothers had peripheral vision. Well, Deke had it too.

The burly cook in the stand placed their hot dogs on the high counter. "Drinks?"

"Grape," Terry said.

"Two."

"Don't forget the salt," Terry whispered.

"And salt," Deke called.

The vendor didn't like giving salt to the youngsters who used it to sweeten pilfered celery and tomatoes. But he handed down the shaker and watched Deke and Terry apply it.

With the fizz of cold grape soda in this throat, Terry took a massive bite of hot dog and watched Deke for a reaction.

"Good, right?" Terry said.

"Not bad."

"Best hot dogs I ever ate!"

"Not bad at all," Deke conceded. Then he reached over and shook Terry's shoulder gently. "A connoisseur right here in the Everglades," he said. "I'm a lucky man."

"I know all the best places."

"Yeah?"

"Sure! What do you want to see?"

"Everything before it's over. The glades. Everything."

"I can show you."

"Really?"

"I really can," Terry said. "I know lots about the swamps."

"Grew up here, did you?"

"Off and on. But I go out to the swamps a lot."

"How far?"

How far? Terry chewed, mind churning. "Thirty miles."

"Umm. Well. Before it's over," Deke said, "I have to go farther than that. I'm writing a book about the Everglades."

Terry slipped nearer, voice lowering. "Deke, I could go with you."

"I don't know —"

"I could help with things. I climb trees good. I can pick up snakes. I can catch a fish with my bare hands."

Deke ignored the sidelong glances of workers coming to take a break.

"I can handle old *Agkistrodon* or even *Crotalus,* with my bare hands."

He'd gone too far. Deke peered at him with a peculiar expression, green eyes narrowed. "Where'd you learn those words?"

"A friend taught me. Long time ago. *Agkistrodon piscivorus* is the cottonmouth water moccasin and *Crotalus* is —"

"I know what it is," Deke said.

"You do?"

"Rattlesnake. Eastern diamondback. Ever see any *Agkistrodon contortrix*?"

"Not here. They like more hilly country. Pinewoods. But I know where some might be, north of Lake Okeechobee."

Terry watched Deke chew, slow, methodical movements. "I only knew one other person who ever knew the true names of things," Terry said.

"You know other things besides snakes?"

"Some."

"Oleander?"

"Everybody knows oleander."

"Say a man were looking for a certain kind of lily?"

"What kind of lily?"

"True name: *Crinum americanum.*"

Hope plunging, Terry said, "I don't know that name."

"Florida swamp lily."

"Sure!"

"A man can't know everything," Deke said. He crumpled the waxy paper left from his hot dog and with a deft overhand pitch threw it into a waste barrel.

"I can learn though, Deke."

"Betcha can. Which way out of here?"

"The long way is down there."

"I'm in no hurry. Let's find the steps."

Terry kept pace as Deke propelled his chair with easy forward strokes of the wheels.

Despite Deke's objections, a couple of men helped him down the steps. Women at the conveyor line stole furtive glances, none smiling. That was Deke's fault. He wasn't smiling at them.

Entering camp again, Terry indicated, "I live right there. It's not so far away that I couldn't meet you anytime."

"So I see."

"I climb trees real good, Deke."

"I'll keep that in mind. But I need a strong back and a weak mind, Terry. Understand?"

"I know where to get that, too."

Deke laughed, a sound pitched higher than Terry expected. "What'll your mother say about you going into the Everglades?"

"She won't mind."

"I won't tolerate lying to her."

"No sir! I don't have to, really."

Terry got out. Deke was on the screened front porch when he spoke again. "You mentioned a strong back?"

"My friend Lamar has a strong back."

"How expensive will he be?"

"He'll help because we're friends."

"Can't beat the price."

"I'll bring him to meet you. You'll see. He's very strong. And he — well — he has a weak mind."

Terry felt Deke assessing him.

"You mean truly weak," Deke said gently.

"His daddy hit him with their car because Lamar was playing in the driveway."

"What will *his* mother say?"

"Nothing."

"You see very sure of this — Lamar."

"Lamar is my friend. He'll do anything I say, really."

A horn blew and Terry saw Mama wave.

"That's Mama."

"Pretty."

"Sir?"

"You have a pretty mama."

Flustered, Terry said, "See you tomorrow then? With Lamar?"

"Why not?"

Terry burst into the house. Easy. Easy. He clamped one hand with the other, seeking control.

"Hi, Mama."

"Hi yourself."

"How was work?"

"I'll learn. Did you do all right today?"

"Yes ma'am."

He was grinning so hard, the flesh burned at the

corners of his mouth.

"That leg coloring doesn't work so good," Mama lamented. Sweat made crisscrossing streaks after all.

She glanced at Terry and paused. "What is it?"

"I met somebody today."

Mama waited.

"He knows about snakes and true names and things."

She was still waiting.

"Mama," Terry said, voice quivering, "he wants me to go in the Everglades with him. May I? Please?"

"This is an adult?"

"A war hero." Tiny lie. Couldn't hurt. Purple heart.

"If he's a responsible adult, I suppose —"

Terry's ears were drumming so loudly, he didn't hear; he couldn't see through watery eyes — he was hugging Mama so tightly she gasped.

At last. Again. He was going!

Six

"TERRY," MAMA SAID evenly, "I'm sure he's very nice. But you can't go until I meet him."

"Mama — he's a *hero*!"

"Nevertheless."

We could go to his house this morning."

"I haven't time this monring."

"It won't take long." Terry demonstrated, "Deke, this is Mama; Mama, this is Deke."

"Not this morning."

"Mama! He might go to the swamps this morning."

"Then he goes without you. Please don't argue about it."

"You said I could go."

"I did not. I said *if* he is a responsible adult."

He followed Mama, snorting. Mama ignored him. When she drove off to work, Terry turned toward Deke's with angry strides. Lamar met him halfway.

"We have a new neighbor," Lamar said.

"I know."

"His name's Deke."

"I know, Lamar."

"He got his legs shot off fighting Japs."

Terry looked up at his companion, "How'd you know?"

"Me and Pa helped him do some work last night."

Terry's tone betrayed jealousy. "What kind of work?"

"He has to hold on to use the bathroom," Lamar reported. "Pa helped him put in some rails to hold to."

Terry halted.

"Pa said Deke would fall in the commode," Lamar said.

Terry continued down "C" Street. The truck was there.

"It didn't hurt," Lamar said.

"What didn't hurt?"

"When the Japs shot his legs off."

"Who told you that?"

"Deke did. He said he didn't feel it at all."

"I don't believe that."

"Pa said it was true, though. Deke said he had to throw away one leg."

The prospect of such a thing made Terry's stomach knot.

"It was hanging there — "

"Shut up, Lamar."

" — so he cut it off."

Terry opened Deke's screened door and called, "Deke? May we come in?"

"Who's we?"

"Me and Terry," Lamar replied.

"Sure. Just in time."

They found Deke atop his lift, putting items in the cupboard over a kitchen counter. "Hand me that box. Lamar," Deke requested. Terry grabbed the package and held it up.

"Didn't you cut off your leg, Deke?" Lamar said.

"Yep. It wasn't any good any more."

Terry felt queasy.

"And it didn't hurt," Lamar confirmed.

"Nope. The pain came later." Deke pointed at another carton. Lamar got to it first.

"Deke, Mama said I could go with you," Terry blurted.

"Where?"

"To the swamps."

Deke looked down at Terry a second. He put things in the cupboard.

"My ma puts her dishes up there," Lamar offered.

"These are things I don't often need." Deke pulled himself to a new position and pointed at another box. Terry was ready this time, lunging to seize it.

"That's a heavy one," Deke cautioned.

"Books?" Terry questioned.

"Seldom read but greatly treasured." Lamar took the cumbersome package and easily delivered it to the counter.

Deke withdrew a book, looked at it, and put it on a high shelf. With less care, he placed other books. After a moment, he withdrew the first, thick tome and handed it down to Terry.

"Take a look at that," Deke said.

The title was *North American Flora: Tropics*.

"For me to read?" Terry queried.

"When you're over here. You can't take it home. It'll teach you about things like *Crinum americanum*."

To Lamar, Terry said, "Florida swamp lily."

"Any pictures?" Lamar asked, looking.

"Good pictures," Terry noted. He looked up at Deke, "Are you going to the swamps today?"

"Nope. Going to get my gear together. Do you know the fish camp at Chosen?"

"Owen's."

"That's where I'm going."

"May we — I — go?"

"What'd your mother say?"

Terry held his eyes level. "She wants to meet you sometime."

"Immediately?"

"Sometimes soon."

Deke laughed, that high but pleasant sound. "Well," he said, "Chosen isn't far and we'll be back soon. You may go if you wish."

"And me!" Lamar added.

"I couldn't go without you," Deke said.

"Maybe he should ask his mama," Terry suggested.

"His pappy said he could" Deke vaulted across the floor on his arms. "Okay, boys, let's get out there before it gets too hot."

The sun was a white glare in a cloudless sky. Terry noticed the canals were lower than usual, exposing roots of aquatic growth, the cattails, sedge and saw grass going brown.

Crossing the Chosen bridge, planks grumbling beneath them, Deke said, "Wouldn't hurt to get some rain."

At the crest of the dike, Terry looked across miles of terrain, broken by clumps of live oak, palmetto and palm. Kramer Island spread away westward, a haven for waterfowl, frogs, and creatures which fed upon them.

Terry was surprised to see that Mr. Owen knew Deke. "Did it come, Charlie?"

"Yesterday, Deke. It's a beauty."

The fish camp owner pushed Deke's chair past covered stalls where fishermen kept their boats with outboard motors lifted. A rich smell of earthworms and bubbling minnow tanks made this a wonderful place. Mr. Owen guided Deke through the store to a wooden pier — an airboat! Deke must be rich, Terry thought, to have a new truck *and* an airboat.

"Think you can handle that, Deke?" Charlie Owen said.

Deke was grinning like a child. "Help me aboard, will you?"

As if to hug Deke, Mr. Owen lifted the legless man and placed him atop a high seat. Behind the seat, enclosed in wire mesh like a giant fan, were the glistening varnished blades of an airplane propeller driven by an automobile engine. There wasn't a hunting or fishing man in the Everglades who didn't aspire to own one of these.

Charlie Owen explained the gears, electrical starting system and steering mechanism.

"Twenty gallon capacity," Mr. Owen was saying, "with a reserve of twenty more — that ought to be ample."

"Excellent!" Deke said.

"This metal hull is faster than wood, Deke," Mr. Owen related. "Take it easy in the turns until you get the hang of it."

"Right."

There was a strap that crisscrossed Deke's chest to hold him in and an "emergency" bar to release it if the craft should flip.

"But don't flip," Mr. Owen warned. "Be cautious."

"Well taken," Deke said.

Charlie Owen got into one of two "jumper" seats lower and on either side of Deke's pilot's chair. Deke pushed a button. With a resounding roar, the vehicle came to life, sending ripples in every direction from the flat hull. Mr. Owen cast off the lines, pushing away from the dock, and as Deke eased the throttle, the blades whack-whack-whacked and then became a blur. The craft was propelled by wind blown backward, maneuvered by rudders which deflected the flow of air left or right.

Gaining speed, people watching from the dock, they turned into the main canal. Terry saw Mr. Owen hook his safety belt and suddenly, with a propulsion that made the viewers exclaim, the boat skimmed away. They watched until the throb of the propeller was a distantly pulsing brrr.

"How fast you reckon?" somebody asked.

"Thirty."

"Forty, by God!"

"He won't know where he is until he ain't," someone commented. Everybody laughed.

Never once in his entire life had Terry been on an airboat.

"It's too loud, Terry," Lamar said.

"I like it."

"Too loud," Lamar said.

Then, from the horizon, a rising hum like a monster mosquito zooming toward them and Deke was back again.

"How about it?" Deke yelled.

"Yessir!" Terry hollered.

"Well?" Deke pointed at the lower seats, motioning, "come on — "

"Too loud, Terry!" Lamar drew back.

"Come on, Lamar!"

"I don't want to."

Charlie Owen held the craft, helping Terry aboard. He hooked Terry's belt.

"How about Lamar?" Deke shouted.

"He's scared."

"Too loud!" Lamar called.

"Come on, Lamar," Deke urged. Lamar pressed against the building.

"Ready, Terry?"

"Yessir!"

The boar shuddered, the blades engaged, the hull rose, and suddenly they were moving. The wind was searing, the water a sheen of reflected sunlight, the canal like a corridor as they flew between tall grasses on either side. Birds rose before them and the boat roared under ascending flocks. Terry's lungs locked, his heart was a hammer in his throat.

Out of the canal and into open glades had taken only an instant it seemed to Terry — he twisted to look back and the canal seemed to flow away over the curve of earth; a whisk of grass flashed as they passed right over. He looked up and Deke was grinning, his black hair blown straight back.

Terry grabbed the side of the boat as, abruptly, they turned, the craft skipping sideways before the airflow shot them forward again. It maneuvered with incredible ease, crossing huge blankets of moist grass. Alligators, caught by surprise, swirled to dive. A water moccasin drowsing on a stump reared his head in alarm as he felt the shiver of the passing boat — but by then they were gone, flying, or as nearly flying as man could be while still touching water.

The roar lowered as the throttle was eased and Deke's

boat drifted. Man and boy looked at one another and laughed.

"What do you think?" Deke shouted.

"Great!"

"Betcha bottom dollar," Deke responded.

Then they were off again, skimming the surface, sometimes actually rising above it, the open glades an endless saucer and Deke in his high chair the tallest object to be seen. It was the most exhilarating thing Terry had ever experienced. Now and then he dared glance up, and Deke, overhead, laughed aloud, barely heard over the din of the engine.

They came to port slowly, the craft put-put-putting along the canal. Deke eased into a stall at dockside, where Charlie Owen awaited them.

"Just one thing, Charlie," Deke said. "It needs a better muffler."

Both men laughed.

"Hey, Lamar," Deke called. "How about helping me?"

"Don't touch the engine," Mr. Owen admonished. "It's hot."

"We have to lick that muffler problem," Deke said. "I can't go over the glades terrifying wildlife and my helper, too,"

"I'll work on it, Deke."

"Think you could lift me to my chair, Lamar?" Deke questioned.

"Yeah. I'm strong, Deke."

"Like your daddy showed you last night, okay?"

Terry saw Mr. Owen reach out, but the man didn't move to assist. Lamar stumbled unsteadily in the boat as it rocked, but hugging Deke as Charlie had done, he carried him to his wheelchair and put him in it. Face red, Deke looked up at Mr. Owen, then lifted his arms in triumph.

"Nothing to it!"

"As it should be," Mr. Owen said.

"The three musketeers," Deke indicated Terry and Lamar. "Thirsty as an Arab, Charlie. How about a soft drink?"

"Yeah!" Lamar said. Then, troubled, "I got scared, Deke."

"No problem, Lamar."

"It's too loud."

"We'll fix that."

"It was scary, wasn't it, Terry?" Lamar said.

"I like it."

"But it's too *loud*," Lamar insisted.

His ears still throbbed with aftereffects of the roaring engine. Terry sipped a Nehi orange drink and listened to Charlie Owen and Deke discuss a muffler system.

"The thing's going to be noisy, Deke," Charlie argued. "The propeller alone will be noisy."

"No doubt. But if you modify that muffler this way —"

It was obvious the two men had known one another a long time. First names, the familiarity with which they laughed and talked to one another. How long? From where?

In the truck, going back to Camp Osceola, Terry asked: "How did you meet Mr. Owen, Deke?"

"We played football against one another when I was in high school."

"You did?"

I grew up in Pahokee. Belle Glade and Pahokee are old rivals."

"I know."

"The Army wouldn't take him, but they took me,"

Deke said, but Terry saw it was a comment to himself. "Well," he said softly, "that airboat has legs aplenty."

Lamar was dozing, slumped against the truck door. Terry gazed out the window.

"Legs enough," Deke repeated. Then, to Terry, "Do you think Lamar will get over being afraid?"

"I don't know."

"I need him," Deke remarked.

"Yessir."

"Ah well," Deke drove down "C" Street, "God has provided so far. It'll work out. Somehow."

Terry swallowed noisily. Mama was getting out of their car, home from work.

"Isn't that your mother?"

"Yessir. She's home early."

"Good. I'll meet her now."

"You could come back later if you want to."

"Now's fine."

Mama turned at the front steps as the truck halted. When Terry stepped out, he detected a change in her expression.

"Mama, Deke wants to meet you."

She rounded the vehicle to the driver's side, smiling, but it wasn't genuine, Terry could tell.

"I'm T. R. Dekle," Deke said. "Everybody calls me Deke, Mrs. Calder."

"Pleased to meet you."

"I hope you won't mind," Deke said, "I took Terry to Chosen with me. I needed some help. He said you preferred to meet me. So I may have imposed a bit. If I did, I apologize."

"It isn't in the swamps," Terry said quickly.

"I know where it is, Terry."

"Where we go swimming all the time," Terry persisted.

Deke's green eyes caught the light and sparkled. "Don't often meet a boy who can recite Latin biological terms."

"He seems to absorb such things."

"I'm doing a book on the flora indigenous to the glades," Deke said. "I could use two good legs to climb for plants, tote and fetch. I could pay Terry a little something. The government is feeling generous toward veterans these days, so when I ask, they give."

"I doubt that is needed to entice Terry into the glades."

"No, apparently not. Perhaps we could sit down over a cup of coffee and discuss it."

"That would be fine."

"Tonight?"

"Not tonight. This weekend, perhaps."

"Good enough."

Lamar was leaning against the truck, head nodding. Terry shook the boy awake and Deke drove on home.

"You disobeyed me?" Mama asked.

"Did you mean I couldn't see him at all until you met him?" Terry reasoned.

"I suppose not."

"I didn't disobey then."

"Deke has a boat, Miss Mickey." Lamar followed them inside.

"You ought to go tell your mama you're home, Lamar," Terry said.

"It's too noisy, Miss Mickey."

Mama kicked off her high heels and sat slumped on the couch.

"Go home, Lamar," Terry growled.

"I'm hungry, Miss Mickey," Lamar said.

"Then go home," Mama suggested.

Alone with Mama, Terry held his silence. Her eyes closed, head back on the couch, Mama said, "I'm too tired to argue, Terry. Don't force the issue. Thank heavens they let us off early."

"Yes ma'am."

"The temperature in that office must've been a hundred."

"Yes ma'am."

She opened her eyes and looked at him. "You got too much sun today. Your nose is going to peel."

"Yes ma'am, Mama."

She closed her eyes again and Terry stood, waiting.

"He seems nice enough," Mama admitted.

"He is."

"Obviously concerned with my feelings about you."

"He is, Mama."

"All right, then. But no swamp trips until I have talked with him."

"You'll like him, Mama."

Her reply was a sigh.

"He's smart and he's handsome," Terry said. He thought he heard a chuckle.

"Mama?"

"What?"

"Do you like men who are shorter than you?"

"Nobody is shorter than me."

Mama awaited an explanation, but Terry dodged. "Want me to go and get Ann from the day-care center?"

"Would you?"

"Sure!"

When the door slammed, Mickey winced. After a moment, she rose, walked to the porch and looked toward Deke's house. Shorter than five feet two inches? Mickey unpinned her hair, letting it fall to her shoulders.

Down the street, his slightly bowed legs churning, Terry was racing toward the day-care center.

So, all right, thank you, God, she thought. After the war-long experience of knowing only men like Burrell Mason who'd been rejected by the military for a physical impairment, this would be good for Terry. Good to have somebody to look up to.

Seven

TERRY AWOKE with a start. Naked, except for underpants, he was clammy with sweat, the bedsheet thrown
aside. It was still dark. Ann snored in sibilant sighs. Ann
could sleep in a furnace.

Primordial wariness had wrenched his abdomen. He
was trembling, ears humming. Then, he realized it was —
nothing. No rumble of diesel or chug of coal-burning
engines; no breeze to give breath to whispering pines.
Gone was the clackety-clack of creaking boxcars, the hiss
of steam and percussion of couplings. From the packing
houses, silence. Terry crossed to a south window and
peered out.

It was so still, he heard the squawk of a bird disturbed
on its roost in a distant tree. Somewhere a dog yelped,
quit. The only constant came from the administration
building. Insects drawn to the security light droned in a

writing funnel, flying themselves to death.

"Psst —"

Muscles quivered, sinews taut.

"Psst —" from the window by Terry's bed.

"Ossie?"

"Can you come out?"

Terry slipped on trousers and a shirt, padding barefoot to the front steps.

From the dark, Ossie emerged, the glow of a cigarette tracing his passage. He took a puff, extended the butt and Terry accepted.

"I got to go throw circulars in colored town," Ossie whispered. "They need somebody else. Want to go?"

"I don't think I can."

"We could be back in a couple hours, working together."

"I'd have to be here before Mama left for work, or else —"

"Make a dollar," Ossie lured.

"I want to," Terry said, genuinely. "But Mama —"

"Terry!"

Ossie darted like a rabbit.

"Are you out there, Terry?"

"Yes, Mama." He heard slippers shuffling in the living room.

"Who's with you?" she asked.

"Ossie. He's going to throw circulars in town. He was asking if I could go."

Long pause. The reply stunned him, "I suppose you could."

"Hey, Ossie?"

"If," Mama said, "Ossie will come in. I won't have him standing out in the dark waiting while you get ready."

"Ossie?" Terry raised his voice.

A shadow rose from the hedge. "You have to come in," Terry said.

"How come?"

"I can't go if you don't come in."

"How come?"

Mama called, "Come on in, boys. I'll cook breakfast while Terry gets dressed."

"We ain't got time," Ossie protested to Terry.

"Either do it," Terry replied, "or go alone." He heard Ossie panting to dispel the scent of tobacco.

The dilemma was simple: Ossie dreaded going to colored town alone as much as he feared meeting Mama. But the vegetable growers were suffering for labor and they would pay well to distribute their handbills which enticed workers with descriptions of wages, benefits, and the condition of crops to be harvested. Few boys would rise before dawn and go into colored town to pass out the circulars. Those who dared earned high pay.

"Smell my breath," Ossie said.

"You stink," Terry admitted.

Ossie was drunk on oxygen. "Well," he said, "she ain't my mother."

Mama whipped eggs in a skillet as Terry and Ossie slinked along a far wall, holding their breath in passing.

"Wash up, boys."

In the bathroom, dressing anew, Terry ordered, "Brush your teeth."

"Hell, I got no brush!"

"Suck some toothpaste, then."

Ossie bent over the lavatory, liquid squishing, cheeks puffing, then threw back his head and gargled. Terry did the same. In the kitchen, Mama paused. *Smoking* —

Hot tea poured, Mama sat with the two boys. "Hmmm,"

she said. "You look pretty good up close, Ossie."

Ossie swallowed toast. He sounded like a bullfrog croaking.

"You notice," Mama said, "I don't have horns. I don't bite."

Ossie stole a glance at Terry and Terry tried to smile.

"I would consider it a privilege," Mama said, "if you come to our house, Ossie. Otherwise, if I ever visit your home I would feel I should stay outside, also."

"You wouldn't come to my house," Ossie replied.

Levity lost, Mickey asked, "Where does your mother work?"

"Glades Café."

"Your father?"

"Ain't got a daddy."

"Nobody seems to these days. Would you like another slice of toast?"

"No."

"All right," Mickey said, rising. "Do a good job, boys." She returned to her bedroom to ease their tension. A moment later, the front door closed gently. They'd left food uneaten.

Taking quick, short steps to stay atop ties between railroad tracks, Ossie muttered, "That's the kind of crap I hate."

He meant Mama.

"All smiles and sweet talk and not a true word in it."

"Hey, watch it," Terry warned.

"No wonder white people lie. They grow up lying and call it being polite."

"Ossie, watch it."

"You know it's true," Ossie concluded.

They crossed a trestle, then doubled back on dirt streets

toward town. Ossie slowed to a walk as they approached the hiring hall. "Hold out for a buck fifty," he said.

"They won't pay it."

"They'll pay."

Sitting at a low desk under a bare light bulb, the "straw boss" chewed his cigar, peering at Ossie from beneath a green visor pocked with holes. The man wore a soiled tee-shirt and khaki shorts, a mosquito feeding unnoticed on his hairy shoulder. Now and then he shifted the cigar between thick teeth and it lifted to burn a new hole in his visor.

"This is Terry," Ossie said. "He'll help me."

"You know what time it is?" the man said.

"We still have time."

"The hell you do. You ain't no better than the niggers, you know that? You come in here begging for work. I say be here at four with a helper and here you come at five with a kid!"

To Terry, "How old are you, kid?"

"Nineteen."

Somebody in the shadows laughed softly.

"I brought him," Ossie alibied, "because he knows where the Bahamians sleep. He knows the best workers. His daddy used to manage Camp Osceola."

"Then he ain't no friend of mine."

"He knows the workers," Ossie reasoned.

"You won't get out five hundred circulars before they're on the streets listening to barkers."

"Working together, we'll get out more than you need," Ossie stated. "And we'll get the best workers."

His eyes never leaving Ossie, the man lifted his voice, "Whatcha think, Louie?"

"Might as well."

"Buck fifty apiece," Ossie said.

"Buck fifty. Jesus! *I* don't make a buck fifty. For a few lousy circulars?"

Ossie stood, impassive, jaw set, face square in the harsh light.

The man eyed Terry. "Your father know you're here?"

"He's in Poland investigating atrocities."

"Investigating what?"

"With the Red Cross."

"That figures," the man in the shadows said.

"Next thing I know, your mama will be down here with the sheriff looking for my ass and you'll have all my circulars."

"She knows we're here," Terry said.

"Shit."

"She fed us breakfast," Ossie said.

"*Bull* shit."

Ossie leaned across the table and blew in the man's face. "Eggs," he said.

"You're wasting time, Mac," the voice from the dark.

"All right, I'm going to give you five hundred circulars each. I expect a thousand black asses to show up this morning. If I find you threw one circular in the garbage or a canal, I'll skin you alive."

"Buck fifty apiece," Ossie persisted.

"After the circulars are delivered —"

"Half now, half after," Ossie bargained.

The man fished coins from his pocket and counted seventy-five cents to each of them. Then with a penknife he cut the sisal cord binding a stack of handbills. He gave half to Ossie, the rest to Terry.

"Put them under every door. If a body stirs, put it in his hand."

Outside, Terry said, "The Bahamian people are at the edge of town."

"Yeah," Ossie acknowledged.

"Want to go there first?"

"No. One blackie is as good as another. Let's work town first."

"Apart or together?"

"Together."

They felt their way up steep narrow stairs of a tenement house. Boards creaked as they moved down a long hall pushing circulars under each door. A wave of roaches skittered through debris, up the walls, and looked down with antennae waggling. Acrid fumes of a "community" toilet and heat trapped in the windowless corridor took their breath. On the third floor, they walked through a large room in which men, women and children slept on pallets, paying for the privilege. On balconies exposed to the elements, men lay covered with newspapers. Anytime they heard voices, Terry would tap lightly and wait.

"Who there?"

"Want a circular?"

The door opened a crack. "Child, where's your mama? She know you here?"

"She knows."

"I bet she do."

Terry blew at the woman. "Eggs," he said. But he wasn't near enough to prove his point.

Outside the building, Ossie said, "Filthy niggers."

"They aren't dirty," Terry said, hotly. "The place where they stay is dirty. My daddy said that's why the camps are important, to help people get out of here."

"If you like Indians, I guess you'd like niggers too."

"Yes, I do. I'm not ashamed that I do."

Standing in an alley, sensing Ossie's animosity, Terry said, "We're going to miss the Bahamians." The sky was growing pale. They still had hundreds of circulars.

"Okay," Ossie conceded. "Let's go."

Soaked by perspiration, their clothes beginning to chafe from body salt, they jogged toward a field at the edge of town. Here, in automobiles, trucks, under lean-tos and improvised tents, the Bahamians segregated themselves from other laborers.

Because of the war, America let them come from the islands to harvest sugarcane and perishable produce. Known for honesty and hard work, these people were sought by growers. Terry liked their colorful clothes, the way they talked — the music they could produce with only empty barrels and the tops of garbage cans. The men liked to tease him about a head of hair "on fy-ahr."

They gathered around smoldering embers seeking refuge from mosquitos. Women prepared meals of "chick-pea" and made "island tea," a beverage that wrenched the belly and curled Terry's tongue. He gave each person a circular, grinning.

"Ah, boy! What say dis?"

Terry paused, listening to the melody of somebody reading aloud from the circular — "hom-pair" for hamper, "ku-wah-tuh" for quarter.

Some offered to share their breakfasts, but Terry saw the tip of the rising sun and he still had circulars to distribute. When he glanced back, down straight and unpaved streets, the air was russet with rising dust as trucks arrived to transport laborers. Ossie was waiting at the edge of the encampment.

"I still have more than half," Terry said.

"Chunk them."

"Remember what the man said," Terry admonished.

"Probably won't pay us anyway. Chunk them."

But Terry carried his handbills, following.

"You show up with those," Ossie warned, "and you ain't going to get paid."

A white man on the rear of an approaching truck shouted, "Twenty cents a hamper — fresh field, good condition — twenty cents a hamper!"

Black and brown and tan faces observed stoically, waiting.

"Twenty-five then," the barker yelled. "Twenty-five a hamper — a bean field never picked —"

A few moved forward but didn't climb aboard.

"Cold water all day," another man called. "Twenty-seven cents a hamper pole beans —"

When the best offer came, the first workers to accept climbed into trucks to sit along either side and on benches down the center. Late comers were left to crowd in, standing all the way to the fields.

"I'm telling you," Ossie said, "you got to chunk them papers or won't neither of us get paid!"

Terry put the circulars in Ossie's outstretched hands. Ossie dropped them in a steel barrel where embers glowed.

To Terry's surprise, the man in the hiring hall delivered their money without comment. Elated, the boys alternately skipped and walked fast toward town.

"Let's go to the Glades Café," Ossie said.

"If we're going to buy something," Terry countered, "let's buy hot dogs."

"Come on," Ossie urged. "We can eat anything we want and it's free."

"Free?"

"Sure. My mom works there."

They ran along a canal, through back lots of stores facing Main Street, then up an alley beside city jail.

"Hey!" a hand waved between iron bars. "Get me a cigarette, eh, boy? Boy!"

They passed crates of refuse swarming with flies and entered the café through the kitchen. Inside, sweating cooks prepared food, waitresses shouted, and a man washing dishes clanged utensils in a double tub.

With practiced ease, Ossie led Terry through swinging doors to a corner booth out front. A cigarette lay burning in an ashtray. Ossie took two puffs, put it back.

Mrs. Knight was serving a table full of men across the room. Laughter erupted and one of the men stroked her back. She bumped him with a hip, and again they laughed.

Ossie glanced at Terry. He pretended not to see. Now the man had an arm around her waist.

"Let's go," Ossie blurted.

"We didn't eat."

"Forget it."

As they reached the swinging kitchen door, Mrs. Knight called, "Hi, Sweetie!"

But Ossie was running now, with Terry following, outside through the alley, back to the canal, and still Ossie loped.

"Ossie, slow down."

Ossie kicked the ground. Terry measured his words. "We could go to the packing house. Get a hot dog."

"They're closed. Switching to beans for tonight."

"How about an orange drink at Poole's grocery? We could get some salted peanuts to go with it."

"No."

"I can make a sandwich at my house. Iced tea, maybe.

Nobody's there."

"Sonsofbitches."

"Or we could pick guavas —"

"Sonsofbitches," Ossie said again. He wheeled and ran. Ossie could run fast and long. Terry didn't try to follow.

That night, with supper finished and Ann in bed, Terry put away clean dishes while Mama wrote to Daddy. Another day and still no mail, but Mama wrote every day.

"Anything you'd like to say to your father?"

"Say I love him."

"Anything else?"

Terry stood, dishtowel in hand, thinking. "It would take too long."

"Tell me and I'll try to shorten it."

Terry opened his mouth, then closed it. "Say I love him, I guess."

After a minute, Mama said, "Anything I could listen to?"

Terry turned quickly, "Mama, if you like somebody a lot and that somebody doesn't like other somebodies you like, what can you do about it?"

"Anyone I know?"

"Ossie."

"Who, besides white people, does Ossie dislike?"

"Colored people."

"Prejudice has confounded men for a long time, Terry."

"He hates black people, white people, Indians —"

"Indians!"

"Indians, too."

After a long pause, Mama said, "Well, I suspect Ossie reflects what he thinks he sees in the eyes of others."

She pulled Terry to her. "I would say," Mama said, "nothing can defeat hate but love. You be understanding of Ossie and maybe Ossie will see others in a different light."

She pushed back his red hair, touched the tip of his nose with a fingertip. "Why don't you go on to bed?"

"It's so hot."

"You could sleep on the porch."

As he carried bedding to the front porch, Mickey read again her letter to Gerald — dull, uninspiring — and worse, she'd succumbed to the anger and frustration of no reply. She tore the letter in squares and dropped it into a waste basket.

Up the street, the new neighbor's truck pulled in. Mickey watched headlights go out. Curiosity drew her into the yard. She heard the truck door slam; the screen door opened. But she didn't see him.

Mickey strolled up "C" Street, pausing for a better look through windows which had no blinds or curtains. She glanced both ways, up and down the row of houses. Not really spying. Just interested.

Ah. He rose into her line of vision, standing at the kitchen cupboard. Odd — the way he moved — Mickey stepped back to the street again for fear someone might see her.

Terry was wrong, she thought. Mr. Dekle wasn't short. He stood at cabinets identical to hers and looked into the highest shelf.

Who knew what formed the impressions of a child?

Eight

"**I COULD GO** with you, Deke," Terry said.

"Not today. I'm going to La Belle."

"I could go," Terry insisted.

"What about your mother?"

"You could talk to her."

Deke leaned against a doorjamb, buttoning his shirt. "Is this a good time for that?"

"Sure."

"Hmm."

Deke rolled onto his back atop a thin mattress he used for a bed. He pulled trousers over two short stumps, buttoned the fly, sat up again, pulling a belt through the loops.

"See, the thing is," Terry explained, "Mama wants to talk to you. Then I can go anywhere. Overnight, even."

He watched Deke roll long pants legs and pin them.

Where the legs of his body met the trousers, he'd sewn patches so the fabric wouldn't wear prematurely.

"After Mama talks to you," Terry urged, "everything will be fine."

"Think so?"

"Sure. And I could save lots of time."

"How's that?"

"Running to get things and stuff like that."

"That'd save time, all right."

"If Mama could only talk to you —"

"We'll see."

That meant "no." Terry said, "She's home right now. Today is her day off. Now is a good time."

"Is she expecting me?"

"She said you said this weekend was fine."

"Yes, I did."

"This *is* the weekend, Deke."

The man balanced himself on extended arms, gazing at Terry with steady eyes. Then Deke pivoted to a mirror leaning against a wall and brushed his hair. Terry heard a crackle of static electricity, watched coal black hair rise with each stroke.

"You need to wet it," Terry observed. Then, "What do you think, Deke? Think you could come talk to her before you go to La Belle?"

"Terry —"

"Please Deke. It won't take very long."

"I'm fairly sure of that."

"Right this minute she's down there."

Again, Deke looked at him with unwavering eyes. The unsettling expression made Terry say, "I could go say you're on your way. Or something."

"Okay."

"Right now?"

"Might as well. Come tell me what she says."

"Right!" Terry raced out and down the street. He ignored Ann's call, beckoning to a palm tree she was trying to climb. Into the house, impatiently he waited for Velma Mason and Mama to take notice.

". . . the radio said over five hundred Superfortresses bombed Kobe today," Velma reported.

"Horrible."

"Fire bombs. I read somewhere that the Japanese build their houses of bamboo, cane and paper. It must burn very quickly."

Terry shifted from one foot to the other. He breathed harder. Sniffed loudly.

"Still," Velma said, "Tojo claims they'll fight to the last man, woman or child."

"Dear Lord," Mickey replied.

Terry cleared his throat, scuffed his feet, inched nearer.

"Terry, what *is* it?"

"May Deke come now?"

"Can't you see Velma and I are visiting?"

"He needs to talk to you now, Mama. He's going to La Belle."

"La Belle? You can't go to La Belle, Terry."

"Mama," fiercely, "why not?"

"I don't know this person, Terry. I have to know him before I —"

"He wants to come now, Mama. He's ready to come right now. So you can know him."

Mama looked at Velma and shook her head. "Who?" Velma asked.

"Your new neighbor. Mr. Dekle."

"Poor man."

"Mama," Terry's voice lifted an octave, "can he come *now*?"

"What do you mean 'poor?'" Mama asked Velma.

"You don't know?"

"Mama," Terry pushed between them. "He's a hero, Mama."

"What, Velma?"

"He lost his legs at Tarawa."

"Dear God," Mickey moaned.

"Burrell said he's a botanist."

"His legs," Mickey said. "How ever will he —"

Terry was trembling. He put a cold, small hand on Mama's arm. "He drives a truck, Mama. He has an airboat."

"How do you know?"

"I see him. He —"

"You've been on this airboat?"

"He's good at it, Mama. He knows how to do everything." Terry's eyes were filling; he dared not blink, "Please. You said you would meet him. He's ready. He's waiting."

"He asked Burrell if Lamar could accompany him," Velma added. "I fret about every little thing, I guess. Over my objections, Lamar is going to help the poor fellow. He needs somebody to lift him in and out of his chair, things like that."

"Oh, Terry," Mama whispered.

"Mama," Terry burst into tearful rage, "he has good arms and he can do anything anybody can do. But he needs somebody to climb trees and —"

"Suppose you get out somewhere and have trouble?" Mama questioned. "Motor trouble. Twenty or thirty miles from anywhere, suppose you can't start the motor.

Then what, Terry?"

"He can fix motors."

"Suppose he can't."

"But he can."

"Terry! Suppose he can not. Then what?"

"We'd —" *walk? swim? how?* "— think of something."

"I hadn't thought of all that," Velma said. "I'd better speak to Burrell about this. But in Burrell's state of mind, with his sympathy for someone afflicted, I don't know —"

Terry demanded, "Can he come? Now?"

"Terry, we're inviting an unhappy encounter we could easily avoid if —"

"You said you would meet him. You promised you'd talk to him. He's waiting," Terry cried. "He's up there waiting."

Velma winced, rising. "I'd better go," she said.

"Have you met him, Velma?"

"Over the backyard fence, so to speak. If you want my opinion, I haven't one. As a matter of fact, you changed the one I had."

"It's not fair, Mama," Terry seethed. "You're doing what Ossie does. You don't know Deke."

"I know that without legs, he is limited in movement, Terry."

"I can help him."

"Yes. But could he help you if the need arises? Terry, I want to say you can go. I want to very much. I want you to be able to do things you wish to do. But out in the depths of the glades, on your own?"

"Lamar will be there, too."

"Don't be too sure," Velma said. "Well. I'm going."

When the front door closed, Mickey took Terry's shoulders and held him at arm's length. "You're a reasonable person, Terry. If you were me, what would you say?"

"I'd say okay."

"Damn it, child! This isn't a game. You are asking me to let you put your life in the hands of a man who may not be able to help himself. Suppose the boat overturned, or caught fire?"

"Mama," Terry whispered, "you said you would."

"I said no such thing! I said if this man were responsible, if he met my approval, then you might go. But I assumed he was physically capable. You surely understand that. But whether you do or not, I must be wise enough not to yield to this pressure."

Terry snatched free and whirled to run. Mickey grabbed, but the boy lurched away and bounded through the back door.

"Terry!"

Across the lawn, through the pines, scrambling up a cinder bank of the railroad tracks, Mickey saw a final flash of shirt as he crawled beneath boxcars toward the packing houses.

Damn. But what else? How else?

Mickey walked to the front door and peered up the street. The truck was there.

He was there. Waiting.

"Mr. Dekle?"

"Mickey heard a thumping sound from within. She called again, "Mr. Dekle, it's Mickey Calder."

"Fair warning," a soft oath, "this place is a mess."

Mickey laughed deliberately. "That's why I couldn't let you come to my house. May I come in?"

More thumping. A lump rose in Mickey's throat.

"Come in, Mrs. Calder." He braced himself in the front door beyond the porch.

She had tried to prepare herself, but Mickey was still shocked. She accepted the firm handshake of this man who came only as high as her waist. He was deeply tanned, with rugged features. He gazed up, enduring her too-light comments before saying, "Come in, please. Forgive my place. Furniture is something I don't use and seldom have need to offer. Can you stand sitting on a bean bag chair?"

"A bean bag chair?"

"Yeah," he said, "I made it to fill a need. Punch it around and make it fit your body."

Mickey did this with an elbow, but she felt her skirt rise and settled for leaning on one arm. There were boxes as yet unpacked, the kitchen cabinets strewn with oddiments, a lamp without a shade. She glanced in a nearby crate.

"Books," she said. "I've been missing people who read."

"Mostly things related to botany, horticulture, cellular structure."

"Interesting," Mickey commented, but her tone said otherwise.

He turned from the door where he'd been, and with a vaulting motion crossed to another sack of beans. He wiggled his hips to settle himself in the bag, and only then did his hands leave the floor.

"You aren't interested in fiction?" Mickey questioned.

"I've had a spate of drama, I suppose."

She unlocked her eyes from his, looked at bare walls. "Could you use some assistance moving in?"

"I'm in," he said. "Burrell Mason from next door has

been helping. His son, Lamar. And Terry."

"Yes," Mickey said. "Terry."

With a gaze she began to resent, Deke stared. "Terry seems to admire you a great deal, Mr. Dekle."

"Could we get on a first-name basis?"

"Certainly. Mickey."

"Deke," he replied.

"Terry has spoken of little else since you arrived."

He waited.

"Terry is fascinated with swamps. The glades. If he had his way, he'd spend every summer in the midst of it."

"A fine boy."

"Yes, he is. A handful now and then. But since his father went overseas, he's been very mature and helpful to me."

Deke nodded.

"I guess every mother worries needlessly," Mickey confessed. "Skinned knees and stubbed toes. But a child has to have certain freedoms, doesn't he?"

No comment.

"We find ourselves trying to channel adolescent energy, guide and direct without being overly protective. Do you know what I mean?"

"Yes."

"I would let Terry climb a tree of reasonable height, knowing that to fall would break an arm, or could possibly be fatal. But I wouldn't allow him to scale a skyscraper. He assumes that permission to climb a tree is also approval to climb the building. Do you see the distinction?"

"Of course."

"What worries me," Mickey plunged, "is safety."

"I can understand that."

"I give Terry tremendous freedom, short of being irresponsible. I suspect he'd take it anyway, if I refused. He's always been headstrong. I yield as much as possible and try to compromise."

"Mrs. Calder —"

"Mickey," she corrected.

"Yes. Mickey. Let me help you. You don't want Terry to accompany me into the glades, is that correct?"

"It isn't that I don't want to," Mickey blustered.

"In essence. That's the point?"

"I — well — I'm afraid —"

"Damn it, say it! You worry that I can't take care of him or of myself, right?"

Face crimson, Mickey said, "Right."

"Well," he said, "I can understand that. I was fairly sure that would be your response. I tried to discourage Terry, taking him where he would always be in safe surroundings, such as the fish camp at Chosen. I would never place him in danger."

"No, no, I didn't mean to insinuate —"

"Nor for that matter, would I place myself in jeopardy. I think we can both get off the hook if you're open to it."

"Yes?"

"Except for those trips I make into the swamps, I could take him along. I like Terry. The truth is, frankly, I like being accepted on an equal basis, which children do — and adults don't — these days. If you have no objections, I will allow him to accompany me, always with safety and his well-being in mind. Otherwise, he won't go."

"Yes, of course."

"We can avoid a conflict here, I think. Terry is a smart child. He knows there are places he cannot go. But anyplace he'd go alone, particularly, he will resent not being able to go with me. Do you agree?"

"I agree."

"There's an element of risk in anything. But beyond the hazards of life and living, I will protect him. Will you accept that?"

"That's fine."

"Make no mistake, I need his young legs. But I won't send him up a tall building."

Mickey smiled.

"I understand your husband is stationed in Poland."

"The last I heard, yes — Poland. Investigating Nazi atrocities. But I haven't heard from him in several weeks, so that may have changed. Gerald — my husband — has such empathy for all people, I dread to think what this experience will do to him. I worry that he isn't writing because he's so miserable."

"After an agonizing day wallowing in the mire of man's inhumanity," Deke said, "he may be too exhausted to write anything but truth. And he wants to shield you from that."

"Probably."

They avoided eye contact for a moment. Then Mickey said, "I guess I'd better go tell Terry the good news."

"What have you read recently?"

She settled back again. "I read everything. They've started printing inexpensive books in soft covers — pocketbooks they call them. I buy every one I can find, good or bad."

"I have a copy of *For Whom the Bell Tolls* you could borrow."

"I've read it. Thank you. Did you like it?"

He hunched his shoulders. "I haven't read it. It was a gift."

Mickey kept her knees together, maneuvering to rise. "Perhaps you'd like to borrow some of my books?" On her feet, she added, "But you don't read fiction."

"My study takes so much time."

"Well. Thank you, Deke. I feel better now."

"Thanks for coming by. Oh, Mickey —"

She paused at the door.

"Tell Terry I'll see him Monday. Today I'm going to La Belle. Unless —"

"Yes?"

"Unless you'd both like to ride down with me? It's a good day for a drive."

"No, I'm sorry. Where in the world are you getting gasoline?"

"Uncle Sam is providing it. Getting your legs shot off has its benefits."

"I'm limited to three gallons a week. Sometimes I get home from work on the fumes."

"I have a grant for research." He thumped toward her, looking past her legs as though at the sunshine. "That includes my truck, airboat, paraphernalia — and gas. The national conscience, that kind of thing."

"You deserve it."

"Don't we all?" He shook her hand, holding it, balancing with his other. "Thanks for coming."

"Won't you drop by some evening? I've been saving my stamps and we're about to trade them all for one good pot roast, if I can find one."

"Great. Let me know."

Mickey walked down "C" Street, acutely aware of his eyes following. He was flirty. She shuddered, as if to shake off an unpleasant situation. But it hadn't been all that unpleasant, had it? He was a gentleman. Thoughtful.

Educated. God knows what he'd endured. Mickey entered her house, eased the screened door shut.

Ann was at the kitchen table smearing peanut butter on a slice of bread. Lamar was eating with her.

"Miss Mickey," Lamar said, "my ma says I can't be friends with Deke."

"Don't talk with your mouth full of food, Lamar."

Lamar closed his eyes tightly, swallowing. "Ma says he'll hurt me. He won't hurt me, will he, Miss Mickey?"

"Oh Lord," Mickey sighed.

"Ma said Pa was wrong. She said Pa didn't know nothing about swamps or anything."

Mickey leaned against a kitchen cabinet.

"Want another sandwich?" Ann questioned.

"Yeah." Then, to Mickey, "Pa cried again, Miss Mickey."

As Mickey turned, Ann was caught licking the knife. Taking the utensil and the jar of peanut butter, Mickey said gently, "Go ask your mother to come see me, Lamar."

"I can't. I can't, Miss Mickey."

"Why not?"

"Ma took Pa to the hospital."

"The hospital?"

"I hit him with a stick, Miss Mickey. I hit him on his head. He was bleeding."

Mickey capped the peanut butter with trembling hands.

"Pa said he was going to kill her, Miss Mickey. I had to hit him. I used Ma's broomstick. Ma said I hit him too hard."

"Lamar, go wash your face and hands," Mickey suggested.

"With soap?" Lamar asked at the doorway.

"Yes. Soap."

Mickey placed the knife in the sink. When she turned, Terry was standing on the back porch.

"I saw Deke," she said. "I think it will be all right for you to go some of the places he wants to go. He and I had a long talk, and he —"

"He can't go without Lamar," Terry said angrily. "Now you've made it so Lamar can't go."

"Pa laid real still," Lamar was telling Ann in the bathroom. "Ma hollered and hollered, but Pa didn't move."

Wearily, Mickey said, "Terry, I have compromised with you and Deke. I can't tell Velma and Burrell what to do with Lamar."

Terry glared at her, turned on a heel, and walked out.

Was nothing simple? Nothing normal?

"Pa cried and cried," Lamar related.

"I cry sometimes," Ann said. "If I hurt myself, I do."

Through the kitchen window, Mickey saw Terry climb toward the railroad tracks, his shoulders bent as if he bore the cares of the world. He wore short pants which he despised because she hadn't done the laundry.

"Miss Mickey — uh Ann cries and I cry and Pa cries. Everybody cries now and then, don't they?"

"Yes, Lamar. Now and then everybody cries."

Nine

MAMA SLAMMED HER CAR door and rolled down
the window. She pushed the starter with her foot. The
motor turned, caught, chugged and died. She tried again,
holding the steering wheel with both arms straight, brac-
ing herself against the seat.

"What's wrong, Mama?"

"I don't know, Terry."

She looked around, hesitated a moment. Then, again,
the motor churning, coughing.

"Oh dear," Mama said softly. "I'm going to be late."

"Want me to get somebody?"

"Who?"

"Deke, maybe."

"No."

She tried again—the motor quit.

"Deke will know what's wrong," Terry suggested.

"Knowing what's wrong and being able to correct it are two different things."

Mama made another attempt. The motor whined, growled, seemed to catch, then stopped.

"All right," Mama conceded. "It isn't going to cure itself. Go ahead, Terry."

He ran to Deke's house. Boy, what luck! If Deke fixed the car, Mama would know he could do anything. He rapped on the front door, his nose pressed to the screen wire.

"Yo!"

"Deke, it's Terry. Mama can't start her car."

"What's the problem?"

"I don't know. I told her you could fix it."

Deke came to the door, looking past Terry down the street. "I'm not much of a mechanic these days," he said. "I can't reach the motor."

"If you tell me what to do, maybe I can help."

Deke pushed himself up on his fingertips, stretching to see over a poinsettia growing next to his porch. From a radio inside, women sang, "Mares eat oats and does eat oats and little lambs eat ivy . . . "

"All right," Deke said. "Get my chair."

Terry hauled the chair outside and held it for Deke to climb aboard. He trotted alongside as Deke propelled himself with smooth strokes of the wheels.

"I'm sorry to bother you," Mama apologized.

"Give it a try and let me hear it."

Lamar appeared on the run. "My pa is coming!"

Burrell Mason lurched toward them on crutches, his legs thrown forward two at a time, in braces.

"We're a fine team," Deke announced by way of greeting.

"Bits and pieces," Mr. Mason said. "It's hotter'n satan's whore and barely daylight."

Mr. Mason had a shaved placed on his scalp. Beneath gauze, Terry saw the black ends of a doctor's stitching.

Deke called to Mama, "Release the hood, Mickey!" Then to Mr. Mason, "What happened to your noggin, Burrell?"

"I hit him," Lamar said cheerfully, "I hit him with a stick."

"Sounds like it isn't getting any gas," Mr. Mason said to Deke.

"He was going to kill Ma," Lamar continued, "so I hit him."

"Maybe the fuel line is clogged," Deke said.

"Do you have gas in this thing, Mickey?" Burrell asked.

"Not much."

"Ah hah," Deke said. He unscrewed the gas cap and locked the wheels of his chair. "Help me rock the car, Lamar."

Lamar rocked it so hard Mama's head jerked back and forth. Deke put his ear to the funnel, listening.

"I think it's empty."

Mama tried to smile. "A fine way to start the week."

"Those tires won't last much longer, either."

"Are you trying to completely depress me?"

"Let me give you a ride to work."

"I knew you'd know what's wrong," Terry said. "I told you he'd know, didn't I, Mama?"

"Deke," Lamar reported, "my ma says I can't go with you anymore."

Burrell Mason growled, "Lamar—"

"Ma said," Lamar mimed, "Not on your *life!*"

"Some problem?" Deke questioned.

"I don't have to tell you," Burrell Mason's lip curled. "You know better than anybody. Damned woman."

"You wouldn't hurt me, would you, Deke?"

"Not for anything."

"I apologize for Velma," Mr. Mason said.

"No need, Burrell. Don't worry about it." Then to Terry, "Get my car keys off the kitchen counter and let's go. Your mama will be late."

In Deke's truck, Mama sat between them clutching her pocketbook, eyes forward, while Deke worked gears and accelerator controls on the steering wheel.

"Did you see that, Mama?"

"What?" *She knew what.*

"He's got everything where he can reach it."

Mama seared him with a glare.

With the rising sun on their left, they drove to Okeelanta. The sugar refinery rose amid an ocean of cane. They halted at the entrance and Mama said to the guard, "They're giving me a ride to work this morning."

Deke gazed at the building looming ahead. "Do they refine brown sugar or white?"

"Mostly white."

Deke eased over a hump in the pavement, a speed break. "You like your job?"

"I know how to do it," Mama said. "Bookkeeping."

They stopped at a walkway leading to the office. Out in the fields, the clatter of machinery was a soft tattoo, the chant of workers a distant harmony. Dust rose on the horizon.

"Do you get all the sugar you want?"

"We aren't supposed to."

"What time should we come to pick you up?"

"Three o'clock, if that's convenient."

"We'll be here."

Mama closed the truck door, paused. "Do you need sugar?"

"I don't use much sugar. I was thinking of a trade for tires—you need them."

"I couldn't do that."

Terry shut his eyes tightly, lips pursed for a kiss. "Be good today," Mama murmured, and walked toward the office with short, self-concious steps.

Terry watched Deke watch Mama's walk. Deke smiled faintly, shook his head. "Bits and pieces," he said.

Driving back toward Belle Glade, Terry tried to penetrate Deke's moody silence.

"Can you still go to the swamps without Lamar?"

"It poses a problem."

"He was afraid of the airboat anyway," Terry said. "Maybe I could find somebody else with a strong back."

"Don't worry about it. Are you thirsty red-on-the-head?"

"The concession stand at the packinghouse is closed," Terry said. "We could go to a service station."

"They don't sell what I want."

Deke turned in at the Silver Dollar Café, then sat there looking at the place, motor idling. Stake-body trucks were lined along a platform, drivers waiting to sell their produce to the packing houses. From the opened door of the Silver Dollar Café came a whine of fiddles. Terry heard Renée laugh.

"They may not let you in," Deke observed.

"Sure they will. I come here lots of times."

Deke got out of the truck, into his wheelchair and Terry held open the café door. Deke bumped hard against the threshold and rolled into the dimly lighted room.

"Don't let nobody play with your legs," Renée was saying, "unless he promises to marry you."

Deke shoved a chair out of his path. Conversation lulled as they approached. He selected a table in the rear and turned to face the room.

"What'll you have, soldier?" Renée asked.

"Terry?"

"Big orange drink."

"And a cold Pabst. Keep your eye on me—I'm going to need tender loving care."

Renée shouted their order and the cigar-smoking owner plucked bottles from a low icebox.

When she returned, Deke dug a purse from his pocket, "How much?"

On the house, soldier."

"No. I prefer—"

But Renée was gone and Deke would have had to shout. He lifted his bottle to the man behind the counter and got a nod in return.

"Where'd you catch it?" A voice from a nearby booth.

"Tarawa."

"Filthy Nips."

Deke sipped beer, gazing at Terry.

"Yellow cowards," the man said.

"Not cowards," Deke replied mildly.

A woman directly across the room smiled at Deke. Deke smiled in return.

"I think she likes you," Terry whispered.

Deke chuckled. "Drink your drink, redhead."

The friendly woman came to join them later. By then,

Deke was laughing a lot and Terry was so full of soda he thought he'd pop. The men talked about how many Americans might still die before Japan lost the war. They talked about firebombs and paper houses. Terry watched the bubbles of the jukebox, imagining houses afire, people burning, bombs waggling down from planes overhead. He'd seen it in the Movietone News, people screaming, babies crying. He wondered how long it took to build a house out of paper.

"Keep an eye on the clock, redhead," Deke advised. "Don't wanna keep your sweet mama waiting."

"It's two o'clock, Deke."

The friendly woman had an arm around Deke's shoulder and was drinking his beer. It was all right, because they wouldn't let Deke pay for anything.

Finally, driving toward Okeelanta, Terry said, "Do you hate the Japanese?"

Deke's head lolled as they hit a bump.

"If they shot off my legs," Terry said, "I guess I'd hate them, too."

At the sugar mill gate, Deke told the guard they'd come for Mama. Then, very slowly they drove on, still in first gear.

"I guess Japaneses soldiers are mostly Nazis," Terry suggested.

"Cut from a weave that seems similar, but fanaticism of a different cloth."

"What does that mean?"

"It means," Deke said quietly, "I don't hate Japanese."

Mama was waiting. "On the minute!" she smiled. But inside the truck her expression altered.

"A nip of spirits," Deke said.

They rode home without another word.

Mama sat on the side of Terry's bed. Ann was already sleeping. "Where did you go today?"

"With Deke."

"But where?"

"The Silver Dollar Café. Are you angry because Deke drank some beer?"

"I drink beer now and then, but not with a child in my car."

"Deke knows a lot about Japanese people."

"I dare say."

"He doesn't hate them. If somebody shot off my legs, I'd hate them."

The only light came from the kitchen through the bedroom door. Mama's face was unfathomable.

"I think he found a girl friend."

"Oh?"

"I think she really likes him. She sat with us. Real close. You know."

"Yes."

"I told Deke she liked him."

Mama didn't make a sound, but Terry thought he felt her laugh.

"Deke didn't believe it either."

"Well, I believe you."

"Don't you think he's handsome, Mama?"

"He's nice looking."

"If he had legs, would you be friends?"

"Terry. It isn't his legs. Adults make friends more slowly than children."

"But if he *had* legs, you'd really like him?"

"Which reminds me. It may make Deke uncomfortable for you to discuss his legs in the presence of others."

"I don't think so. If people would leave him alone, he'd

be fine."

"Leave him alone?"

"Trying to push his chair. Things like that."

"People want to help, Terry."

"He can do it by himself."

"But he needs help now and then. We all do."

She kissed him, adjusted the top sheet.

"Mama—Deke needs Lamar. He may not be able to go in the swamps without Lamar. Please don't mess it up."

"Terry, really now!"

"Deke can do everything anybody else can do, except getting in and out of his airboat. He needs Lamar for that."

"Terry, I think you do Deke an injustice by insisting he is altogether capable when he is not. Then you turn around and say he can't do his work without Lamar. Deke has an educated mind; he can do many things. Perhaps he excels at some of them. But Terry—he has no legs. He has *no* legs. Nothing can change that. Please stop pressuring me as if I were responsible for his predicament. Deke is smart—he'll work it out for himself or see that he must change his plans."

After Mama left the room, Terry stared unseeing at the ceiling. Somewhere were two legs without a body. Deke had thrown one away, he'd said. Like garbage?

Would they have a funeral for just legs? How much had to die before everything was dead? He tried to imagine the absence of his legs. Then arms. Torso? Head? Nothing dead but head. No, that *was* dead.

In a movie once, he saw a lady get her head cut off by an axe—the king made them do it. She was the queen. He was angry about something, so they cut off her head.

Which did they bury?

Probably all of it.

He rolled his head on the pillow, bodiless.

Like that.

No.

It couldn't be good. The more that dies, the worse it had to be. He reassembled himself and sighed.

Still, it seemed a shame not to bury any of the parts without a funeral. Maybe, for the queen, two funerals.

Ten

"MOSTLY MAMA LIKES flowers," Terry said.

Deke drove with one wrist on the steering wheel. He'd been in a bad mood since they left Camp Osceola.

"Anytime anybody gives her a flower," Terry said, "she pushes it around in a vase with her finger. You know."

"Um-hm."

Terry sat on his legs, an arm out the window of Deke's truck. They passed the black migratory labor camp where most employers went to hire colored people. Deke said he still needed a strong back if Lamar couldn't go to the swamps.

"There're lots of strong backs at Camp Okeechobee," Terry had suggested, but no, Deke knew somebody, he said. So now they drove toward Pahokee.

"In a movie once," Terry tried again, "I saw a man give a lady some flowers she pinned on her dress. I bet Mama would like that."

They drove slowly, Deke gazing through smoke haze caused by muck fires. "Milleniums of compost burning needlessly," Deke had said. "We need rain."

He was talking about the muck. The dark soil of the Everglades was nothing but rotted vegetation. When it was dry and caught fire, it could burn for weeks. Sometimes it burned underground where nobody could reach the flames and put them out.

"Any little thing would do, Deke," Terry persisted. "It wouldn't have to cost much. Maybe draw a picture is all. Mama likes that kind of thing, pictures you draw yourself."

They turned off the paved highway, following a rutted road, dust rising behind them. Here and there, in patches cleared of brush, tiny houses had been built with old metal signs: *Grapette* and *RC Cola* and *Eat Merita Bread*. Some of the dwellings had only tar paper siding and roofs of dried palmetto fronds.

"Here we go," Deke said, turning onto a more narrow lane leading to higher ground. They stopped under a huge oak that sheltered a pine "slab" house built atop stilts. A gray and white barred Dominecker hen and her biddies scratched in a hard sandy yard.

"Eileen!" Deke yelled, still in the truck. The sound of his voice brought a hound up from a nap in a dust hollow, rushing out in full cry, only to halt with hind legs passing the front when Terry stepped from the truck. When he approached the ferocious animal, the dog rolled on his back, licking his lips.

"Ho, Eileen!" Deke hollered again.

"Yessir," the reply. "Who that?"

Deke laughed and sat, waiting.

"Mr. Deke, that you? Bless my soul and body. Is that you?"

"Sure is, Eileen."

"Lord God, Mr. Deke!" The woman came out of the somber recesses of her home, shading her eyes. She put a hand on her knee, coming down each step carefully, chuckling to herself, "Lord God, Mr. Deke."

"Arthritis still troubling you, Eileen?"

It was obvious. She moved with halting steps, knobbed elbows and knees in narrow black sheaths of legs and arms.

"Giving me fits all the time, Mr. Deke. Lord God! Is it sure enough you?"

When she reached the truck, she lifted two trembling hands and Deke leaned out to be kissed and awkwardly hugged.

"How come you don't get down a spell?" she asked.

"I didn't want to shock you, Eileen."

Her smile vanished, brown eyes darting, seeking. She said, "Oh no, Mr. Deke."

"I got hurt a little, Eileen."

"No, Mr. Deke."

He shoved open the truck door and her eyes widened, stared, closed.

"Nothing I can't handle, Eileen. It could've been worse."

"I member this boy running with the wind," Eileen said, eyes still closed. "I member how he jumped and he ran, God."

Deke swung himself out on the harness and lowered into his chair. With each move, the black woman writhed, holding her stomach, and tears glistened on her cheeks.

"Hey, hey now," Deke said softly. "Let's get in a cool

place and have something to drink."

"I lost my boy, Jake," she wept.

"I know, Eileen."

"Lost my baby, Joe-Nathon."

"I heard, Eileen. I'm sorry."

"Last day before the Germans was whipped. I lost my baby boy," she said. She brushed an eye with swollen knuckles. "Reckon God forsaked us all, Mr. Deke? Reckon we being punished for some kind of sin?"

"Do you have anything to drink, Eileen?"

"Got no ice."

"How about some corn squeezings?"

She laughed through tears.

"I seem to remember you had the best," Deke grinned.

"Used to," she acknowledged. "Sugar got so precious though, we been making rum with cane."

"That's fine."

She looked at Terry, then said to Deke, "That your boy?"

"No. A friend. Terry, this is Mrs. Eileen Johnson. She raised me from the crib."

"Sure enough did," she said. "Him so sweet I could of kissed him to death."

Terry shifted under their gaze and then Eileen said, "Reckon you could fetch me a chair, boy?"

"Yes ma'am."

"And boy — on the table in the kitchen, a jar what still got the top on it. Bring us that."

"Yes ma'am."

Terry took her the chair first, and she eased into it, Deke near enough to take her hand gently. She still had tears in her eyes.

"I heard that Michael is home, Eileen."

"Gone to town but he be home directly."

"That's good. Does he plan to finish college?"

"Got him a year to go."

"He should do that."

"I know, Mr. Deke. But white folks don't know what manner man is coming home from these wars."

Walking through the house, Terry saw a flag with three stars to show how many from this home had gone to serve. A pillow on the couch had a bumble bee insignia and the words, "Fighting Seabees." He paused at the fireplace mantel and looked up at two pictures with black ribbons draped on the frames. One was a pilot! The pilot stood next to the fuselage of a fighter plane; he wore a leather hat with earflaps that marked his profession.

Between the pictures, a papier-mâché Virgin Mary held a swaddled child. A halo sprinkled with gold glitter ringed her head, and on the wall hung a plaster crucifix with drops of blood dripping from the hands and feet and thorn scratches on Christ's forehead.

"How about it, Terry?" Deke called.

"Coming!"

The kitchen was cool, dark. Terry could see the ground through knotholes knocked out of the pine slab flooring. A wood-burning stove stood on iron legs. On the table were several jars, but only one was capped.

When he returned with the jar, Eileen said, "Bless me, I forgot the glasses, boy."

Terry got the glasses. The same kind Mama used, after the jelly had been eaten.

They sat outside under the oak, in long periods of silence which Terry dared not interrupt. Deke had agreed to bring him with the condition, "Stay out of the way." That meant, don't interrupt.

"Michael say he ain't going to stay home, Mr. Deke. He say the GI Bill lets him to go school and he ain't nobody's nigger. He talks like that down to Pahokee!"

She took a sip of amber liquid, her lips making tiny folds and creases like a withered prune. "Going up north, he say, and I hope he do, before he gets in trouble."

At the sound of a motor Eileen lifted watery eyes, listening. Terry heard the rattle of a fender as an old truck jolted into the yard and stopped.

"Michael," Eileen said, scared like, "Michael, look here Mr. Deke!"

The soldier was tall, muscular, his Eisenhower jacket unbuttoned. He wore a row of medals across his chest. He took Deke's hand, unsmiling.

"I see they got your legs, Deke."

"It could've been worse, Michael."

Michael turned to a light-skinned woman and a pig-tailed child. "This is my wife, Juanita. My daughter, Marylou. This is Mr. Dekle."

"How do you do, Mr. Dekle?" She talked like a white woman.

The child stared at Deke and pursed her lips. When Deke reached for her, Marylou pulled away, behind her mother.

They brought out cane bottom chairs and for a time nobody spoke.

"Well," Deke broke the silence. "Here we are home from the wars, Michael."

"Praise God," Eileen lifted a hand, let it drop to her lap.

Deke spoke to Michael's wife. "You aren't from around here?"

"Toledo."

Then, to Michael, "You were a prisoner, I was told."

"Nineteen months."

"Get through it okay?"

"About as good as could be expected." Michael glanced at his wife and she looked down at her hands. "Tell the truth," Michael said, "the Krauts treated me as good as the white folks in Pahokee a little while ago."

"Mr. Deke," Eileen said quickly, "looks like you needs some more squeezings."

"I can't stay much longer, Eileen."

"Come into New York," Michael said. "All that confetti and band music and marching — I guess I forgot what it'd be like down home."

The child, Marylou, skipped away through the house; her braids were so tight they didn't bob.

"When I got to Atlanta, the white folks were kind enough to remind me," Michael said.

Terry saw Deke's fingers intertwine and press one another.

"This family lost Jake and Joe-Nathon. I spent nineteen months in a German hell hole."

"Yeah," Deke said gently.

"Sonsofbitches," Michael rasped. "Damn them."

"Now Michael," Eileen said, "Mr. Deke come out here looking for some help and we obliged to try."

"I'm writing a book on the Everglades," Deke said. "I have to go out into the swamps. I need help getting in and out of a boat — somebody to carry supplies."

"A nigger to fetch and tote," Michael said evenly.

Deke cleared his throat. "Without help, I can't do the job, Michael. I hoped you'd know somebody."

After a long pause, Deke said, "I can't pay much."

Michael laughed suddenly, but it didn't sound funny. He stood up, fists clenched. His wife said, "Michael —"

"I got a message for you, Deke," Michael leaned closer. "Thousands of men are coming home — *men* — and they aren't the same sambos that stood around shuffling their feet afraid to look you in the eye. They fought for their country. They've paid their dues. You understand?"

"Yes, Michael. I understand."

"These Bahama blacks come over here and get a dime a hamper more for picking the same beans me and my brothers picked. Well, I got news for you, Deke. The army taught us how to defend ourselves!"

Deke's fingers quivered and he clamped them against his body.

"Look at my mama," Michael said. "Bent up with arthritis. Hurting all the time. Living like — like —" he swept an arm, indicating the house and yard.

"Well, Deke, you pass the word," Michael said. "Things are going to change."

"As it should be, Michael."

"You damned right as it should be."

"What say, red on the head?" Deke tried to smile, but his lips slipped. "About ready to go home?"

"You mama was always good to me, Mr. Deke," Eileen said.

Michael twisted away, standing with his back to them.

"She was a good white woman," Eileen said.

Returning to Belle Glade, Deke kept swallowing and sighing. Terry tried to think of something to say.

"Are you mad, Deke?"

"Not at you."

"At Michael?"

"No. Not really. But I felt the ground tremble."

"Sir?"

Deke sighed.

"Are you mad with Mama?"

Deke looked at him hard. "Why would I be angry with your mother?"

Terry hunched his shoulders. "I don't know."

"Well, I'm not angry," Deke said angrily. He slapped at his rolled pants leg, teeth exposed in a grimace.

"I could go with you to the swamps," Terry insisted.

"No, you can't."

"I could help you get in and out of the boat, honest I could."

Deke looked like he might cry. It frightened Terry. They missed their turn in Belle Glade.

"Where are we going, Deke?"

"I'm not going *anywhere*."

"This is the way to Clewiston."

Deke nodded grimly. He circled a block, going back the way they'd come. Now he turned toward Camp Osceola. But when he reached the Silver Dollar Café, Deke pulled in and parked.

"You'll have to walk from here, Terry."

"I'll stay with you awhile."

"No, you won't. Go home."

Watching Deke swing into his chair, Terry waited.

"I said go home, redhead."

"I was only going to open the door for you."

"I can do that. Go home."

"Deke — please — did I do something wrong?"

But Deke didn't answer, snatching open the café door, rolling at the threshold so hard his chair tilted, then backing off to hit it again. Somebody came to help and Terry heard Deke said, "Get out of my way, goddamn it!"

Terry walked past the icehouse — idle.

He missed Bucky Dallas. He wished he could find Mr. McCree.

He followed the railroad tracks toward Camp Osceola, stepping on ties because the rail was too hot for his exposed feet. He passed an engine, steam whispering, the boiler banked with coal enough to keep it ready when needed.

When he reached the house, Mama was home. Terry heard Velma talking. He stood under the kitchen window, listening.

"I told Burrell he's risking Lamar's life, Mickey. I told him and he doesn't listen."

Mama didn't say anything.

"Know what he said?" Velma asked. "He said, 'I'm a cripple. Would you tell Lamar he can't go with his own father?'"

Still, Mama said nothing.

"What can I do, Mickey?"

After a long time, Mama said, "I don't know, Velma."

Eleven

"HE'S A HERO, Ossie," Terry said. "He got his legs blown off."

"Half a hero, you mean." Ossie walked a rail without extending his arms for balance.

"He needs help getting in and out of his boat," Terry explained. "You and I together could do that, couldn't we? He needs us to fetch and tote."

"Nigger work."

"No it isn't!"

"White man's work," Ossie said. "Either way, I ain't interested."

Terry crawled under a boxcar, following.

"See the thing is," Ossie said. "*Phantom of the Opera* is a scary movie."

"You saw it?" Terry skipped to keep up.

"Not all of it. They caught me sneaking in. Anyway.

You saw the posters at the theater, didn't you?"

They were under the Blue Goose packing house, cool moist soil on bare feet, keeping silent as they passed beneath a guard overhead. Beyond the guard, Ossie said, "How many boxes you got?"

Popcorn boxes from the theater. Ossie had told Terry to save them. "Three. Ossie, what do you say? Let's help Deke."

"I got three myself. That's about all we'd get in with, anyway. Okay, about the movie. This guy gets his face messed up with hot wax or something. Then he hides in a big opera house. Anyway. He gets horny and starts trying to catch him a girl. It's scary as hell."

Into blinding sunlight again, down a graveled alley between three-story buildings. At the rear, an iron ladder outside rose toward a small open window in the packing house loft.

"That ladder is hotter'n a two-dollar pistol," Ossie said. "Use your sack like this." He pulled a burlap bag over his arms, making a glove-in-common for both hands.

"If you don't climb fast," Ossie warned, "you won't make it before your feet start to burn. I seen a kid jump from halfway up once. Drove his ass between his shoulder blades."

Heat from the building radiated as if from an oven. Grabbing each rung with both hands, humping higher to grab again, they moved upward.

"Awful high, Ossie."

"Don't look down."

His feet searing, Terry thought about the boy with an ass between his shoulders. "Hurry, Ossie!"

Inside, they fell to the floor and rubbed their feet, Terry howling, "Ow, ow, ow —"

"Burned little criscrosses," Ossie observed clinically, examining an upturned instep.

"What do you say, Ossie?"

"About what?"

"Helping Deke!"

"I said, no."

"Then I'm not going to help you with this," Terry said. The temperature was suffocating. He moved to the window, arms trembling, and gazed across Camp Osceola; in the distance he could see the dike at Chosen, a shimmer of heat rising from rooftops far below.

"I ain't going to say I'll work for somebody I never met," Ossie said. "I'd have to meet him before I could say yes."

"Okay," Terry agreed. "I'll introduce you." He peered down the blistering ladder. "How will we get down?"

"First," Ossie said, "let's catch the bats."

"You'll like Deke," Terry insisted. "He likes everybody. Indians and colored people — even Japanese and they shot off his legs!"

Every move stirred silt. Rising dust was visible in the stabbing shafts of sunlight entering holes in the walls and roof. Sheet metal cracked and popped as steel expanded, nails yielded, beams warped under the sun.

"Ever catch a bat before?" Ossie queried.

"No."

"They hang upside down."

Terry knew that from vampire movies.

"Do they suck blood?"

"Not if I can help it." Ossie stooped. "Watch your head."

Then, his eyes adjusted to the dark, Terry saw them in symmetrical rows, like fruit on a vine. The bats were smaller than he'd expected. Some with wings closed, others seeking relief from the heat let their arms fall open.

"Will they start flying?" Terry asked.

"They can't see in the light. Watch." Ossie pushed open a shutter, then another. The bats made peeping sounds. Ossie lifted another and another. Not a bat had left its roost.

"Now," Ossie said, "I'll catch them. You hold the sack."

He climbed a beam, reached up and plucked a bat from the rafter. Terry saw needle teeth and a red tongue.

"Open the sack," Ossie commanded. He thrust the mammal inside, went for another.

When they had six, Ossie closed the shutters. With dark restored, a restless stir in the rafters brought goose-bumps to Terry's shoulders, prickling down his arms.

"Ready?" Ossie said. "Let's go."

No need for secrecy now. They climbed down to the next level, ran through the loft and with a whoop, Ossie leaped to a pile of crocus sacks in a bin below.

"Hey!" the guard yelled. His voice reverberated, "Outta-here-outta-here."

They dodged crates, hopped over dollies, ran under conveyors and through a boxcar with the guard close behind. They cleared the building, laughing, and heard the guard swear from the platform.

"We're going tonight?" Terry yelled.

"Tonight! Bring your boxes."

Terry halted at the camp entrance, watching Ossie jog on. "First show or second?"

Ossie replied without looking back, "First!"

Grinning, Terry ran for home.

They sat in an alley behind the theater, waiting for the right moment. Ossie shared a mentholated cigarette with Terry. The six popcorn boxes moved now and then as the occupants stirred.

"What you do," Ossie instructed, "is go in the bathroom. When there's nobody there, I'll pass the boxes through the window."

"What about you?"

"I'll sneak in and meet you in the balcony."

"You think they'll let me go through the lobby with six boxes of popcorn?"

"No, stupid! Take a couple boxes at a time, go up in the balcony and hide them under a seat. After a minute, go back for a couple more."

Terry blew mentholated smoke through his nostrils. It made his eyes water.

"We'll watch the movie all the way through," Ossie said. "Then we'll turn them loose and run for it."

Ossie puffed, inhaled, blew twin plumes through his nose. He made spitting sounds to get tobacco off his tongue. He thumped the butt with the nail of his forefinger to tamp it.

Terry waved away the cigarette. "I don't like menthol."

"It was all I could get. My mom is dating a dumb fruit that smokes with a cigarette holder. He smokes these."

Long silence. Terry asked, "What happened to your daddy?"

"He's dead."

Terry watched Ossie blow more smoke, nares flattened. "He was old when I was born," Ossie commented.

"What kind of work did he do."

"There ain't a lot Indians can do, except gig frogs. Skin gators. Hunting is ruined because of white people."

Their backs to the theater wall, they could hear eerie music through the vents. Ossie chuckled, "We'll scare shit out of somebody."

"How come you left the reservation?" Terry asked.

"Mom."

"She didn't like it?"

"It's against the law — Indian law — for a woman to go with white men. If she got pregnant or something, they'd kill her."

"Kill her! Who?"

"The old men. Usually. Sometimes they let you do it to yourself."

"Why doesn't somebody call the police?"

"Cops can't mess with Indian law on a reservation. Anyway, we didn't want to stay. Living in a chickee. Eating sofkee made from grits. Sofkee is supposed to be made from coontie roots. You ready?"

Terry stood up.

"Remember what I told you. Couple boxes at a time."

Terry waited in a line of town kids buying tickets. The serial this week was Lash LaRue. Last Saturday, with a fuse burning right up to the dynamite, Lash LaRue was left struggling to get untied.

"Don't you camp brats ever take a bath?" a boy said. A girl in a white dress giggled.

Terry stared straight at the ticket booth.

"Or wear shoes?" another one said.

Terry's coins were slick in his hands. With peripheral vision he assayed his adversaries: older, bigger, trousers creased, brown and white oxfords.

"Stay upwind," somebody farther back called. Everybody laughed.

Wait. Dumb fruits. Just wait.

Terry pushed through the crowded foyer, into the rest room. A man at the urinal bent his knees and broke wind. He spit, flushed, and stood there. In a compartment where pants and feet indicated another adult, a man called, "Any paper out there?" Nobody responded.

To hurry them along, Terry looked in adjoining booths. No paper in any of them. He heard the hapless man swearing under his breath.

"Hey, redhead, go ask the manager for some toilet tissue." He could see? Yes. Through cracks where the door joined the wall.

Terry found the manager. "A man in the bathroom needs some toilet paper."

"We don't have any."

"But he's on the toilet."

"Listen, kid, there's a war on. We don't have any."

Terry returned, reported this. Now there was only the trapped man and himself. He pulled a trash can to the window, climbed up. Ossie was there.

Quickly, Terry took the six boxes, hid them behind the trash can, and took two up to the balcony. He had trouble finding a place where he dared leave them. Back to the rest room and with barely restrained excitement, through the lobby and upstairs again. When he returned for the last boxes, the manager and the man on the toilet were arguing through the wood door.

"Sir," the manager said, "there's a paper shortage."

"Bring me something, goddamn it."

Terry washed his hands. No towels. He eyed the manager, stooped for his boxes and eased toward the door.

"Hey, Red," the manager said — but Terry bolted and ran.

He missed all of the news films, two Tom and Jerry

cartoons, and Lash LaRue was out of one mess and into another before Terry dared settle back and relax. No Ossie.

Maybe Ossie got caught. Maybe the manager had him down in the office right this minute threatening to put Ossie in jail. Terry watched ushers walking slowly up and down aisles below. What if Ossie didn't show up at all? What then? Leave the boxes unopened? Would the bats smother, starve? Terry put a hand on the top box and felt a reassuring movement as the bat within flexed his wings.

Lash LaRue was about to jump out the window of a burning building. The floor collapsed, sending him down to a fiery death — continued next week.

"You got 'em?" Ossie whispered.

"Where've you been? I thought you got caught."

"I come through the front door. The manager and some guy are having a brawl in the bathroom. Walked right in."

Just in time. The *Phantom of the Opera* was about to begin.

They saw it twice. It didn't cost any more to do that. Then, just as the withered face of the awesome phantom was about to appear, Ossie released the bats.

At first, nobody seemed to notice. They were shrieking and hollering as the phantom dragged himself from one side of the screen to another. Then, somewhere below, a different note rose from the audience.

"Bats!"

Terry heard Ossie muffle a laugh.

"Jeeze!" A man now. "Bats!"

Most people probably missed the best part, where the misshapen phantom — who really was sort of pitiful —

lunged from the shadows to seize the woman he loved. The woman didn't love him, though. She *did*, but she didn't recognize him because his face was all twisted and burned with hot wax or something.

"Bats! God! Bats!"

The balcony moved *en mass*.

"Let's go, Ossie."

"In a minute."

"They'll catch us," Terry warned. "They've caught you before."

Ossie rose, begrudgingly, and they reached the stairs as the film ground to a halt and house lights came on. Now there really was screaming.

The manager loomed in the crowded stairwell, trying to push past. "Run," Ossie suggested.

Over seats, down the aisle, below the projectionist booth, blocked! Terry turned as the manager extricated himself, coming for them on angry strides.

"Run," Ossie repeated, more sincerely.

"Where?"

They parted as the manager recognized Ossie and went after him. Terry darted by, reached the stairs and met an usher head-on. "Bats!" Terry screamed.

"Take it easy —"

"Bats! Bats!" Terry squirmed free and vaulted to the next landing. He heard Ossie, "Bats! Bats!"

More ushers. Terry shrilled, "Bats! Bats!" and they let him pass.

The sidewalk and street were filled with people. A policeman was getting out of his car. Terry slipped along a wall, cleared the crowd and walked deliberately toward an alley.

A door at the end of the building flew wide and Ossie

emerged on pumping legs. "Bats! Bats!" he yelled. Terry halted, watching as an usher lunged, missed, sprawled.

Nobody could run faster than Ossie. Especially when Ossie was scared. Terry turned and took another route toward home.

"Everybody comfortable?" Mama asked.

"I am," Ann said.

Mama adjusted her light and very carefully slit an air-mail envelope.

"How many letters, Mama?" Terry questioned.

"Only this one. It was forwarded from Birmingham."

Ann scratched her upper lip with her lower teeth, hands clasped behind her head, waiting.

"Ready?" Mama said.

"Ready."

Mama read, " 'My Darling Babies and Mickey: I know it is summer there, but here in —' " Mama studied the word and said, "I can't read it." She continued, " 'the air is cold and it feels like autumn. Poland is a beautiful country with a tragic past. Foreign armies have pillaged the lands, enslaved the citizens and subjected the Poles to hardships we cannot imagine. But now, an even more horrible thing has happened on Polish soil —' "

Terry saw Mama's eyes dart ahead, gauging the material. Mama read, " 'You must forgive me as I write this. I am weeping. I considered sending you a cheerful letter, filled with stories of folklore and legend. I tried, too. But my heart is sick this night, my family, and never have you meant more to me than at this moment. Now, after much thought, I feel nothing would be better than to tell you the true horror of what I have seen. Mickey, please read it all. Perhaps our children — the hope for the future — will be so moved that they will never allow such to occur ever again.' "

Terry's stomach fluttered, muscles taut. Mama's eyes scanned the letter. She turned the page reading the flip side.

"Mama?"

Mama looked at Terry with a strange wildness. She started again, voice odd, " 'Here where the hills roll gently, in a land famous for poets, patriots and hard work, I have been one of a team of men assigned to document a terrible thing. In all the history of our world, nothing more inhuman has ever been undertaken by one people against another.

" 'Today, you have never heard of Auschwitz, Treblinka, and Chelmo. But soon, the world will speak these odd words with the same ease they now use in talking of a baseball pitcher or a famous movie star.' "

Mama's eyes darted ahead and Terry implored, "Mama?"

" 'My babies, something awful has happened here. Men and women and children, starved until they were skin and bones, worked in bitter cold without proper clothing or rations. They were beaten, tortured, the victims of terrible medical experiments, then forced to watch their friends and relatives die at the hands of men who must surely have been mad. They arrived in railroad cars in spring, summer, fall, and sub-zero winter, like cattle packed together. Then the weak, the elderly and the lame were separated from the able-bodied men and women —' "

Mama sucked a quick breath, reading ahead.

"Mama."

"Daddy," Mama's fingers trembled, "Daddy — was

upset. I don't think he would really want me to read this letter to you."

"Mama, please."

Mama looked at Ann, lying with blue eyes wide, staring up at the ceiling.

"Mama, Daddy said so."

"Terry — he —"

"I don't want to hear it," Ann declared.

Terry sat up, "Mama, please —"

Ann shut her eyes tightly.

Mama put a quivering hand on Ann's forehead, stroked away a stray hair. "Sleep, baby," she said.

Jaw set, Mama jerked her head, motioning Terry out. Together they went into the kitchen and sat at the table.

"I don't want you to read this," Mama said fervently. "But if you insist, absolutely insist, I cannot read it to you. You must read it for yourself."

"All right."

"You insist?"

"Yes, Mama."

She pushed the first page to him.

Twelve

"MA SAID ME AND DEKE can go camping," Lamar said.

Terry saw the two bedrolls, canned goods, an infantry trench shovel. "May I go, Deke?"

"Afraid not, Terry. We'll be gone a couple of days."

"Where to?"

"Big Cypress. Be careful with the equipment, Lamar."

Lamar placed an armful of boxes in the truck.

"Mama might let me go for a couple of nights," Terry said.

"Better not this time, Terry."

He watched Lamar stow supplies. "What're you going after?"

"Specimens," Deke said. He checked a microscope, placed it back in a wooden container.

"Why do you need that, then?" Terry questioned.

"There's more to identifying species of plants than looking at leaves and flowers," Deke replied. He moved nearer the truck to check Lamar's packing.

"If I'd known you were going," Terry pressed, "I could've asked Mama before she went to work this morning."

"There'll be other times, redhead."

"We're going to build us a campfire," Lamar said.

Terry knelt beside the man. "I'm real good at building campfires, Deke. I know how to get moss and keep away mosquitos. I've done it lots of times."

Deke checked items on a list.

Lamar spoke to no one in particular, "My ma said, Oh, all *right*!"

"Lamar gets spooked easy, Deke," Terry whispered. "He's scared of swamp gases because he believes in ghosts."

"I'll watch it," Deke said.

"What I mean is," Terry labored, "he starts crying. I know how to make him quit. Lots of times when he cries, I talk to him real easy and he stops."

Deke's gaze shifted from one side of Terry's face to the other.

"It wouldn't hurt to have two helpers," Terry persisted.

"Not this time. I wish we could, Terry. But not this time."

"Let's go!" Lamar hollered from the front seat.

"Deke?"

"Yeah?"

"Are you going to need some help loading your boat?"

"I don't think so."

"I could walk back from Chosen. I do it all the time."

After a moment, Deke said, "Okay. Hop in."

"Dibbies on the window!" Lamar cried. Terry crawled over him.

They left Camp Osceola, driving through thick ground fog. It was like a boat stirring vapors that swirled and closed behind them.

Lamar peered out his window. "I can't see the road, Deke."

"We're all right, Lamar." Deke glanced at brittle cattails and brown water grass. "We could use some rain."

"Deke?"

When he didn't respond, Terry leaned nearer. "You know where the canal at Chosen widens? Right where the levee ends?"

"Yes."

"I could ride your airboat that far. I can walk back along the dike. I've done that a lot of times."

"It would be better to leave you at the fish camp, Terry. It's tricky beaching an airboat along a canal bank."

He felt Deke's arm muscles flex as they topped the dike. Below them, in the last mauve shade of first light, lay Owen's fish camp, oaks on Kramer Island, and a few palms rising from a world enshrouded with night fog. Atop the earthly cloud, a single tousled head bobbed under the bridge — Ossie. Going fishing, perhaps.

"If I were going with you," Terry confided, "we wouldn't need all those heavy cans of food. I know what you can eat in the swamps."

Getting out, Deke said, "Take care with things, Lamar. Don't drop it."

Terry followed Deke's chair toward the bait store. "We got a letter from my daddy."

"Good news?"

"Deke, what's an incinerator?"

"Something in which to burn trash. Morning, Charlie."

"Ready to go?" the fish camp owner pumped kerosene into a Mason fruit jar. A black boy waited with his hands tucked into the bib of his coveralls.

"That's what they did with people," Terry said.

"Ought to wait for the fog to lift, Deke," Mr. Owen advised. "Logs floating in the river, stuff like that."

"I know, Charlie. We'll go slowly."

Mr. Owen gave the jar to the black boy and waited as the child unknotted one corner of a bandana where he'd tied his money.

To his customer, Mr. Owen asked, "How's your mama, Son?"

"Still sick, Mr. Owen."

"Did she go to a doctor like I told her?"

"No, sir."

"She ought to go. Tell Mamie I said I'll carry her to town to the free clinic if she'll go. It won't cost her anything."

"Yessir." The boy gave Mr. Owen four cents.

"Is she taking medicine?"

"Kerosene and poultice."

"Tell her what I said," Mr. Owen stated. He watched the boy lope toward the bridge.

"Now," Mr. Owen faced Deke, "what can I do for you?"

"Wanted to tell you, I'll be gone until Friday."

"What am I supposed to do with that information? What could anybody do if you don't show up?"

"I'll show up."

Mr. Owen's expression looked none too sure. Then he bumped Deke's shoulder with a fist.

Following Deke back to the truck, Terry said, "That's

what they did with people, Deke."

"What?"

"Burned them in incinerators."

Deke stopped, staring toward Lamar down the dock.

"First they starved them," Terry said.

Still looking off, Deke reached out and pulled Terry to him.

"Know what I wish, Deke?"

"What?"

"I wish I could go with you."

"Wish you could, redhead," Deke said. "But not this trip."

"Wish I could, though."

"Me too."

"Then," Terry asked, "why can't I?"

"Too far. Too long."

"If I'd only known —"

Deke squeezed him and Terry threw his arms around the man's neck. Then, despite his best effort, Terry sobbed.

Deke's voice was distorted. "Go ask Charlie when the fog will lift."

"Soon as the sun comes up, Deke."

"Tell him I need a left-handed monkey wrench."

"Okay."

Terry wiped his eyes, walking. He told Mr. Owen and he said, "I'll look for one in a moment."

The motor roared and waterfowl rose. Mr. Owen pushed the boat free and Terry's hair blew askew as the propeller whipped fog and canal froth to the rear. He ran to the bridge seeking a better view.

Lamar saw Ossie and half-stood, shouting, "We're going camping, Ossie!" Deke motioned Lamar down again.

Responding to the thunder of the craft, birds beat upward, the sky filled with whites and yellows, reds and brown. As they reached the light of rising sun, the flocks churned crimson and gold, catching the rays broadside, then seeming to disappear when they wheeled as one. From land to sky to lake and back, the motor echoed in overlapping waves.

Ossie came up to the bridge and stood beside Terry. "Who's he?"

"That's Deke. He's the hero who got his legs shot off by the Japanese."

"Yeah?" Ossie put his elbows on the bridge rail. He held a knife, his hands and forearms bloodied.

"He took Lamar," Terry said.

"I saw him."

"I can't go, because of my mama."

"Listen," Ossie said, "want to help me clean some frog legs?"

"I don't think so."

"They're paying forty cents a pound at the icehouse. You and me could go gigging. I'm going again tonight."

"I don't think so, Ossie."

"Four-tee-cents a pound!" Ossie enunciated. "I caught so many last night I couldn't hardly tote the croker sack."

"I don't have a gig or a light."

"I'll loan you one."

"Anyway," Terry said, bitterly, "my mama wouldn't let me go."

"She let you throw circulars, didn't she? You could ask. Forty cents a pound! Hell, I got one frog that weighs mighty near a half pound."

"You do not."

"Come see. I mean, with his legs on, he did. Most of

the weight gets thrown away when you cut off the legs."

Terry's stomach churned. Ossie scratched his nose with one filthy finger. His chest and face were dappled where he'd been slapping mosquitos with bloody hands.

"What's the matter?" Ossie questioned.

"I don't feel too good."

"On account of the guts and stuff?"

"I don't know."

"Hey!" Ossie shifted his knife and put a brotherly arm around Terry's shoulder. "Everybody gets sick at first. Come on. You'll get over it. Just think — forty cents a pound!"

Terry followed, under the bridge to a ramp used to read water levels of the river. Ossie laid on his stomach and reached down to swish his knife in the canal. Then he uncovered a washtub full of dead frogs.

"Light me a cigarette," he said. "A few puffs and it'll settle your stomach."

"Menthol?"

"No. I bought these. Don't drop the matches, it's all I have."

Terry lit the cigarette — a brand he'd never heard of — and fumes seared his mouth. He placed the cigarette between Ossie's lips and sat to watch. Distantly, the broken hum of the airboat faded away.

"That's how you could make some big bucks," Ossie said around the smoking butt, eyes squinted. "If we had us a *pile-putki.*" He jerked his head up, surprised for having used the word. "That's Seminole for 'airboat,'" Ossie said.

"I know."

"Oh, yeah. Anyway. If we had us one, we could go after gators and frogs out in the glades where they get really big! You know what a gator hide is selling for now?"

Terry accepted the cigarette, puffed, returned it to Ossie's lips. Ossie had wet it.

"No telling," Ossie answered himself. "But you can go so fast in a airboat you're right on top of a gator before he knows it. You got him before he sinks."

Shifting abruptly, Ossie laughed in a high-pitched cackle, "We scared them shitless, didn't we?"

"Yeah."

"I heard some lady snatched out handfuls of her own hair." Ossie laughed again and the cigarette wiggled dangerously near his nose.

"Did he come see your mama?" Ossie questioned.

"Who?"

"The manager of the theater."

"Why should he?"

"You know why."

"But he doesn't know me."

"He does now. I had to tell him. It was either that or get my ass blistered, which I don't take for nobody."

"You told them?"

"He recognized me," Ossie said. "From the time I put a dead skunk in the fan shaft. Anyway, he come to see my mom at the café and they come home madder than a raped drake. I had to tell them, that's all."

"Ossie!"

Ossie flipped frog legs into a bucket, reached for another. "Maybe he won't come," he said.

"Ossie, my mama will kill me."

"Not like my mom if I hadn't told her when she asked me."

"What happened?"

"He was one more mean sonofabitch," Ossie said. "He come to the house ready to put me in jail."

"What happened?" Terry demanded.

"My mom told him I was just a boy." Ossie pinched the cigarette between two sanguine fingers, examined it, and threw it in the canal. "My mom is smart about things like that."

"Ossie! What happened?"

"Mom asked him if he ever did anything like that when he was a boy. She got him to laughing and teasing. Anyway. He gave me a permanent pass to go to the movies anytime I want, for free. How's that for smart?"

"Then why did you tell him about me?"

"Because," Ossie said evenly, "it was my mom who asked me, that's why. If my mom asks me, I have to tell. Either that or she'd beat my brains out for a year."

"Ossie —" Terry stood, hands clenched.

"Anyway, Mom and this guy plan to go to the American Legion dance next Saturday, so I reckon he's okay. He's better than the mentholated fruit before."

"You shouldn't of told. You should've made up somebody."

"It was my mom," Ossie snapped. "My mom!"

"You could've told her anybody, Ossie. She wouldn't have known any better."

"She would've known."

"How? Why?"

Ossie tilted his head sideways, looking up with one eye shut against the glare. "I don't go with anybody but you."

"No telling what Mama will do," Terry worried.

"If it'd been cops or the manager only," Ossie said, "they could've driven bamboo splinters under my fingernails and burned them."

They saw that in a movie where the American got his face operated on so he'd look Japanese. But the Japanese caught him anyway.

"They could've tied me on a bench and dropped water in my mouth until I swole up and exploded."

Same film.

"But it was Mom. She knew before she asked. Who was it? She knew. Couldn't've been anybody else but you."

"I have to go home," Terry said.

"How about some gigging tonight?"

"No."

"Want to go see *Phantom of the Opera* again, on my pass?"

"No! Not with you."

Ossie threw his knife in the bucket and leaped to his feet, teeth bared. He threw Terry on the ground. Terry's eyes bulged as Ossie gripped his throat.

"I couldn't help it," Ossie seethed.

"Ossie, let go."

Ossie shook Terry fiercely. "I couldn't help it. It was my *mom*!"

Dark eyes brimming, Ossie held Terry a moment, then backed off. He returned to the bucket and his frogs.

"I'll ask my mama," Terry said.

Ossie nodded.

"She might let me," Terry said.

Ossie nodded again.

Mama said no. It didn't matter. Ossie didn't come by to find out.

Thirteen

"I DON'T WANT Terry to cook my eggs," Ann said.

"Why not?"

"His nose is skinny."

Terry crossed his eyes, examining.

"Peeling," Mama explained. "He'll keep his nose away from your eggs, Ann. Go on, Terry."

Sitting at a vanity, Mama brushed her hair, listening to the morning news. "Four million New Yorkers lined the streets to give a tumultuous welcome to General Eisenhower. . . ."

"Don't get skin in my eggs," Ann warned.

From the radio, "After a grueling eighty-two day battle, Okinawa has fallen to the U.S. Tenth Army . . . ."

Terry heard Mama grumble, "Is there no news from Europe?"

Hot grease popped in the skillet. Terry pushed Ann

back. "Go sit down."

"I won't eat it if it has skin in it."

Mama dialed another station, ". . . the Japanese city of Kure, on Honshu Island, battered by a fleet of 450 Superfortresses."

Terry put Ann's plate on the table and she poked at it with a fork.

"Six o'clock, Mama!"

"I see skin," Ann said.

Terry looked out back toward the Australian pines. Ossie wasn't there.

"Oh dear," Mama stared down at her blouse. There was a spot on it.

"Want me to take Ann to the day-care center, Mama?"

"Would you, Darling?"

"I'm not going to eat it," Ann cried.

Terry stood in the bathroom door, watching Mama use a washcloth and cold water to scrub the spot.

"Mama," Ann hollered, "I'm not going to eat it!"

"All right, Ann. But that's it."

"I'll give it to Lamar," Ann suggested.

"Lamar is gone," Terry said. "He and Deke went to the swamps."

Mama paused, began scrubbing again.

"For two nights," Terry added.

"What time is it now?" Mama asked.

"Five after six. Mama — why can't I go with Deke if Lamar can go? Lamar isn't as much help as I am."

"We've been through that."

Ann's voice rose in disgust, "Look at that skin!"

Terry spun and shouted, "There's no skin in your eggs!"

"That's enough, you two," Mama said mildly.

"If you aren't going to eat," Terry demanded, "get

ready to go to kindergarten."

"School," Ann corrected.

"No," Terry snapped, "kindergarten. Get up!"

Mama appeared at the door. "That's enough."

Terry stood at the sink, breathing hard. He mumbled something and Mama said sharply, "What?"

"Nothing."

"What did you say?"

"Nothing."

Mama glanced at the clock. She hesitated. Then, "Get ready for school, Ann."

"I'm hungry, Mama."

"Ann," ominously. "Get ready. Now."

Ann started to cry and Mama grabbed her shoulder, taking the child to the bathroom. "Brush your teeth. Wash your face and hands."

"Mama, I'm hungry!"

"Hey," Mama stooped, holding Ann's arms. "Enough."

"But, Mama —"

"I'm going to bite your nose off," Mama threatened.

"Mama —"

"You'll look like a baby pig, if I do. Snorting and oinking."

Ann ducked her chin, giggled.

Mama came up behind Terry, pulled him against her. "Please, let's not argue."

"I still don't see why —"

"Terry," Mama said gruffly, "*please!*"

Walking through camp, Ann dawdled, taking deliberately short steps, soiling her newly polished white shoes by kicking up dust.

At the day-care center, Ann postured, one foot lifted, eyes tightly closed, lips pursed for a kiss. Terry watched her skip toward a smiling black lady who monitored the playground.

Because he had no purpose, Terry walked without direction. He wandered through the metal shelter section of camp, ducking under clotheslines draped with garments that smelled of lye and chlorine. From a community washhouse, he heard a woman crooning, a thumping agitator her metronome. A naked boy and girl, bellies distended, watched with wide eyes as Terry passed.

"Hi," Terry said.

Their mother sat on concrete steps, smoking. Her dress made a shallow valley between bony knees and she wasn't wearing underpants. When the children moved to follow Terry, she said softly, "Never mind —"

At the edge of camp, he halted. Hitch a ride on a train, maybe? The packing houses were closed. Terry peered down his nose. He tried to peel skin with a thumb and forefinger, but it made his flesh burn. Gnats hummed in darting speckles, seeking moisture.

He wondered what Deke and Lamar were doing. Camping in a hammock, probably. Surrounded by sedge and water that flowed without evidence of motion. There would be snails and snakes and alligator hollows if anybody knew where to look. Deke probably knew where to look.

Aimlessly, he followed the canal, crossed a culvert gushing water at a pumping station, and ambled toward town. The Bahamians were gone. To harvest potatoes or tomatoes or anything else getting ripe farther north.

Walking through colored town, Terry stopped to press his face to a window, cupping his hands against the glare to watch men play pool. The owner came out to ask Terry what he wanted.

"Nothing."

"Best move along," he said.

"I was only looking."

"Best move along," the man said.

He stopped at a sign of a hand. It stood outside a door with a curtain made of beads. Trying to see inside without stepping nearer, he leaned forward.

"Come in." It was a whisper, but Terry jumped anyway.

"Come-come," the voice purred. "Come tell Sister something she doesn't know."

A hand appeared, the beads tinkled, and a ringed finger beckoned, "Come-come."

"I don't have any money," Terry said.

"Then we'll trade."

"For what?"

"What have you?"

"Nothing."

The finger crooked, drawing him. "Then," she said, "what would you have?"

"I don't know."

"Don't know?"

"I could think of something."

"Yes?"

"A bicycle."

"More important than your father overseas?"

"Oh."

"Or someone to befriend you?"

He said again, "I don't have any money."

"We'll trade."

"What for what?"

"What you want, for what I want."

The finger bore a long nail, painted red, and a ring shaped like a finger. "Come-come."

The beads parted musically, tiny pieces of glass tinkling. "Are you afraid?"

"I'm not afraid."

"Then come inside."

The room was a box, like a booth, with no entrance but the front. There was a small table, two chairs and a candle. Splinters of light from the beads danced on the walls.

She had eyes as dark as Ossie's, skin as smooth and brown. She smelled good. On every finger was a ring. On some fingers there were two. She wore a turban and the front of her dress was cut so low Terry could see the curve of almond breasts. Not black. Not Indian.

"Gypsy," she said.

"Ma'am?"

"You wonder, so I tell you. I am Gypsy."

Then it struck him and Terry fell back a step. "Are you the conjure woman?"

"I am what you wish me to be."

"Did you kiss Mr. McCree on the mouth?"

Tiny flickers of light made her pupils look elliptical, like a cat's eyes. "McCree?" she said.

"The snake man. Did you kiss him on the mouth?"

"Why do you seek this — snake man?"

"He's my friend."

"He was old."

"He could climb trees."

"He is like the wind," she said. "He flows all over."

"You mean he's dead."

"Nothing dies but that it lives."

Terry felt breathless. "Are you sure?"

She pointed at one chair and sat opposite him. "Give me your right hand."

"I really don't have any money."

"Your hand," she said.

Terry wiped a palm, extended it. She turned it, squeezing his fingertips. "Good thumbs," she said, "persistent. You keep your room neat."

Terry stared at his hand between hers.

"Apex central, Mount of Mercury. You are a good speller; you love reading."

"Yes ma'am."

"Poetry in this soul," she said. "Like McCree."

He wasn't sure what it meant, but it pleased him.

She traced his palm with a fingernail and a shiver rippled up Terry's spine. "You will live for a long time."

"I wish Mama knew that."

She looked at him, then back at his hand. "But your fate is uncertain. This you will make for yourself."

"What does that mean?"

He saw himself reflected in her dark eyes. "What becomes of you is your own doing. You may be what you wish, but you will have to work hard. It will not come easily."

A moment later, she added, "Success may come late."

"Is Mr. McCree really dead?"

"Listen — you can hear him whisper your name —"

Terry heard the tinkling of the bead curtain, people clapping hands rhythmically to give music to a tap dancer down the street.

"Do not mourn for him. He is with you always."

"Can you make my daddy come home?" Terry questioned.

"He is coming."

"When?"

"Soon enough. All things in time."

"Will he have to fight the Japanese?"

He felt her hand tense. "No," she said. "That will be over."

"Who will win?"

"Nobody."

"Ma'am?"

She tapped his palm with a fingernail. "Here are all the secrets of your universe. The past, the present and the future. But there is something missing."

"What?"

"Your wish."

"I don't really need a bicycle." And she'd already said that Daddy was coming home. Terry met her gaze. "I wish Deke would take me with him," Terry said.

"Tell me about Deke."

"He's a hero. He got his legs shot off by the Japanese." Her eyes were unwavering, waiting.

"Can you make legs grow again?"

"I did not take them, so I cannot create them."

"See, the thing is, Deke can do what anybody else can do. But Mama thinks he can't. So when Deke goes out camping, she won't let me go. But he takes Lamar —"

"Who?"

"Lamar. His daddy hit him with a car and Lamar is still a baby."

"Ah yes, Lamar."

"Could you make him grow up right?"

"Is he not happy?"

"He doesn't know any better."

"Who wishes him different? You? Or Lamar?"

"Not just me! His mama and daddy and my mama and —"

"But it is not Lamar. How can you ask me to change him when Lamar is happy? When he wishes to change, let him come and ask for himself."

Terry watched her knead his flesh.

"Now," she said. "If you could wish a single wish, the most important wish of your life — what would it be?"

"Forever?"

"Yes."

"I have to think about it."

"That is wise."

"You can make it come true?"

"Yes."

"I got a lot of little wishes."

"Just one. The most important."

Terry pulled his hand and she let it go. "How much will it cost?"

"We'll trade."

"What for what, though?"

"That depends on your wish."

"How about two little wishes and a medium-size wish instead?"

She held up one finger.

"I have to think about it."

"Come back when you have decided."

Terry stepped outside and stopped. Maybe he could *pay* for a tiny wish and still trade for a big one. He turned, calling, "Ma'am?"

Terry parted the curtain, "Ma'am?"

But the booth was empty.

Mama sprinkled flour and rolled dough for biscuits. Terry leaned against the counter. "How can nobody win a war, Mama?"

"What do you mean?"

"How can a war be over and nobody won?"

"If both sides quit fighting, I suppose." Mama cut circles with a baby food can and tapped dough onto a cookie sheet.

"Mama? If you could wish for anything, one big wish, what would you wish?"

"That your father would come home. Move, Terry, you're in my way."

"He's coming home," Terry declared.

"In one piece, then," Mama said.

Unnerved, Terry suddenly realized the conjure woman hadn't specified that! Still, surely, she would've told him.

"If Daddy had no legs," Terry questioned, "would I not be able to go some places with him?"

"Terry!" Mama turned angrily. "What kind of game is this?"

"I'm sorry."

Before he reached the door, Mama said, "Terry, when are you going to let go of this business with Deke?"

"I was only asking, Mama."

"Look at me!"

Resentfully, he did so.

"The issue is settled, understand? There is no margin for debate. No pressure will work. It is completely and irrevocably settled. Do you understand that?"

"Yes, Mama."

"Then we will not discuss it again."

"Yes ma'am."

When the porch door shut, Mickey closed her eyes.

What kind of parenting was this? No patience, no understanding — *damn it*!

She placed biscuits into the oven and went to the sink.
She gazed out the window, rinsing her forearms. She saw
Ossie Knight, a motionless part of shadow patterns
beneath the pines. But when she blinked, he was gone.

Ann in the front yard asked, "Why is Mama angry with
you?"

"I don't know," Terry replied.

Mickey massaged her temples. One wish?

She wished she could sleep until the war went away.

Fourteen

... TODAY'S-THE-DAY-TODAY'S-THE-DAY ...
Friday.

Sides aching, Terry could not hold himself to a walk. They wouldn't come until late, common sense told him that. Still, he ran.

He darted off the pavement, in parched grass, to let a car pass. Dust rolled and Terry ran through the cloud.

... today's-the-day-today's-the-day ...

A mindless chant timed to the fall of his bare feet on ground.

First, see if Ossie would go swimming or something. Like Deke and Lamar had nothing to do with it. Maybe fish under the bridge. Terry had a dime Mama had given him. That would buy two cold drinks at Owen's fish camp.

He cut across the road, down a bank, through bamboo

and over the canal to Ossie's house. In the thicket it was dark, cool, rich with humus. He slowed to catch his breath. Ahead, rising on stilts, shutters open, Terry saw the flicker of a kerosene lamp. He ran again.

Recklessly, so excited he didn't listen, up the steps, onto the porch, shouting, "Ossie! Hey, Ossie!"

As he reached the door, caution overtook him but too late. Hands came out of the dark and yanked him inside.

"It's all right!" Mrs. Knight screamed.

His feet left the floor and like a rag, Terry was shaken so violently his teeth snapped. Mrs. Knight shouted, "Let go! It's all right!"

With a shove, Terry was sent sprawling and he scooted under a table. Mrs. Knight, voice quivering said, "It's all right, Papa Night Song — he's a friend of Ossie's. It's all right."

Terry could see baggy trousers and Mrs. Knight's bare legs. She blocked the man's advance and Terry scampered backward to a wall.

"Tell my grandson to come here."

"He's gone, Papa."

"No longer can he wait; I am old."

"Terry," Mrs. Knight said without turning, "this is Ossie's grandfather, Joe Night Song. It's all right. Come on out."

"Osceola must learn to track."

"Papa Night Song —"

"He knows nothing of snares. He knows only white man's things."

"Now, Papa, you know how boys are —"

"When the white man is gone, how will Osceola know to stalk the deer and fish the streams again?"

"Terry," Mrs. Knight coaxed, "come on out."

"Too long we have waited. My days are not enough and already my mind cannot recall some things he must know."

"He is learning other things, Papa."

"White man's school."

"Yes."

"There he learns to cheat and lie."

"He learns what he must, to survive."

"When the god of sky and the god of earth hurl men into the sea, where will the white man be then?"

"Ossie can fish, Papa. He hunts frogs and —"

"Is his gig of steel?"

"Yes, but —"

"When there is no steel, can he do this with bamboo?"

"I don't know, Papa."

"He cannot," the man avowed.

"Papa, it's a new life we lead here. We do not live the old ways. It isn't necessary."

"I look about and not one basket do I see woven in the true way."

"Papa, we buy baskets. They are cheap. There are better ways than palm fronds."

"These white men will pay for plundering nature."

"Perhaps, Papa. But until then, we must live with them."

"Never!"

"Sit on the bed, Papa Night Song."

"The gods will win," he said. "The storms will come. The earth will heave and the rivers will flow again."

"Sit down. Sit down, now."

"Their buildings will go and all that has scarred the land will be overcome. You will see. It is only a matter of time. Then our children must know how to care for their children."

She untied his brogans, pulled them off.

"How many white men know such things?" he asked.

"Lie back, Papa."

"They will starve when their stores are closed and the crops are drowned. Then we will win."

Mrs. Knight loosened his blouse. She got a cardboard fan with a scene of the *Last Supper*, and fanned the old man's face.

"The white man will learn the laws of the spirits," he said softly.

"Until then, Papa, we must live by the white man's law."

"They dam our rivers and drain the lakes. Even now the sky glows red from muck fires and where are the wild things to run? Crimes. They have committed crimes."

"Go to sleep, Papa Night Song."

"My grandson, the son of my son —"

"Sleep, Papa."

"Osceola must learn. He must be ready."

She fanned, making a humming sound, sitting on the bed beside the man.

"I have killed them before. I shall kill them again."

"That was long ago, Papa," Mrs. Knight soothed. "In your father's time and his father's." She said something in their language and Terry heard Mr. Night Song sigh.

"What will Osceola know of souls and spirits?" he asked. "When the wind blows I hear their voices say, 'What of us now, Night Song? What of us now?' "

Under the table, hugging a wall, Terry heard the old man make a blubbery sound as Mrs. Knight fanned his face and gently creaked the bedsprings, rocking him.

"Papa, why do you come here only like this?" she questioned tenderly. "It isn't good for Ossie to see you like this."

"He does not listen to me."

"He listens more than you know."

"He nods only to fool me. I am not fooled."

A few minutes later, Mrs. Knight covered him with a quilt. She crossed the room and stooped to look at Terry under the table. "He is old," she said. "When he drinks he imagines himself young again. He dreams of wars he thinks he fought."

"Did he really kill people?"

"He thinks he did."

"Is he going to hurt you?"

"No."

She beckoned and Terry crawled out. He followed her gaze to the sleeping man.

"Will you tell your mother?" she asked.

"About what?"

"Your mother will not understand."

"I won't tell."

She put a hand on each side of Terry's face and kissed him on the mouth.

"When Ossie heard his grandfather," Mrs. Knight said, "he ran."

"I'll find him." At the door, Terry leaned in again to look at the unconscious man.

"What happened to his ear, Mrs. Knight?"

She pushed Terry gently, "See if you can find Ossie."

"Did somebody cut it off?"

"Run find Ossie. I must go to work."

"Mrs. Knight?"

"Yes?"

"I sure would like to meet Mr. Night Song sometime."

More sternly, she said, "Go play with Ossie."

"I never talked to a real chief before."

She shoved Terry gently, "Go!"

Terry ran toward Chosen.

Ossie sat on a piling, feet close to his buttocks, hugging his knees, watching a blue heron on a far bank. When Terry appeared, he extended his cigarette without greeting. Terry took a puff. "That's awful!"

"Cuban," Ossie noted. "They like things strong. You ever drink Cuban coffee?"

"No."

"Like yaupon tea — black drink — makes your belly ache."

"You're going to itch sitting on that creosote," Terry observed.

"Indians love to suffer," Ossie said.

"What do you mean?"

"Drinking black drink to prove what men they are. It makes you vomit."

The blue heron took a step, toes folded, and stood on one leg watching for minnows.

"They've always been dumb," Ossie said. "Before a battle they stayed up all night dancing and vomiting, then went to war sick to their stomachs and dead tired."

"I went by your house," Terry said.

Ossie drew on his cigarette.

"Your grandfather was there."

"You know I know that," Ossie said.

"I sure would like to meet him sometime."

"Didn't you meet him?"

"I meant, I'd like to talk with him sometime."

"He's crazy," Ossie said.

"You really think so?"

"Claims he fought in the last Indian War and that was a hundred years ago."

"His daddy might have."

"Gets drunk," Ossie said, "and pushes my mom around. Got his ear chopped off for telling about an Indian still. Disgraced himself and now he makes out like me and Mom are disgracing him."

"Who cut it off?"

"The man who owned the still. One ear. The other ear got chewed off in a fight. He has to wear a headband to keep his hat from falling over his eyes."

Enthralled, Terry looked up at Ossie silhouetted against the morning sky.

"One minute he bitches because we don't live by Indian ways. Next minute he's screaming because, down at Dania, they sell to tourists and let white people take their pictures. He's crazy."

"You think he ever killed anybody?"

"Says he killed his first baby."

"Why?"

"It had six toes."

"You believe that?"

"It's what he says."

The heron rose on long sweeping wings, feet up, rising to glide along the canal.

"Wish I could fly," Ossie said softly.

"You're going to fall off," Terry cautioned, "if you aren't careful."

Ossie repositioned himself. "How do you reckon birds keep from falling off a limb when they're sleeping?"

"When they bend their legs to perch, it locks their toes shut."

"It does?"

"Sure. When a hawk dives on a rabbit, his talons sink in when he hits, because his knees bend."

"How do you know that stuff?"

"I read about it."

"I never studied in school about birds' knees."

"I read it at home. I have a book you could borrow that tells about things like that."

Ossie jumped down. "I got better things to do than read books."

They walked along the dike, Ossie looking for pebbles he could use in a sling.

"Ossie, if you could wish anything and know it's coming true — one wish — what would you wish?"

"I'd wish all my wishes would come true."

"I don't think that'll work."

Ossie examined a stone, discarded it.

"I guess I'd wish I was somebody else," Ossie said.

"Who?"

"Somebody who ain't black or Indian or yellow."

"White, you mean?"

"I didn't say that."

"What else is left?"

Ossie looked at Terry. "I wouldn't mind being you," he said.

"Me!"

"Why not?"

"But, why?"

Ossie put a pebble in his sling and swung it round and round his head. "Watch that tree," he said. The stone made bark fly.

"Why me?" Terry asked.

"You got a crazy granddaddy?"

"My granddaddies are dead."

"Your mom ever sleep with men you don't know?"

"No."

"People call you nigger?"

"I wouldn't care if they did."

"Like hell. You get pissed off when somebody calls you 'Red.' "

"Depends on how they mean it."

"When they say 'nigger,' " Ossie said, "they don't mean nothing good."

"People ought not to do that," Terry allowed, "even when a man is colored."

"You like black people and Indians and — hell, everybody! You got no cause not to. You're white. You'll probably grow up and be some kind of a big shot. Watch that next tree."

The sling whirred and the stone flew. It nicked the trunk.

"Ossie, colored people get called 'nigger' and they don't like it either. You know how it feels. So how come you call them that?"

"They call me whitey."

"But you're Indian."

Ossie grunted. "The Indians call me 'American.' It's an insult when one Indian calls another Indian *American*."

They swam awhile and fished awhile. They let the fish go, so they wouldn't have to clean them. Ossie tried to teach Terry to use a sling, but Terry whacked himself behind his ear and decided to quit. All morning, Terry dreaded the moment when Ossie might suggest they go elsewhere. He didn't especially want to admit he was waiting for Deke.

For lunch, Ossie ran home for saltine crackers, but they were soggy. "Eat them anyway," Ossie advised. "They swell and you feel like you ate."

Terry spent his dime for a can of potted meat to put on the crackers, and a big orange drink which they shared.

Later that afternoon, when Ossie paused to hear a distant motor, Terry realized his companion was also waiting.

"What time do you suppose it is?" Terry questioned.

Ossie studied the shadows, the sun. "Four o'clock, maybe."

"They ought to be here about dark, don't you think?"

"If they're coming."

"Deke said Friday."

"Well," Ossie conceded, "it's Friday."

They picked wild limes and challenged one another to a longest-sucking-without-wincing contest. Ossie won. They laid on their backs under sighing pines, watching clouds meld from one identifiable form to another. They talked about girls Ossie had known intimately and Terry listened in awe.

Terry told Ossie again about catching fish with his bare hands, but when he tried to demonstrate, dropping frothy spit into the water as bait, nothing happened. Ossie dismissed it, forgivingly, but Terry could see his friend thought it was a lie.

Then, somehow, the airboat was in sight even before they heard the thumping propeller.

Terry and Ossie ran to the bridge and Lamar waved. Deke had whiskers. They hurried to the fish camp dock to join Charlie Owen, waiting.

"Safe and sound, I see," Mr. Owen remarked, taking a

rope Deke threw.

"We went camping," Lamar yelled.

"Hi, Deke."

"What say, redhead?"

"We cooked on a fire," Lamar reported. The boat lurched as he jumped for the dock. Deke jolted and accepted a hand from Mr. Owen.

"We saw ghosts," Lamar confided.

"How'd it go, Deke?" Mr. Owen asked.

"Not so good."

"I was afraid of that," Mr. Owen said gently.

"Look what I got." Lamar pulled a shell from his pocket.

"It stinks, Lamar."

"It stinks," Lamar said, "because the thing inside died."

"Throw it away."

"No."

"I've got to make other arrangements," Deke said to Mr. Owen.

Deke spoke to Terry. "Who's your friend?"

"Ossie," Terry said.

"Indian?"

Ossie stared.

"Ossie," Deke mused, "meaning 'Osceola,' right?"

Face set, Ossie returned his gaze unblinking.

"Osceola?" Deke asked.

"Yeah."

"Related?"

"No."

"They live across the dike, Deke," Mr. Owen said. "Mrs. Knight works at the Glades Café."

Man and boy studied one another and Deke asked, "Which tribe?"

"Seminole."

"Brighton or Big Cypress?"

"Cypress."

"Ah," Deke said. "Mikasuki. Do you speak Hitchiti?"

"Some."

"Easy with the equipment," Deke shouted at Lamar. Still in the high seat of his airboat, Deke turned again to Ossie. "How strong are you?"

"What do you need?"

"Think you could help me down from this thing?"

"I can try."

"Don't drop me."

Face searing, Terry watched Ossie accept the man's embrace and turn to put him on the dock. "Good enough," Deke said, extending a hand. "If you are a true descendant of the Mikasukis, you're good enough for me, Ossie. I never knew a Mikasuki who couldn't whip his weight in wildcats. Nor one I wouldn't trust with my life."

Terry tried to take a breath, but nothing came. He saw Deke hold Ossie's hand a minute, smiling.

"My great-great-grandfather was Arpeika," Ossie reported.

"Then you are royalty, young man," Deke said softly. "I am honored to meet you. What would your mother say about you working with me?"

"She wouldn't care."

Deke looked at Charlie Owen and the man nodded.

"Well!" Deke grinned. "I pay a dollar a day, Ossie."

Terry heard somebody call his name, but he was running, eyes burning, chest constricted, teeth clamped —

Fifteen

"I DON'T WANT a haircut, Mama."

"But you're going to get one," Mama said pleasantly.

"It makes me crawly and itchy."

"Don't roll up the windows, Terry," Mama instructed, parking the car. "It's too hot."

"I could come next week when you're at work. I don't see why I have to mess up a whole Saturday."

They eased past children gazing into store windows. Outside the courthouse, on wooden benches, old men chewed tobacco, talking, watching passers-by. "Trading day," country folks called this, and they crowded the sidewalks.

"All week long I sit around with nothing to do," Terry protested. "On my best day I have to do this!"

Mama halted beneath an endless, revolving red stripe of a barber's pole. She took a quarter from her purse. "Here," she said. "Tell him to make it short."

"Mama, it'll stick up!"

"Short," Mama replied mildly.

"Where will you be?"

"First at the post office to buy stamps and a savings bond. Then to the dime store for material to finish Ann's new dress. Finally at the grocery store. But if you don't find me, go back to the car and wait. Don't wander off."

"Why can't I walk home?"

"I want to be the first to see how handsome you are."

"Mama!"

She waved at the barber, Mr. Cantrell, then gently shoved Terry toward the ordeal. The shop was packed with waiting customers. Six barbers' clippers whirred, scissors snipped, and the floor was a blanket of fallen hair.

"Move over, youngsters," Mr. Cantrell called. The already crowded boys squeezed some more and Terry hooked one buttock on an edge of the bench. All the comic books were taken. A boy next to Terry blew bubble gum, engrossed in *Superman*. Terry examined a page over the boy's shoulder. He'd read it before.

"Next!" Whap! A flick of a pin-striped cloth sent hair flying. Terry hated this.

Across the street at the dime store, yellow flecks of popping corn danced in a glassed cage. The lady selling it was handing a tall sack to a black girl. For a nickel it was twice the popcorn you could buy at the theater.

"Next!" Whap! Hair everywhere.

A man in a chair at the far end of the room folded his newspaper. The headline said, US-BRITISH CARRIERS BOMB JAP MAINLAND.

"Next!" Terry held his breath. Whap!

"Ouch!" a boy cried. "Just a little nick," the barber soothed.

At an adjacent chair, a mother stood beside a screeching child. The boy was so short he had to have a "booster" seat placed across the arms of the chair to elevate him. With each swipe of clippers, she told the barber where to cut next. Behind them, two other barbers exchanged grins. Whap! "Next!"

"Stop shoving!" somebody cried, and the entire bench jolted. Mr. Cantrell peered over his spectacles at the guilty boy.

Terry saw Mama looking in a window at the dime store. Her faded dress hung limply, her hair was pinned in a severe bun that reminded Terry of an old-fashioned photograph. Then, from the store, a black cowboy hat came through the crowd. Terry sat forward. Chief Night Song!

He wore a bandana rolled and tied around his forehead to keep his hat up, and a bright red blouse with baggy sleeves. His trousers drooped at the crotch but were so short in the legs Terry could see his brogans were not laced all the way to the top. Mr. Night Song sat on the curb, right next to Mama, who was unaware. He was doing something to his walking cane — Terry rose slightly to better see, and Mr. Cantrell said, "Don't lose your place, young Calder."

"That's Chief Night Song," Terry told the boy chewing bubble gum. But the boy continued reading *Superman*.

"Will it be all right if I go see my mama, Mr. Cantrell?"

"You'll lose your place," the barber warned.

But Terry didn't care. He crossed the street, darting between the cars waiting for places to park. Mama had gone inside the dime store.

Now he could see what Mr. Night Song was doing. The old man held a narrow roll of crepe paper. One end was pinned with a thumb tack to the bottom of his cane. Very carefully, he wound the red paper around his walking stick like the stripe on a barber's pole.

"Mr. Night Song?"

The Indian did not take his eyes from his task.

"I met you at Ossie's house, remember? You shook me around some."

"Then I apologize."

"It's okay. Listen. You want to meet my mama?"

"For what purpose?"

"She's never met a chief before."

"I am not a chief."

"Ossie said you were."

"No more."

Mr. Night Song checked the tensile of his crepe paper, adjusted it. From a pocket he withdrew a pair of blunt scissors, the kind Ann used to cut paper dolls, and snipped with care.

"I've been wanting to talk to you, Mr. Night Song."

"What about?"

"Swamps. And things."

The Indian turned his cane slowly between dark hands stained red by crepe.

"I sure would like to learn about the swamps."

"Ask your father."

"He's in Poland investigating atrocities." Terry sat on the curb. "That looks nice," he said.

Mr. Night Song placed a finger here, there, checking the symmetry of spacing. Somebody bumped him from behind and Terry shouted up, "Be careful!"

The intruder replied with profanity, but Mr. Night Song didn't respond. "Could I come visit you sometime, Mr. Night Song?"

"You know where I live?"

"Big Cypress. Caloosahatchee River, on the old dry lake bed," Terry added. These and other camps, he knew.

"I go where the wind blows and the fish swim."

"Yessir."

Mr. Night Song gazed skyward with moist eyes, both hands on his cane which he'd placed between spread legs.

"See, the thing is," Terry said, "I know a lot about swamps already. Coontie flour and *asi* drink. I can catch fish with my bare hands sometimes. Things like that." Mr. Night Song didn't believe it either.

"I did once, anyway," Terry revised.

Night Song rose, appraised his gaily wrapped cane.

"It really looks good," Terry said.

The Indian walked, reaching out to prod anybody who blocked his way. Terry followed. "I want to learn about the soul and spirits, Mr. Night Song."

Night Song stopped at the popcorn machine. Children were laughing, kernels snapping, fluffy corn jumping behind glass.

"Want some popcorn, Mr. Night Song?"

"I have no money."

"I do! One big popcorn," he told the lady. She reached for a bag already filled and Terry said, "Can we have a bag of just-popped?"

"Ain't none of it more than a minute old," she said.

"Please. Some of the just-popped."

Black hairs on her upper lip crawled over muttered words. She scooped fresh popcorn, filled another bag and extended it. Terry gave it to Mr. Night Song.

"We could get a cold drink, too," Terry suggested. "I still have some money."

Mr. Night Song walked and ate without offering to share. As they drew near colored town, the crowded walkways changed tempo. More laughter, brighter garments, a tantalizing aroma of frying fish, hot bread, and a cauldron of simmering beans for sale at a penny a cup.

"If you want a big orange," Terry offered, "we can get it at the pool hall."

The Indian poked his festive cane, prodding people so they would step aside. Several people waited to see the conjure woman. Two boys danced as a blind man played a banjo. Mr. Night Song stopped when they reached the pool hall, munching popcorn, waiting.

Terry swallowed his trepidation, entered, and stretched for attention at a bar where men drank beer. The click of billiard balls, a deafening roar of a jukebox, made it necessary to shout.

"One orange drink!"

"No kids," the bartender said.

"One big orange drink," Terry insisted.

The black man leaned across the bar. "I can't sell to no white boy. Go someplace else."

Terry pointed toward a solitary figure in the doorway. Night Song ate popcorn, his cane crooked over an arm. "For him," Terry demanded. "One big orange."

The bartender shot a glance at several men watching, then got out an orange — not a Nehi, a small one!

"Hey," Terry yelled, "not —" But it was open and on the counter now.

"Ten cents."

"A dime? It's a little one and it costs a nickel!"

"Ten goddamned cents, boy."

"That costs a nickel."

He snatched away the drink, but Terry screamed, "Okay! Ten cents." He slapped a coin on the counter and angrily carried the drink to Mr. Night Song.

Not once did the Indian make comment. He did not respond to questions, he did not look down as Terry followed, tentatively trying to gain a favorable audience.

When, at last, Mr. Night Song walked toward the railroad trestle, Terry knew he'd been dismissed. Bewildered, he fell back and watched the old man go. Only then did it occur to him to think of Mama and the haircut money he'd spent.

"Spent your money on what?" Mama snapped.

"Popcorn. A cold drink. I —"

"You didn't stay at the barbershop?"

"No ma'am. Mama, I saw Mr. Night Song and —"

"Then you disobeyed."

"No ma'am. I mean, yes ma'am. But Mama, I saw Mr. Night Song and I went to meet him."

"Terry," Mama's voice quavered, "you disobeyed, didn't get your hair cut, and left me sitting here with groceries that are ruining in this heat."

"I'm sorry, Mama."

Mama seized his hand and pressed a quarter into the palm. "Get in there and get your hair cut, young man. This instant. And then, come straight home."

"Yes ma'am."

"And Terry, it had better be short and you'd better come straight home."

"I will, Mama."

Terry took a seat on the waiting bench. In the barber's wall mirror he saw Mama back out and drive away.

"Next!" Whap!

Already Terry began to itch.

The oleo margarine had melted. The precious pork roast was bleeding. That child! Mickey shut the refrigerator door with a hip. Then, as her coffee began perking, she sat at the kitchen table to look at the mail.

Not one, but six letters from Gerald. Two had been forwarded from Birmingham, but the airmail envelopes of the other four were addressed to Camp Osceola.

She savored the moment, a mix of anticipation and dread that always came before she opened a letter from Gerald. One never knew what awful turn of events might have transpired. Carefully, Mickey slit the envelopes. No hurry. It might be days before another letter came. The coffee smelled good, ready, waiting. Afar, she heard Ann's shrill voice, playing with children down the street.

Finally, with almost ritualistic delays dispelled, she placed the letters in order of their dates and began to read very very slowly:

". . . there is talk of a United Nations . . . our best hope for global peace . . . rumors of Churchill having tough going in upcoming elections . . . a commission to try war criminals . . . dreadful atrocities . . . entire communities wiped out . . . genocide . . . personal and national destruction. . . ."

Oh God, Gerald, is there nothing good? Come home!

Next letter — banalities, trivia, names of people she didn't know, tedious reporting of intra-agency bickering . . . civilian relief. . . .

The next: "The new Polish government of national unity sitting in Warsaw has been officially recognized, finally. Governments are agonizing in their slow ways. . . ."

The letter spoke of "Russian interference . . . puppet states . . . American lack of firm resolve. . . ."

Who cared? Who at home could possibly have cared? Mickey ached for the words that finally came in Gerald's fluid firm strokes: "My Mickey, my baby, how I love you. I dream of you each night. I awake to turn and you are there only from my dreams. I pray for the day when I can —" the thought must've been interrupted; the sentence ended with, "there's a rumor that allied forces will be withdrawn from this theater."

What did that mean? Coming home at last? Withdrawn to where? Being sent where? Mickey sipped coffee from a cup held by shaking hands.

Ann romped in, saw Mama reading, and quietly withdrew. Mickey went to the next letter, and the next.

Anger was futile. Frustration was normal, she told herself. Gerald did not manipulate his life these days. They were not alone in their loneliness, their deprivation, the often insane delays by bureaucratic governments.

"I'm home, Mama," Terry announced from the porch.

"All right."

"Letters from Daddy?"

"Yes, Terry. Let me read them alone, will you?"

"May I read them?"

Mickey pushed the first letter across the table.

"Did Mr. Cantrell cut your hair?" she asked.

"No ma'am. Another man."

"Well," Mickey said, "it's short if nothing else."

She saw resentment in the boy's eyes. Terry took the letter and began reading, lips synchronized to the script, one finger tracing the page.

"Not much to interest you, I'm afraid."

"I want to read it anyway," he said.

She turned to the final letter, a single sheet.

"My babies," Gerald had written, "I am in Rome now.

I hope permanently. Until time to return home, anyway. The worst has passed, I pray. People are digging out, planning for tomorrow. Now and then I hear the laughter of children, a clap of hands, and music in the night air. The war in the Pacific is on all our minds. We are awaiting word on which of us will go there. I confess, my American zeal is waning. I wish only to come home. But the quasi-military word is, a million casualties will be suffered if we must attack Japan's mainland with invasion forces. That is more than the entire war has cost us thus far. Pray for a miracle. The U.S. is trying to get Russia into the Pacific fight, but Stalin doesn't seem to be up to it."

Mickey turned the page. Nothing. Had something been censored? Omitted? What? She looked in the envelope. No second page. No "Love, Gerald."

Terry looked up, "What is it, Mama?"

"I think part of this letter is missing."

Terry mirrored her distress and Mickey realized how distraught she must appear. She tried to smile, but her face pulled.

She went into the bedroom, shut the door, and lay face down across her bed. It was a disease, this loneliness. A cancerous, eroding, debilitating disease.

Terry tapped lightly on the closed bedroom door.

"What is it?"

"Want me to bring you a cup of tea, Mama?"

Long pause.

"I'll make it the way you like it," Terry offered.

"All right."

Terry stirred in sugar and took it to the room. Mama propped against the headboard, Terry sat at the foot of the bed, hands in his lap.

"We'll make it through all this," Mama said huskily.

"Yes ma'am."

"Then this will all seem like a dream."

Terry nodded, watching her hold the cup without drinking.

"Who is Mr. Night Song?" Mama asked.

"Ossie's grandfather."

"Is that Ossie's true name? Night Song?"

It hadn't occurred to Terry. "I guess so."

Mama looked at him soberly, then laughed.

"What?" Terry questioned.

"Did Mr. Night Song cut your hair?"

"No!"

She laughed again. "Well. I think you've been scalped."

"It looks terrible."

"It will grow."

Mickey reached for his hand. "I love you," she said.

"Mama, may I talk to you about Deke?"

Mama's jaw set.

"He is going to pay Ossie a dollar a day to go with him, Mama."

"What happened to Lamar?"

"I don't know. I heard Deke tell Mr. Owen at the fish camp that he had to make other arrangements."

"What will Ossie's mother have to say about that?"

"She won't care."

"If she knows what's involved, I don't believe that."

"Indians live in swamps, Mama. Ossie could get out by himself if he had to. That's what Mr. Night Song wants them to do — go back to living in the swamps."

"What is your point?"

"Please, Mama. With Ossie, even if Deke couldn't help,

I know we could get out of there alone."

"Terry," Mama put her tea on a bedside table. "I've tried to explain the hazards, the intolerable hazards of such a venture. I'm not being overly protective. I'm being sensible! Don't tell me that you don't know this. You wouldn't expect me to let you walk a board between two tall buildings, would you? Yes, you might make it. Yes, if the wind doesn't blow, if the board doesn't twist, yes! But *if* something went wrong, the consequences are too great. The probability is death. Death is final. I cannot, I will *not* allow you to place yourself in danger."

He glared at her.

"I don't like the expression on your face, Terry."

"May I go camping then, at Kramer Island?"

"With whom?"

"With Mr. Night Song."

Exasperated, Mickey swung her legs off the bed, rising. "How long is this going to continue?"

"He is an Indian chief, Mama," Terry said. "He has his legs. He knows all about swamps. I've camped at Kramer Island before with the Boy Scouts, remember?"

"You went along; you did not do it alone."

"I'll be with Mr. Night Song, Mama!"

"I don't know this man —"

"He's Ossie's grandfather. I wanted to introduce you to him today, but you were in the dime store."

"Terry, dear God, Terry!"

"Mama!" Terry leaped to his feet. "I want to go with Mr. Night Song. May I?"

It was as near rebellion as she'd ever seen him. Eyes darting, face livid, he stood with fists clenched.

"No."

"Why not?" Terry screamed.

"For all the reasons listed before. I don't know him."
Terry walked from the room, then turned to look back
down the hall. Mickey felt her heart skip a beat.

Her son, that moment, hated his mother.

Sixteen

AT BEAUDRY'S GASOLINE station in colored town,
Deke stopped to get air in his tires. Terry said, "I need to
go see somebody, Deke."

"Don't be long."

He ran to the sign of a hand and stood outside the bead
curtain, mustering courage.

"You have decided?" asked a whispery voice.

"I need to ask something."

"Come in."

"Listen. If I wish somebody would like somebody, is
that a big wish or a little one?"

"You wish this someone to like you?"

"That my mama would like Deke."

The beads rippled, tinkling.

"Come in," she said. "We will talk."

"I can't. Deke's waiting for me."

"Do you mean like, or love?"

He looked up at his eyebrows, considering. "A lot of like would be all right."

"What of your father?"

"He won't care."

"You're sure?"

"I don't think he would."

"Is this what your mother wishes? Or the man?"

"I don't know."

"It is not yours to wish, then."

"It isn't?"

"They must wish for themselves."

Terry heard Deke's truck horn. "Ma'am?"

"Yes?"

"If Deke wished it, could you make it come true?"

"If it is his wish."

The horn blew again, longer.

"How much would it cost?"

"That is for him to discuss with me."

"Okay." Terry skipped away sidewise. "I'll tell him."

Driving out the Pahokee highway, Terry said, "Deke, if you could wish one wish and knew it would come true, what would you wish?"

"I'd have to think about it."

"I know somebody who can make it happen."

"Oh?"

"The conjure woman."

"Conjure woman," Deke said. He turned off the pavement, past a tent with a sign reading, REVIVAL.

"She can make any wish come true," Terry reported.

"Think she could grow me some new legs?"

"She did not take them, so she cannot create them."

Deke looked at him, then shifted gears. "I imagine such

a service isn't cheap."

"You might could trade."

"What for what?"

"What you want for what she wants."

"Like what?"

"That's for you to discuss with her."

Deke looked at him again, this time with his chin down.

"Anyway," Terry reasoned, "it depends on the wish. You could pay for a little wish."

They crossed another bridge following a firebreak through a cane field.

"Mama already likes you," Terry labored. "A little more is all we need."

Deke stopped, dust overtaking them. He leaned on the steering wheel peering ahead. "I must've made a wrong turn."

They drove back toward Belle Glade.

"That my book would be the definitive reference of tropical Florida flora," Deke said.

"Sir?"

"I would wish," Deke said, "that my book would be the best ever done on the subject."

"She can do that for sure."

Deke gazed out his window.

"She might give cut-rate for two wishes at once," Terry said.

"Sounds reasonable."

"Want to go?"

Deke looked out his window again.

"One thing you could wish," Terry counseled, "just so it would be easier: that Mama likes you more. She already *likes* you, so it ought not to cost much. You could tell her that."

Terry wiped his hands down his trousers. Past the
revival tent, over the bridge. Terry said, "What do you
think?"

"About what?"

"Going to the conjure woman."

"Sure," Deke said. "Why not?"

Terry trembled as Deke got into his chair. Then they
wheeled up to the curtain of beads and Terry said,
"Ma'am?"

"Come in."

He pulled back the beads and Deke rolled inside.

"You are Deke," she said.

Terry saw Deke's gaze drop to the low-cut blouse,
linger. She didn't look old.

"Give me your right hand."

She squeezed his fingers, looking at calloused knuckles
made because Deke moved as he did. She massaged his
palm.

"Nothing bad, I trust," Deke remarked.

"Much strength of will."

She clasped his hand and their eyes met. "Do you wish
for fame or fortune?"

"My needs are more immediate than that."

She looked into his eyes a moment. "We can arrange
that, too." Then, to Terry, "It is best we are alone. You
can wait outside."

"In the truck," Deke said.

Terry got into the truck, perfectly willing to wait as
long as required. But in a distressingly short time, Deke
appeared, looked both ways, and came rolling out.

"Is she going to do it?" Terry cried.

"Do what?"

"The wish!"

"I expect she would."

"Does it cost much?"

"That remains to be seen."

"What'd she say?"

"About what?" Deke started the motor.

"Deke," Terry shrilled. "The wish!"

"What wish?"

"Deke!"

Deke held Terry's knee, shaking it, laughing.

"What'd you wish?" Terry demanded.

"Wouldn't that mess it up, telling?"

"Would it?"

"I should think so," Deke said. "If you tell a wish, doesn't that stop it from coming true?"

"She didn't tell me that."

"What did you wish?"

"I haven't wished yet."

"When you do, maybe you shouldn't tell anybody."

Terry seized Deke's arm. "Is she going to do it?"

"When we came to terms on price, she said she would."

"Wow, wow! That's great."

"It's been a long dry spell," Deke said softly.

"Yeah," Terry agreed, "we could use some rain."

"Can I have a cold drink?" Ann asked.

"*May* I."

"May I?" Ann said.

"We'll see."

Ann stood behind the front seat and whispered in Terry's ear, "Does that mean yes?"

"It means," Mama said, "we'll see."

They drove into Beaudry's gasoline station. Terry could see the conjure woman's hand sign. "May I go visit some-one, Mama?"

"No." She waited for the owner to complete business with someone else.

"I won't be gone long."

"No, Terry."

"Afternoon, Missus Calder." Mr. Beaudry shifted tobacco in his cheek, touched the brim of his hat.

"Mr. Beaudry, please look at my tires."

He put his hands on his knees and bent. "Thin."

"Worn out, Mr. Beaudry."

"Yessum."

"Three weeks ago you said you could get tires."

"Yessum. You got your stamps?"

"You have my stamps."

"Oh, yessum. I recollect."

"Mr. Beaudry, the threads are showing on one tire. I must have it. Now, I gave you my stamps and —"

"See, Missus Calder," he said, "everybody needs tires."

"I realize that."

"— a set of tires is mighty dear these days."

"Mr. Beaudry, we've been through all that."

"I could sell a full set of tires for a hundred dollars a tire."

"A hundred dollars! That's outrageous. They're listed at eighteen, Mr. Beaudry."

"According to the government. But what the government says something is worth and what something is worth may be two different things, Missus Calder."

"Hey!" Terry shouted. "There goes Deke."

"Terry," Mama snapped, "you're interrupting." But she

glanced at Deke's truck driving into colored town.

"See, Missus Calder, it's a case of supply and demand."

"Mr. Beaudry, my husband and I have been doing business with you since we came to Belle Glade."

"Yessum. Appreciate it, too."

Terry put his arms on the dashboard, gazing through the windshield at Deke's truck. It stopped at the hand sign.

"I've been told you received your full allotment of tires. Is that correct?"

"Near about, Missus Calder."

"So now it's a matter of who gets the tires."

"I tell you," Mr. Beaudry shifted tobacco, "it's a lot like sugar, Missus Calder. Sugar sells for four cents a pound. The government says so. But if I had it, I could sell a thousand pounds for a thousand dollars."

"Trade sugar for tires?" Mama said.

"You have sugar to trade?"

Mama stared toward Deke's truck turning a far corner. "That's black market, Mr. Beaudry."

"Look, Missy," Mr. Beaudry leaned on the car, "the war's nearly over. In a year or two you can buy all you want for eighteen dollars a tire. But right now there are a hundred people with threads showing. Out at Okeelanta they cut sacks so they can give sugar to their people."

"It isn't supposed to be so."

"But it *is* so."

"Then you won't sell one tire?"

He spit out the wad, eyes flashing, "Yes, ma'am, I'll sell you one tire. Come back tomorrow."

Mama was shaking as she drove out of the station. At a stop sign, where the street joined an alley behind Main Street stores, they met Deke's truck.

"Hi, Deke!" Terry leaned out, hollering.

Deke waved, looked away.

"Hey," Terry said softly, "he's got the conjure woman."

Deke passed in front of them, going down the cluttered alley. Mickey saw raven hair and dark eyes when his companion glanced their way.

"Who?" Mama questioned.

"The conjure woman," Terry said.

Mickey shifted gears, eased off the brake. Any minute these tires might —

"She can make a wish come true," Terry reported.

"I dare say."

"You can pay," Terry said, "or trade."

"What kind of trade?"

"What you want for what she wants."

When they reached Main Street, Mama said, "How do you know her?"

"She's the conjure woman. Everybody knows her."

"I don't."

"Most people."

"I don't," Ann said.

"You don't go down to colored town, either."

"What are *you* doing wandering around colored town?" Mama demanded.

A moment later, Mama said, "Not that it matters."

"Ma'am?"

"It doesn't matter. I was wondering, that's all."

"I threw circulars with Ossie, Mama."

"Yes, of course."

"Paddled my ass," Ossie said. "Just wait. We'll fix him."

Terry watched Ossie stretch the neck of a prophylactic over a catsup bottle and upend it, letting tomato paste flow into the condom.

"Where'd you get those?" Terry whispered.

"Found them."

"Found them where?"

"Never mind," Ossie said. "Give me a rubber band." Ossie secured the prophylactic, but not tightly. He examined his work, nodded. "It's got to look like blood," he said, putting the first one aside to begin the next.

"It won't be long before I go to the swamps, Ossie." Ossie shook catsup into another condom.

"I went to see the conjure woman."

Ossie paused. "You did? What for?"

"To make a wish."

"For what?"

"For Mama and Deke to like one another."

"You did? Why'd you do that?"

"So I can go with Deke to the swamps, that's why." Ossie shook the bottle, watching red ooze. "Does your mama mess around with men?"

"Mess around? No."

"She want to?"

Terry stood up, hotly. "No!"

"Before now, you mean. She can't resist the conjure woman. You may have a daddy with no legs before it's over. Okay. Two for you and three for me. Remember what to do, right?"

"Right."

"Don't squeeze it until you get inside the washing machine. Then, mash hard. Come out kind of staggering. Be sure the guard is close up before you let the catsup trickle out of your mouth. Got it?"

"I think so."

"Act it up a little," Ossie directed. "Kind of vomit, then let it flow."

"Okay."

They had reached the loft by way of the outside ladder behind the packing house. From there, past sleeping bats, they descended to the second floor looking down a long conveyor.

"When you hit bottom, those rollers are going to be screaming bloody murder," Ossie advised. "Don't get shook up. Ride it all the way to the washing machine. When I see you coming, I'll throw the switch and start the motor."

"What about you?"

"Depends on what the sonofabitch does. If he tries to grab you, I'll jump out and show him this —"

Ossie had his arm bent and only his elbow protruded from a short sleeve. Catsup dripped from the nub.

"That looks good," Terry said.

"First I'll bang on the side of his office," Ossie explained. "Then when I reach the master switch, come on down."

The guard could be seen behind glass, feet on his desk, leaning back in a swivel chair, a hat pulled over his eyes. His mouth was open.

"Is he the mean one?" Terry asked.

"Mean as a snake and sneaky as a weasel. You ready?"

Terry positioned his wooden crate, prepared to push off. One of the guard's arms slipped off his chest. But all he did was shut his mouth for a moment. Ossie crept from pillar to post, machine to machine. He shot a glance at Terry, got "thumbs up" and ran across an open space to crouch under windows of the guard station. Terry tensed, ready.

Ossie banged the wall and the guard flung forward, hat flying. Ossie ran in a stoop and reached the switch that controlled current for the entire floor. Terry, nestled in the box, pushed off.

Whing! Rollers whining, the box gathered speed and screamed into the first turn.

"What the —" the guard yelled, coming as fast as his weight would allow. Whing! Terry smelled wood burning as friction seared the box. Still gathering speed, he rushed toward a long sloping ride to a washing machine where vegetables underwent a rinse before shipment. Whing! The guard bellowing, Terry flew overhead, arms tucked inside, and Ossie threw the switch.

Lights came on, then dimmed as huge motors drained the surge. Wheels began to turn. Terry flew past an ascending belt. The guard looked this way, that, and settled on Terry now going into the final glide that would send him into the washing machine.

For one instant, Terry thought he had not enough speed to make it, but momentum carried him off the rollers, onto a belt and he was drawn through hanging flaps which kept spray inside. He was immediately drenched, pushed and pulled through jets of water before emerging. He mashed the prophylactic and red oozed.

Coming on thundering footfalls, the guard showed his teeth. Terry stood, turned, and the guard hesitated but kept coming. It wasn't going to work! Terry leaped to a far side of the washing machine and his heart stopped. Blocked by hampers, blocked by boxes, blocked by —

Ossie jumped out, mouth wide, tongue extended, catsup trickling. He waggled the short arm, staggered, and screamed.

The guard halted, blanched, sat down hard. Ossie

shrieked, short arm flipping, and the guard's eyes rolled as
he fainted and fell on his back.

"You think he's all right?" Terry raced beside Ossie.

"Yeah."

"What if he had a heart attack or something?"

"People with heart attacks don't chase that good."

When they reached the safety of Terry's house, Ossie
said, "That'll teach him to paddle my ass for catching
bats."

Seventeen

"I GOT YOUR NOTE," Deke said.

"Come in."

Mickey held the screen door as he mounted the steps backward, turning to vault his body on straight arms.

"Do you need your chair?"

"Leave it out there," he directed. "I'll sit on your couch, if that's all right."

"Fine."

Deke rolled onto the sofa, sat up and braced himself in a corner against the back and arm of the furniture. He met her eyes with an unsettling directness.

"Well," Mickey clasped her hands. "Would you care for tea, or coffee?"

"Coffee, if you have it."

"Freshly perked. How do you take it?"

"Black."

Mickey served the beverage from a low table between the couch and her chair. "I hope you won't consider this an imposition," she said. "I have a problem and I need to discuss it."

"Your note said Terry," Deke acknowledged.

"Yes. I considered talking with Velma Mason. She's the closest friend I have here. But Velma has a simplistic approach to things. I mean, she does or doesn't do something. It's black or white and no shades of gray with Velma."

"I don't believe I can fault her logic."

"No," Mickey agreed. "The psychology of a situation or the subtleties of personal relationships don't clutter Velma's life. Perhaps that's a blessing. Anyway, she has allowed Lamar to accompany you, against her better judgment and because Burrell forced the issue. It was a choice of leaving Burrell or relenting, so Velma relented. I can't see any point in producing more friction in that household by worrying aloud about Terry to Velma."

"I can sympathize with that."

"You knew about their argument?"

"Fight," Deke corrected.

"Yes."

"I knew." Deke sipped coffee, green eyes welded to Mickey's face. She sipped coffee too, stalling.

"I have given this a great deal of thought, Deke."

"Apparently."

"It is obvious that nothing short of absolute candor is required here. Blunt. To the point."

He waited, sipping.

"I confess I have been observing you from a one dimensional view," Mickey said. "I have allowed your lack of legs to be the focal point. I have considered you only in the realm of what you can not do, rather than what you can. I apologize for that."

"I was guilty of the same thing for a long time."

"I don't know why that should surprise me," Mickey stated.

"As a matter of fact," he said, "I've become accustomed to that — syndrome. I spend my life these days fighting off people who are trying to be helpful, but by their solicitous behavior constantly assault my self-image."

"Yes, so Terry has said."

"Smart boy."

"Obviously we've all been misguided where you're concerned. But most damning of all, I admit I have allowed your lost legs to dominate my assessment of you. I did that without realizing I was doing it. Terry brought me up short a day or so ago."

"Oh?"

"He asked me a question that has haunted me ever since," Mickey said. "He asked me, if his father came home without legs, would I not allow him to go some places with his father?"

"I think Burrell used the same logic. In any event, touché."

"Touché indeed. It brought me face-to-face with my argument. I don't want Terry to go with you into the swamps —" she faltered, "— because in the event of trouble, a motor that wouldn't start, the boat overturned, whatever, you would be more of a liability than a help in safely getting my child home again."

"Don't you think I know that, Mickey?"

"I haven't changed my mind. But when forced to examine my reasoning in the light of, 'What if this were Gerald?' a quandary evolved."

Deke laughed sardonically.

"If it were Gerald, I asked myself, would I tell father and son they could not go to the swamps together? Like Velma, against better judgment, I would yield."

Deke grunted.

"Therefore," Mickey said, "since the same hazards would exist if it were Gerald, am I being wise to alienate my son by persisting in this objection?"

"Have you reached a conclusion?"

"It's a contradiction in logic. Since it is you, I have no reason to ignore the dangers and tell Terry he may go. If it were his father, the weight of parental relationships would make me yield despite the dangers."

"All right."

"There is where Terry saw the illogic of my reasoning. I would let him go with his father if Gerald had no legs, and not letting him go with you now seems arbitrary in Terry's opinion."

Deke was smiling. *Damn him.* "What would Velma say?" he asked.

"What has Velma to do with this?"

"Because her response is the only answer. It is, as you stated, 'simplistic.' Having told Lamar he can go, she accepts that. Your problem is, you want to show a little boy the responsible, adult reasons why he cannot do what he wants to do. Simplistically, you should say, 'You can't go because it is dangerous. Period. That is that. End of discussion.'"

"How dangerous is it, truly?"

"Very. Snakes, bogs, quicksand, forty miles from the nearest human being. I'd be a fool to deny it. Nobody knows the danger of going out there with me more than me. A hundred things can go wrong. It is, literally, a life or death gamble. I know it. But, selfishly, if I didn't take Lamar for his strength, and now the Knight boy for his maturity and willingness to follow my orders, I couldn't go. I don't need Terry. I could use him, but I don't require him. Understand?"

"Yes."

"Using Lamar alone to help me in and out of the boat, I was baby-sitting. He's a child mentally younger than your daughter."

"I know."

"He is afraid to climb a tree, afraid of the night sounds, but blithely unaware of real danger. Seeing that, and having now discovered Ossie Knight, I can take both boys. Ossie is an Indian boy; he knows the dangers, and they are a calculated risk he's accustomed to facing. I believe he could get out of the glades alone if he had to. But I still need Lamar's strength."

"Why do you want to go at all?" Mickey questioned.

"To write a book is the simplistic answer. But the reason for the book is complex. A man in my condition has a short life expectancy. That makes me think about today, tomorrow, and what I might accomplish with the time I have left. A book is a stab at extending life.

"Everyday in the hospital, doctors and psychologists and therapists came walking up on their good legs to tell me how I needed to get a grip on reality. Very pat answers for what was wrong. In fact, nobody could help me but me. When I realized that, I applied for a grant. The government couldn't afford to turn me down. Using my lack of legs, I got a truck when nobody can get a truck. And unlimited gasoline, oil, tires, *et cetera*. By being selfish, pushing, demanding, and thinking only of what I wanted, I made moves. Had I thought of others, the war effort, I'd still be doing exercises and utterly depressed in Forest Glen, Maryland."

"That — is human enough."

"See, Mickey, I'm down to the basics of self. If I let it, the world will destroy me in my own eyes. If I don't allow it, I can produce a book, hopefully, that will extend my life beyond this one. Fifty years from today, somebody will pick up my book and my voice will ring in his ears as he reads the text. Survival. That's what it's all about."

"I understand, Deke."

"But as it is," he said, "I don't need Terry to survive. And I want to help you with him. Even that is selfish."

"What do you mean?"

"If the problem didn't exist, would we be having coffee?"

"You can have coffee anytime you please," Mickey offered.

"Oh, God," Deke said, "don't go back to platitudes. Do you know how long it's been since I had a one-on-one adult conversation? An intelligent discussion with words longer than two syllables? And as for facing my stumps, no other adult has been able to bring himself to say it — Hey, Deke, you're crippled. Permanently, you poor bastard! And frankly, it's a pain in everybody's ass and —"

Deke's gaze dropped away and Mickey reached for his arm.

"The truth is," he said, "I'd like to admit it is a real pain for me, too."

"I know that."

"It isn't my nature to take advantage of people," Deke said. "But if I don't, with these youngsters, then I might as well go hole up and die, Mickey. I'm not after sympathy, goddamn it. I am being blunt, as you said, and to the point. I am sorry for myself. I am crippled physically. But I am *trying*. I fight the self-pity. I take advantage. I push and shove and I will continue to do so because it is essential. For survival."

"Maybe I should reconsider this," Mickey said.

"Oh, damn it!" Deke shook off her hand. "Mickey, For God's sake! If Terry were my son I would flatly tell him he couldn't go. That's all you can say. No. That's it! No."

"If you can bear with me, Deke, I'll meet you on your terms. I'll overcome the natural inclination to — pity you. I will try to face your — stumps. I will do it, given time."

"It's all a man can ask."

Mickey watched the pained expression ease. Deke said, "Are you lonely?"

"Excruciatingly so."

"So am I. There's precious little laughter in my life these days. What we all need is a good laugh. Normal, natural, laughter over normal things. Nothing forced. I'd give an arm for that — and that's a real sacrifice for me." He leaned forward, "Look, let's get off the negatives. Let's see what we can work out that is positive. I think we both see the problem in all its human complexities. Now to find some compromises."

"That's what I need."

"First of all, my work isn't confined exclusively to the deep glades. I am cataloguing the flora native to South Florida. That means I can take Terry to a good many places where he'd be a real help to me. Kramer Island, for example."

Mickey poured more coffee for both of them. "Terry loves the outdoors, Deke. He loves wild things. Insects, flowers, trees, water, the sky — and he's observant. It's a very important thing to him. We went to Birmingham when Gerald left for Europe and that was a terrible mistake. Aside from my own unhappiness there, I watched Terry wither. He spent his days in a nearby cemetery because that was the closest thing he had to woodlands. He reads constantly. Have you seen his books? What you have to understand is his intimacy, the necessity apparently, of his association with nature. Like oxygen, he requires it. When he was six-years-old he wouldn't go to school — running away to spend time with an elderly man who prowled the swamps in search of seeds and things he sold to botanical houses."

"He told me."

"I don't want to destroy that," Mickey said. "So I can't say, 'No, and that's final.' "

"Compromise," Deke concluded. "I'll make trips to Kramer Island for awhile. The glades are suffering from drought anyway, so it isn't inconvenient."

"Thank you."

"No," Deke amended, "thank *you*. It has been a long while since I had a verbal exchange above the oh-oh-look-at-Johnny-go level."

Mickey laughed. Surprised, she recognized it as genuine. Deke turned, eased himself from the couch, and bumped toward the door.

"It wouldn't hurt to get everybody together socially," Deke suggested over his shoulder. "Let Terry see we aren't enemies. Maybe with Velma and Burrell — more importantly, let Lamar and Ossie join us. Part of our problem has been a lack of communication."

"How about dinner tomorrow night?"

"Excellent! But my pull with the government doesn't extend to meat. What can I bring?"

"Yourself." Mickey watched him negotiate his chair.

"What time?"

"Six?"

"I look forward to it."

He wheeled up the street. Ann ran out to greet Deke and he returned the waves of several children playing hopscotch.

Deke was right — they all needed some normalcy in their lives. That included the interchange of intelligent minds. "Oh-oh-look-at-Johnny-go —" Mickey laughed softly, rinsing cups.

Mrs. Knight repeated Terry's words, "Come for dinner?"

"If he can," Terry related.

"Sure he can." She put a hand on Ossie's shoulder. "Does your mother know about this, Terry?"

"She sent me, Mrs. Knight."

"Sure he can then," Mrs. Knight smiled at Ossie. Ossie wasn't smiling.

"Deke's going to be there," Terry told Ossie. "We're having a pork roast and biscuits and gravy, which my mama makes good."

"How come?" Ossie queried.

"Ossie, it isn't polite to question a dinner invitation."

Ossie asked again, "How come?"

"I don't know," Terry admitted. "But who cares? Mama makes the best biscuits you ever ate and you don't have to eat anything you don't want. I asked about that."

"My, my," Mrs. Knight shook Ossie's shoulder gently, "maybe we'd better think about what you'll wear."

Seeing Ossie's expression, Terry said quickly, "Any old

thing is fine, Mrs. Knight. I'm going without shoes."

"Oh, we can do better than that," she said.

"I ain't going."

"Of course you are, Sweetie!"

"I ain't wearing shoes just so I can eat."

"Sweetie! It wouldn't hurt you to dress up now and again. You need a new suit anyway."

"Suit!" Terry cried.

"Now I know I ain't going."

"Yes," Mrs. Knight said, smile fixed, "you are going. Tell your mother he'll be there, Terry. And tell her I deeply appreciate it."

Not sure why Mrs. Knight would appreciate it, Terry related the conversation to Mama.

"Good," she said.

"She's going to make him wear shoes, Mama."

"There's nothing wrong with that. You can do the same."

"Shoes! To stay home and eat?"

"It wouldn't hurt you to dress up now and then."

Fuming, Terry left the house. He dared not mention the possibilities of a suit. He threw himself on the steps, angrily. "It wouldn't hurt to dress up now and then —"

All mothers must think alike.

One of Mrs. Knight's boyfriends brought them to the house, but before Mama could be summoned, Mrs. Knight let Ossie out and they drove away.

"Lookit this shit," Ossie seethed. "You done this."

"I didn't tell her to do that!" Terry protested. He looked at Ossie's shorn head and winced, "Who cut your hair?"

"You know what I got under all this?" Ossie indicated his starched shirt, string tie, jacket and trousers, new shoes buffed.

"What?"

"Undergoddamnedwear, that's what. Nothing's hanging like it ought to."

"Ossie?" Mama said from the porch.

"Yes ma'am," Terry confirmed.

"My goodness!" Mama held out both hands, "You are positively handsome!"

Ossie cut dark eyes suspiciously and Terry said, "Can he take off his coat now, Mama?"

"It is a bit warm."

"And the string."

"His tie? The tie makes him look very sharp, I think."

Under his breath between set lips, Ossie said, "Jeez-*us*."

"Come in, come in," Mama urged. "I don't think Mr. and Mrs. Mason have met you yet, have they, Ossie?"

Again, on a higher note, "Jeez-*us*!"

"You know Deke, of course." Mama presented Ossie to her guests.

"Hey, Ossie!" Lamar yelled as though they were acres apart.

"Ossie, this is Mrs. Mason, and her husband, Mr. Mason."

Burrell Mason sat up with effort, legs stiff and straight before him. He shook Ossie's hand. The sides of Ossie's head were gray where the hair had been cut.

"You are very handsome in that suit," Velma said.

Ossie nodded grimly. "Cost fifteen dollars with the shirt."

"Well, it's handsome."

"Every man needs a good suit," Deke grinned. "How are you, Ossie?"

"Okay, I guess."

"Lamar," Velma suggested, "why don't you run home and put on your suit so you'll be as pretty as Terry and Ossie?"

Terry saw Ossie's eyes roll.

"I didn't know we were going formal," Velma said.

"I think Lamar looks fine," Mama stated.

"He does," Terry and Ossie said in unison.

"Not as pretty as you, though," Ann observed.

"Mrs. Calder," Ossie said, giving the title the sound of "miseries," "would you mind me taking off some of this? I'm choking half to death."

The adults laughed, Mama nodded, and Terry took Ossie into the bedroom. Ossie snatched loose the collar button, removed his coat.

"My balls are hurting," he said, fishing inside his trousers.

"Nobody can see the underwear, Ossie. Take it off."

Ossie did that. Then, shaking each leg alternately, he settled into his clothing. Still glaring, he followed Terry between talking adults and out to the back steps.

"Want to play some football?" Lamar asked.

"No."

"Want to pass some?"

"No, Lamar."

"Throw it to me then."

"No."

Ossie cut his eyes one way, then the other. He kept his head motionless and looked up, then down.

"What is it?" Terry asked.

"Look at my head. That's what it is. I'm skint. Skint! I

can feel every stir of air. Bugs keep trying to get in my ears. All I can say is — the food better be worth it."

Terry heard Deke say something that caused the adults to laugh.

Ann appeared at the rear door. "Know what Deke told me? He said I had pretty red hair just like Mama."

"Uh-huh," Ossie murmured, knowingly.

More laughter from the living room and Terry squirmed under Ossie's penetrating gaze.

If Mama and Deke hit it off — that had to help. Mama needed to know Deke better. That's all.

Responding to Ossie's stare, Terry said, "Stop it."

"Hey. I didn't do anything — you did!"

Eighteen

"YOU'RE GOING TO *work*, Terry," Mama cautioned.

"I know." He wrapped his bedroll, secured it with a belt. He checked the knife, fork and spoon Mama had provided.

"Do exactly what Deke says," Mama instructed.

"I will." Terry grinned and repeated, "I *will*, Mama."

At the door, when he reached up to kiss her good-bye, Mama said, "Be careful."

"We will. Bye."

"Bye yourself. Have fun."

Terry ran as best his cumbersome bundle would allow. Deke, Lamar and Ossie were already at the truck, waiting.

"Are we taking the airboat, Deke?"

"We're driving. Kramer Island is a peninsula, not an island."

"I know," Terry said.

They stopped at Owen's fish camp and while Deke and Ossie bought supplies, Lamar and Terry wandered over to watch several men working on an outboard motor.

"What say there, Lamar?" one man said.

"Hey uh — Mr. Wyman. Is your motor broke?"

"Sure is Lamar." Wyman winked at his companions.

"What's the matter with it?" Lamar queried.

"I was hoping you'd tell me, Lamar." Wyman turned to the others. "Watch this."

"I don't know what it is," Lamar admitted.

"Trouble is, Lamar, the little light inside the motor is burnt out. You could turn it on for me."

One of the men spit in the water, chuckled softly.

"Lamar," Terry said, "come on back."

"I can help?" Lamar asked.

"Why sure you can," Mr. Wyman said. "Grab this wire with one hand and pull the starter cord with the other hand. That ought to make you see the light."

Two men laughed. Lamar fingered the spark plug wire. "Hold this?"

"And yank the cord."

"Lamar," Terry said sharply.

Lamar gripped the wire, pulled the cord and screamed as electricity shot through his arm.

"Did you see the light, Lamar?" Mr. Wyman laughed.

"That's not funny!" Terry shouted. He grabbed Lamar's arm, started rubbing it.

"It hurt me, Terry."

"Lamar," Mr. Wyman hooted, "how come you're so dumb?"

"His daddy hit him with a car when Lamar was a baby. That's why he's like he is."

Wyman glanced at the other men, but they were looking away. "Get out of here," Wyman growled.

"It hurt me, Terry," Lamar cried.

"You shouldn't have done that, Mr. Wyman."

"Get out of here," the man said.

"He's not dumb, Mr. Wyman. You're dumb. You ought
to know better."

"What's going on out there?" Charlie Owen hollered.

"When you know better and do something stupid, that
makes you dumb."

"It hurt a lot," Lamar said. "He was teasing me, wasn't
he, Terry?"

"I told you to come on, Lamar. You didn't do what I
told you."

"It hurt me."

Terry inspected Lamar's scorched finger and shouted at
the men, "Dumb! That's what you are."

Motor whining in low gear, they lurched over dips and
bumps, the road a vague route through a tunnel of foliage
higher than the truck. Deke gripped the steering wheel
with perspiring hands, eyes riveted to a nonexistent lane.
Disturbed by their approach, grasshoppers, katydids and
milkweed bugs catapulted, becoming a wave of specks
reflecting a relentless sun. Deke drove with windows
closed to keep out the horde of insects, undergrowth
rasping against the vehicle.

In the enclosed rear, holding onto things to keep his
balance and to stop the shifting of goods, Ossie was
drenched by perspiration. Deke slowed for a turkey buz-
zard eating carrion, and Terry looked down at the tuber-
cular neck and curved beak of the creature.

Deke caught Terry's eye and they grinned.

Wild bananas, the fruit pithy and small, grew in clusters beneath dusty fronds. A red-shouldered hawk sat on a bare limb of a water oak, head turning but not frightened enough to fly.

"You enjoy this?" Deke asked.

"Sure do."

On higher ground, tropical ferns gave way to oaks, hickory and palmetto. Deke shifted gears and the whisk of underbrush quickened.

"Osprey," Terry pointed.

The "sea eagle" plummeted, snatched a fish from the lake and ascended with his silvery trophy locked in razor-sharp talons.

"Okay," Deke announced, "roll down the windows."

Rain crows, mocking birds and bluejays swapped insults in a blackberry bramble. The road curved along Lake Okeechobee and Terry saw egrets sprinkled like white blossoms across a mangrove.

A yellow blanket of sneezeweed bordered the lane, the dried leaves once used by early settlers as snuff. Here and there, Queen Anne's lace, its roots a wild carrot.

"How much longer, Deke?" Lamar questioned.

"We could camp there." Deke spoke to Terry, "What do you think?"

"That's a good place."

Slash pine sheltered a low dune beside the lake. It was a place where Indians from Brighton Reservation sometimes came to camp when fishing.

"So be it," Deke said. He pulled close to the water and cut off the motor. In silence, for a moment, they listened to the subtle sounds of unmolested wild things — a murmur like foam from an ocean wave dissolving on a sandy beach.

"First we set up camp," Deke instructed. "Then we go to work."

They erected a tent for Deke. Ossie dug a hollow for the fire they'd need tonight and banked it. He gathered "lighterknots" rich with pine sap, and dry kindling to start it. Lamar unloaded Deke's microscope, cot and several thick books.

"What are we after?" Terry asked.

"Plants native to this area," Deke said. "It's like solving a gigantic mystery — a puzzle with parts in different countries."

"What do you mean?"

Deke pointed to a plant. "Know what that is?"

"Alligator apple," Ossie said.

"Pond apple," Terry stated.

"Both right," Deke said. "*Annona glabra* is the true name. It grows here. But it is also found in the Bahamas, West Indies, tropical America and tropical Africa. The question is, did it start here? Or somewhere else?"

"But how will you know?" Ossie asked.

"That's where the detective work comes in." Deke loosened his pants and sprinkled sulfur powder to keep off redbugs and ticks. "First I have to list every plant that grows in South Florida. Then I have to study lists of plants from other nations. Then we look for fossil proof of which country had the plant first. Where did the plant begin?"

"That will take forever!" Terry cried.

"That's the specter that haunts me," Deke said jovially. He glanced around the terrain. "No good for the wheelchair here," he said.

"Want me to carry you?" Lamar brightened.

"We need my canvas stool, Lamar. It's in the rear of the truck."

Hugging Deke to his chest, Lamar stumbled through vines and briars, heaving Deke around like a bag. Then, at Deke's command, Lamar put the man here or there and Deke moved along by himself. So low to the ground, his arms and body prey to every insect predator, Deke had tied kerosene-soaked rags around his wrists, with liberal applications of sulfur powder in his neckline and trousers. Even then, he was soon a rash of red welts.

Sweating, pushing, dragging himself, every moist patch of leaves soaked his bottom. Gnats circled his head but his hands were too busy to brush them away. He sent Ossie up a tree for a vine leaf, Terry to the trunk for basal foliage. Then Lamar seized his slippery package and lunged to yet another spot. Everything was tagged and put into envelopes or boxes for later classification.

"Wait a minute, Deke," Ossie said, and picked blood ticks from Deke's neck.

Terry carried the notebooks, Ossie the low canvas-bottom chair Deke used at every stop. When the boys brought him a specimen, Deke made note of the location and date. He saved leaves, stems, roots and always any fruit or blossoms.

Lunch was sandwiches and lukewarm tea taken without complaint. Then into late afternoon they worked.

"See that fern out there?" Deke pointed at a bog rising from the lake. "Think you could bring it to me, Ossie?"

"Yes."

"Watch your step," Deke cautioned.

The boy waded out, quickly immersed to his waist. He looked back and grinned. "Feels good," he said.

"Careful," Deke warned.

With another step, Ossie was chest-deep and they heard him gasp as cold water reached his armpits. "Ossie," Deke called, "never mind, let's —"

Ossie disappeared.

Ripples undulated. Suddenly Ossie thrashed and Deke threw himself from his seat to water's edge, looking. Out of the murky lake rose a hand, like a claw grasping.

"Ossie! Jesus! Ossie!"

Terry started to run out and Deke seized him by an arm and threw him back. "Ossie! Ossie!"

The hand opened, fingers quivering, and sank. Deke screamed, "Ossie!" He splashed out a few feet, halted, voice contorted, "Dear God — Ossie!"

Once more, Ossie's hand emerged, shuddered, and disappeared. Deke slapped water, churning, and suddenly fell forward, fighting for balance, gasping.

Ossie slowly rose, eyes closed, and spurted water in a long stream from pursed lips. Lamar and Terry fell on the ground laughing. Ossie looked back, grinning, and his smile vanished.

Deke was thrashing the water, spanking the surface with the flat of his hands. Terry heard him choke — and then Deke turned bottom up.

Ossie shoved water aside, half-swimming, half treading, struggling toward the helpless man.

Terry jumped in, too. But Ossie got there first, grabbing Deke. Instantly, Deke locked himself to the boy, coughing, wretching.

"You all right, Deke?" Ossie asked.

"Ossie —" Deke made a vomiting sound as Terry reached them. They dragged the man toward shore. "Ossie," Deke cried, "goddamn you!"

"Hey, I was only kidding."

"Damn you!" Deke pushed away and whirled, up to his chest and elbows in water. "You think that's funny? You think this is some kind of joy ride, for God's sake?"

Stricken, the boys stood mute.

"Lamar," Deke heaved toward land. "Get me, damn it. Lamar, damn it, come and get me!"

Stunned, Terry and Ossie stared at one another.

Ossie and Terry built a fire, cutting two Y-branches to hold a suspended kettle. They had spoken only in low voices since returning to camp. In his tent, Deke sat by the light of a lantern making notes, looking at specimens they'd gathered.

"I think it scared him," Terry observed.

"I was only kidding," Ossie seethed.

"He didn't know."

"Piss on him."

Lamar was dozing on his bedroll, mouth agape. Ossie moved around the campfire banking embers with moss to drive away insects. He knelt beside Terry, waiting for water to boil.

In the tent, Deke murmured to himself, "Well, well —"

"The water's about hot, Deke," Terry called.

They saw his shadow, head lifted, pausing. Then, back to his notes.

"Hardest work I ever done for a dollar," Ossie grumped.

"I like it."

"That's because you're stupid," Ossie replied.

"If you hadn't scared him," Terry accused, "you wouldn't be so unhappy."

"Got no sense of humor."

"He thought you were in trouble, Ossie. You can't blame Deke. You saw he can't swim good and he was still going to try and get you out."

The fire danced in Ossie's eyes. The kettle made a tentative groan. Terry glanced at Deke's silhouette again.

"I never thought about him not being able to swim," Ossie alibied.

"Let's forget it," Terry said.

"Ended up, me saving his ass," Ossie whispered.

"So, okay, let's forget it."

The lantern in the tent went out and a moment later Deke appeared. He positioned himself next to the fire and diced meat and potatoes into a pot. He poured water from the kettle, added onions, salt and pepper.

"Hope you fellows like stew," he said.

"Suits me," Terry replied. Ossie stared at the fire.

"You saved my neck today, Ossie," Deke stated. "That gives me great confidence in you. I apologize for losing my temper."

Ossie shrugged, still looking at the fire. A lighterknot popped, sizzled.

Deke made coffee in a saucepan, the aroma rich and pungent. Terry declined and Deke poured a cup for himself, another for Ossie.

"Ya-ho-lo, Ossie," Deke said quietly.

"Ya-ho-lo," Ossie rejoined, and they lifted their cups to one another.

Lamar smacked his lips. Terry reached over and killed a bloated mosquito feeding on Lamar's ankle. He covered the boy's legs with a blanket.

"You look after him, don't you?" Deke noted.

"Sometimes he looks after me."

"Fair enough," Deke said. Then, to Ossie again, "Ya-ho-lo."

Ossie grinned. "Ya-ho-lo," he said.

Crickets fiddled, frogs croaked, and the lake made licking sounds on the shore. Shadows of pine trunks wiggled away from the fire. The snap of burning wood and a hiss of hot sap were music. Terry sat next to Lamar, gazing across the lake.

"I saw a ghost," Lamar gasped.

"No you didn't, Lamar."

"Yes I did, Terry. He's over there."

"It's the campfire," Ossie said.

"No, Ossie," Lamar insisted, "it's a ghost."

Terry put a hand on Lamar's leg, patted, still looking across the lake.

"I wonder how many men have sat here in the thousands of years past," Deke mused, "wondering how many men had sat here before them?"

"How long have people lived here?" Terry questioned.

"Florida was shaped by glaciers, and dinosaurs were probably hunted by the first men to arrive from Asia."

"Indians?" Ossie asked.

"That's right. Do you know how remarkable it is, Ossie, to know your forefathers came from right here on this continent?"

"So what?"

"Most Americans don't know a thing about their families past the grandfather, or great-father."

Lamar whispered, "There went the ghost."

"It's shadows, Lamar."

"No," Lamar shivered, "it's a ghost."

"Lamar had me chasing ghosts all over the Everglades last week," Deke said.

"He keeps peeking at me," Lamar reported.

"You believe in ghosts?" Ossie asked Deke.

"Do you?"

"I don't know."

"I don't think their purpose would be to frighten people," Deke said.

"Terry," Lamar squeaked, "I see him!"

"Show me, Lamar."

"He went behind that tree."

"Come on, let's see."

"No."

"There is *no* ghost, Lamar," Terry stood, looking.

"I wouldn't mind seeing one," Deke remarked. "It
would be proof of ever-lasting life."

Terry cried aloud and nearly fell over Lamar.

"What is it?" Ossie questioned.

"I think I saw him."

Ossie laughed. He lifted his arms, hands limp and made
a wailing sound.

"Okay, okay," Deke said, "let's not get shook up."

Terry reminded himself of swamp gas, phosphorous
glowing; it had to be something that simple.

"Deke," Terry said evenly, "there's something out
there. It may not be a ghost but it's *something*."

Ossie rose, cupped his eyes to kill glare from the fire.
He looked where Terry pointed. "Where?" he demanded.

Out of the shadows appeared a form and Ossie yelped,
stumbled backward and fell over Deke.

"Hey, boys," Deke said.

"Oooooh-seee-ooooooh-la —"

"What the —" Deke lifted himself on his fingertips.

"Oooooh-seee-ooooooh-la —"

Ossie shot a glance at Deke, then Terry. He swore
under his breath.

"Who is it?" Deke hollered. "Come over and join us."

"Oooooh-seee-ooooooh-la —" The warbling voice had

Lamar wrapped around Terry's legs like a strangle vine.

"It's my grandfather," Ossie said.

"Your grandfather?"

"Ooooo-seee-ooooooh-la —"

"Yeah!" Terry cried. "It is! Hi, Mr. Night Song. Come on over."

But the Indian evaporated, leaving four sets of wide eyes peering into the night.

Deke stirred the fire, added another lighterknot and lit a cigarette with a hand that shook visibly.

"Can I have one of those?" Ossie asked.

"You smoke?"

"Yeah."

Deke gave a cigarette without debate. Terry considered asking, but Deke would probably mention it to Mama.

Out of the dark came a drumming of a bough on a log. Low chanting moans arose. Ossie stared at the fire, smoking rapidly.

"You could invite him in for coffee, Ossie," Deke suggested.

"He wouldn't come. Crazy old man."

"Beloved old man," Deke replied without rebuke.

"Not him. He's crazy. Ain't he, Terry?"

"I don't think so."

"Then you're crazy."

"What's he doing?" Lamar cried.

"Trying to drive away the white man," Ossie said. "Old fool."

"Not a fool," Deke said. "A pity the Indians didn't manage to do that a hundred-fifty years ago, Ossie. Then all this land would've remained theirs."

In mesmerizing litany, Mr. Night Song lamented. Long after the boys and Deke had retired, the old man's voice echoed across the lake — "Away, away, away, away —"

Terry lay staring up at the wink and blink of distant stars, listening.

"Terry?"

"What, Lamar?"

"Can I sleep with you?"

"Sure. Pull up close."

"— away, away, away, away —"

"I'm scared, Terry."

Terry put his arm around Lamar's thick neck, and with the boy's breath against his face, Terry patted and stroked.

"He's a good old man, Lamar," Terry whispered. "He knows about souls and spirits. That's who he's talking to now, I'll bet you. Souls and spirits."

Mr. McCree, maybe.

But Lamar was breathing easy, sleeping.

Somewhere out on the lake, the putter of a motor . . . a breeze stirred the trees.

Terry listened for his name, but the wind died.

The chant of Mr. Night Song ebbed and flowed.

"— away, away, away, away —"

Nineteen

TERRY AWOKE SHIVERING, damp from the dew. Lamar had all the covers. He tugged gently, but Lamar groaned, turned, securing the blanket for himself.

Terry knelt beside the campfire and blew; ashes swirled, but the last embers were dead. Sitting with hands over the charred soil as if to warm them, he listened to the call of a chuck-will's widow. A flock of birds twittered, fussed, fluttered and settled.

His legs itched from insect bites. Gingerly, lest he step on sandspurs or touch stinging nettles, Terry went to the lake and waded up to his knees. He rinsed his arms, rubbed viscid mud over his wounds. He sniffed: something cooking. Mr. Night Song probably. He waded in that direction.

In the half-light of dawn, a raccoon fished the shoreline, up to her chin, forepaws probing, chirping with anticipation. Startled, the creature froze. When Terry advanced, the raccoon splashed ashore and turned to stare before ambling away.

A column of smoke rose in a spire from Mr. Night Song's fire. He was talking. To himself. But then, Terry heard the Indian say, "I must take this. My need is great."

Night Song pushed aside tiny white flowers of a "healing" croton. He broke branches, saying, "No more than I must." He bled the sprigs of sap, dropping the liquid onto his scratched arms. The sap would form a sticky bandage and help kill pain. Terry moved nearer.

Night Song soothed the bush, giving thanks. When he turned, Terry was there. If he had surprised the old man, Night Song did not show it.

"May I come to your camp, Mr. Night Song?"

"I have not enough for two."

"That's okay." Terry inched closer.

Night Song squatted beside the fire, stirred it with a stick. He wore no shirt, a rope bunched his trousers at the waist. Terry smelled food but saw none.

"Where is Osceola?"

"Asleep."

"I call and he does not come."

"Want to go to our camp?"

"No."

"We have coffee," Terry offered.

"I have coffee."

When Night Song did not look at him directly, Terry stooped on the opposite side of the fire and said, "You remember me, don't you?"

The Indian poked the embers.

"Ossie's house," Terry reminded. "In town; popcorn and orange drink?"

Night Song brushed away coals and uncovered fish wrapped in the leaves of wild banana.

"That's a good way to cook fish," Terry noted.

"I have only enough for one."

"I'm not hungry," but his mouth watered.

Elbows on his knees, Night Song peeled away banana leaves, shifting the hot parcel from hand to hand. He had garnished the fish with wild lime and onion sprouts. Terry swallowed saliva.

"I told Deke there were lots of things to eat all around us," Terry said. "But he brings cans of food anyway."

Night Song blew on the fish.

"Mr. Night Song? Why do you talk to the croton?"

"Because I must hurt it."

"It has spirit?"

"All things have spirit."

"Rocks?"

"All things."

Terry watched him eat. The flesh of Night Song's throat, like the wattle of a turkey, quivered with each deliberate chew.

"I bet that's good," Terry said.

"White men do not know of such things." He meant spirits.

"No, sir. But I'd like to learn."

"They come to destroy."

"I don't."

"White men care for things, not people. Indians care for people."

"I do."

A vireo cried, *chicka-per-weeoo; chicka-per-weeoo.*

"They have much to pay."

Eating fish, gazing past Terry, Night Song chewed

slowly. "Much to pay," he said.

"Yessir."

Without turning his head, Night Song called, "Osceola!"

"Hello, Grandfather." Ossie stepped into the clearing.

"Sit with me, my grandson."

Ossie spoke to Terry, "What're you doing here?"

"He was telling me about spirits, Ossie."

"Sit with me, Osceola. Are you hungry?"

"No, Grandfather." Ossie sat with legs folded Indian fashion.

"I will share," Night Song said.

"No, thank you, Grandfather."

The old Indian sucked his fingers and smiled. "Like bamboo, you grow."

Ossie nodded, eyes down.

"Many times I call but you do not come, Osceola."

"I'm sorry, Grandfather."

"Does the white man tie you to a tree?"

"No."

"Perhaps I am no longer a beloved old man."

"You are beloved, Grandfather. I'm sorry."

"Perhaps you did not hear?"

"I will not lie, Grandfather. I heard you."

"You have not learned the white man's lies?"

"I would not lie to you."

"That much is good." The old man touched Ossie's face. "What happened to your head?"

"I got the haircut."

"For what purpose?"

"Mom told me to."

"I must speak to her."

"Thank you, Grandfather."

"Osceola," Night Song said, "you did not come to the Green Corn dance. Why is this?"

"I had to work, Grandfather."

"White man's work?"

"Gigging frogs."

"You work now for the short one?"

"Yes."

"He comes to kill things which mean no harm, Osceola. I have watched. Why does he kill things?"

"He's making a list of plants which grow here."

"Must he kill them?"

"He needs the whole plant," Terry said. "He has to look at leaves and roots and —"

Ossie silenced him with a gesture.

"What of the spirit?" Night Song questioned. "What of the pain he does to these things?"

"I don't know."

"It grieves me."

"Yes, Grandfather."

Night Song ate fish, sucked his fingers. "Always they kill, Osceola. They killed the deer and panther and the bear. Gone are the otters from this lake."

"Yes, Grandfather."

"They fear the panther and bear, perhaps. But they killed the deer because of ticks they said would hurt their cattle. All things have ticks. Even snakes. Would they kill all but their cattle?"

"I don't know, Grandfather."

"They cut off the antlers and left so many deer the vultures could not consume them."

Ossie stared at his hands, rubbing a forefinger with his thumb.

"At Cedar Key," Night Song intoned, "they cut trees

until not one cedar remained. Even now, with food in a can, they come without hunger to kill the cabbage palm. Why do they do this?"

Ossie looked at Terry and stood. "We have to go."

"It has always been so," Night Song said. "They killed our women and children, took skin from our warrior's thighs to make pouches."

"Who?" Terry demanded.

"*Jacksa Chula Harjo.*"

"Andrew Jackson and his soldiers," Ossie said.

"Skinned them?" Terry cried.

"That was long ago, Grandfather."

"My father knew of such things."

"His father, perhaps," Ossie said gently.

"Is that so long ago?"

"People don't do that any more, Grandfather."

"Osceola," Night Song insisted, "sit with me!"

"Grandfather —"

"I have *asi*. Drink with me."

Ossie sat again, legs folded. He watched the old man dig a pot from beside the fire. His hand wrapped to avoid a burn, Night Song poured black liquid into a tin cup.

"*Ixchay linus tcha*, Osceola."

Ossie said, "Ya-ho-lo, Beloved One."

Night Song swallowed and sat a moment, looking at the boy. Then Ossie took the cup with both hands and lifted it.

"*Ixchay linus tcha*, Grandfather."

"Ya-ho-lo, my grandson."

Ossie took a swallow of the bitter liquid and sat impassively. When he did not wince, the old man chuckled, "Good, good."

Ossie stood up. "We must go. Come on, Terry."

When they left, Terry said, "What did that mean, Ossie, *Ixchay linus tcha*?"

"It means 'to your health;' why did you go over there?"

"I don't know. To talk to him, I guess."

"I hope you're satisfied," Ossie said.

"I don't think he likes me."

Ossie pushed aside the leaves of a poisonwood tree. "It's a wonder he didn't scalp you."

"Aww, Ossie!"

"Probably get a dollar for a redhead."

"Ossie, I'm trying real hard. What can I do to make him like me?"

"Nothing, most likely."

"How come?"

Ossie halted. He put an arm around Terry's shoulder. "You are white," he said emphatically. "He doesn't *like* white people."

As they continued, following the crescent of the shoreline, Terry heard Deke shouting.

"Here we come!"

When they arrived, Lamar stood to one side, eyes wide, hair thatched from sleeping crooked. Deke wore no shirt. His chest and belly were an ugly mass of raw welts.

"Where the hell've you been?"

"To see Mr. Night Song, Deke."

"How is anybody to know where you are?"

"We weren't gone long."

"Don't walk off like that again, you hear me? Never again!"

"Yessir, Deke. I'm sorry."

"I've been yelling my lungs out."

"We didn't hear you," Terry explained.

Neck muscles corded, Deke struggled back to camp.

"We hunted and hunted and hollered and hollered," Lamar said. "Deke's mad."

Terry went to Deke's tent and stood outside. "Deke? Do you have some calamine lotion?"

"Yes, do you need it?"

"I'll rub some on your back if you want me to."

Long pause.

"Okay. I'd appreciate it."

Terry pulled back the flap. Deke turned face down on his cot. "They ate me up," he said.

Terry poured lotion, applied it to the rash from ivy, nettle and insect bites.

"They get you because you're on the ground," Terry advised.

"Nothing much I can do about that."

"Ossie and I could fetch things. You don't have to go yourself."

"Out of my element," Deke grunted.

"If you show us a plant, couldn't we get it?"

"I'm sure you could."

Terry examined the lotion, cracking as it dried, like glaze on an old vase. "You need to smear lipstick or axle grease on chigger bites, Deke. Lotion won't kill them."

"I don't mind the bites," Deke said, "but I wish they wouldn't pull up such a pile to sit on."

Terry grinned and Deke said, "Thanks, redhead."

The sun burned utterly white, etching black shadows beneath trees. Gnats swarmed in search of sweat, earwax and saliva. His mouth and nose masked with a hand-kerchief, Deke had smashed so many mosquitos his face and hands were shingled with flecks of his own blood.

Terry delivered a lily and collapsed in the shade.

"Is that the whole root system, redhead?"

"I think so."

Deke made a notation. He clipped the plant, putting pieces into envelopes for later scrutiny, then looked at Lamar. "How about it, partner?"

"I'm tired, Deke."

"Think you could carry me to those trees?"

"I'm real tired."

"We're almost through," Deke said amiably.

Lamar sighed heavily, hoisted Deke, and dropped him.

"Be careful!" Terry screamed.

"I didn't mean to! He's slippery."

"It's all right," Deke said. "It wasn't your fault, Lamar. Hey — give me a smile."

Lamar peered over his bandana with tearful eyes.

"Are you smiling?"

"Yes, Deke."

"Let me see."

Lamar lifted the handkerchief and bared his teeth.

"Good boy! Terry, grab my notebook and canvas chair."

Holding Deke under the arms, Lamar heaved him again.

"Easy, Lamar," Terry urged.

They crossed a sandy rise, descending to a parched lowland of grass. A sudden whirr made Ossie yelp. The sound, like crushed cellophane, crackled around them. "Fleas!" Ossie yelled.

Lamar dropped Deke and instantly a writhing mass enveloped the man. Lamar slapped at his legs, screaming; from the knees down he wore stockings of biting insects. "Lamar!" Deke hollered. But Lamar was running.

Ossie grabbed Deke by the shirt and Terry joined him. Together they hauled him toward the lake. Deke clamped his lips, eyes shut tightly. They tore away his shirt and trousers, heaping mud on the shivering man. Then Terry and Ossie ripped off their own clothes and ran into the water. He and Ossie smeared mud on themselves and one another.

"Help me, Terry!" Lamar cried from the shore.

"Get in the water," Ossie shouted.

"Help me, Terry!"

Terry sat him down and smeared mud. Finally, wading out up to their chins, Ossie and Terry looked at one another. They watched Deke ease himself into the lake.

"He's going to get killed," Ossie said.

"I want to go home, Deke," Lamar whimpered.

"We're going."

"I'm tired."

"We're going, Lamar."

"Tell you one thing," Ossie whispered. "There ain't no way he could do this by himself."

Deke stopped his truck at Owen's fish camp long enough to report, "We're back."

"How'd it go this time?"

"They're good workers."

"I helped, didn't I, Deke?"

"Sure did, Lamar. Couldn't do without you."

"I'm strong," Lamar said.

At Ossie's house the boy climbed out and stood holding the truck door open.

"I don't know when I'm going again, Ossie," Deke said. "I'll get in touch, though."

"I don't reckon I'll go next time."

"Oh?" Deke flushed. "Why not?"

"Ain't enough money."

"Dollar a day?"

"Ain't enough. I make more gigging frogs."

"I see." The vehicle pulsed in time to the idling engine.

"Worked our asses off," Ossie said.

"I don't care, Deke!" Terry offered.

"Well, I do," Ossie rejoined.

"How much then?" Deke asked.

"Double."

"Two dollars a day, Ossie?" Deke was smiling, but he looked pained.

"Two dollars," Ossie said.

"How about a buck-fifty?"

"Look, Deke. It's hot and hard work from sunup to sundown. I can do you a good job and you know it."

"Yes, I think you can."

"If you get in trouble, like the lake or the fleas, Lamar ain't no help. You can depend on me. That's worth double Lamar."

"I still need Lamar."

"So take him."

"If Mama will let me go, Deke, I'll do it."

"Me," Ossie spit between his feet, "I got other ways to make money besides messing around in a swamp."

"All right," Deke said. "Two dollars a day and I want a handshake that you'll stick with me until I finish this job."

"How long's that?"

"I don't know."

"Hell, I might be forty years old."

"At least until the end of next year," Deke said. "I'm not

going to train a good man and overpay him just to have him get lazy."

Ossie's lips pulled sideways, trying to quench a smile. "I reckon," he said.

Ossie and Deke clasped hands. Then man and boy grinned. "Deal," Ossie concluded.

"And well bargained."

As they pulled away, Terry said, "You should've held out, Deke."

"Maybe."

"He can't make a dollar a day steady, gigging frogs. It's so dry now, the frogs have all dug into the mud waiting on rain."

"I know." They bumped across the bridge into Camp Osceola.

"Why'd you let him get you then?"

"Like most transactions," Deke said, "the reason involves more than mere commerce."

Lamar got out at Terry's house and trudged homeward. Terry held the truck door open as he'd seen Ossie do. He spit between his feet.

"Know what you could do, Deke?"

"What?"

"If you make my mama like you enough, she'll let me go with you free."

"Free."

"Sure."

"Hello!" Mama called. "How are the intrepid explorers?"

"Your son is a future botanist."

"You're telling me," Mama said as she reached the truck.

"He works diligently and efficiently. A good man."

Mama put an arm around Terry's neck, but he eased away so Deke wouldn't see what would've come next: she'd send him to take a bath. "Guess I'll go take a bath," Terry preempted.

"Hey," Duke said, "you cut your hair, Mickey."

"Yes," Mama smiled. "Do you think it's too short?"

"Not at all. It's very stylish."

Behind Mama, Terry gave Deke the thumb to forefinger air force pilot sign for "Okay."

Standing on the porch, he heard the truck motor stop and Deke laughing. Somehow, in a vague way he couldn't explain even to himself, Terry felt cheated. He thrust a hand in the pocket with the two dollars. He got what he'd asked — he'd been allowed to go.

Nonetheless, he felt cheated.

Twenty

TERRY SAT BESIDE ANN on her bed, looking at the photograph of Daddy. "His eyes are really blue," Terry said.

"Those are brown."

"I know. But the people who colored the picture made a mistake. His eyes are really blue."

Ann examined the portrait. "He has big teeth," she said.

Mama and Deke were listening to the news in the living room. Velma was knitting, the click of her needles a quiet, steady rhythm.

". . . President Truman raised the U.S. flag in Berlin," Walter Winchell reported, "saying that the primary American goal now is to bring peace and prosperity to the world."

Terry heard Mama complain, "Is there no news of Europe?"

"Berlin is in Europe, Mickey," Velma noted.

"Rome," Mama amended.

"Doesn't he have big teeth?" Ann questioned Terry.

"Pretty big."

"Those two." Ann touched the incisors.

"Meanwhile," Walter Winchell continued, "warships of the Pacific fleet continue to bombard the Japanese mainland, striking deadly blows at the islands of Honshu and Hokkaido. . . ."

"Hooray," Velma said, needles purling.

"Psst, Terry!" Ossie at the bedroom window. Wearing a tie!

Terry fell across his own bed, face near the screen. "Where're you going?"

"Want to go to the revival?" Ossie queried.

"Church?"

"Yeah. Revival."

"I don't think so, Ossie."

"Holy rollers," Ossier whispered.

"I don't think so."

"They get to jumping and hollering, the women go into ecstasy and fall down rolling around kicking their legs. Sometimes their dresses come up to here."

Terry glanced at Ann. "I don't believe I want to go, Ossie."

"Ever heard anybody speak in *other* tongue?"

"What's that?"

"Mumbo jumbo, the spirits talking through them."

"I don't think so—"

"Best part is," Ossie enticed, "they pick up poisonous snakes with their bare hands. Men, women, children, passing around rattlesnakes and moccasins."

"In church?"

"Revival. In a tent. Like a circus, but with pews. Out the Pahokee road—how about it?"

"They pick up snakes in *church*?"

"Hand them around to one another. Last year I seen a lady get bit right on the titty."

Aghast, Terry slipped nearer.

"See," Ossie expounded, "if they get bit, it means the devil's in them. If they don't get bit, they're holy. Something like that. Want to go?"

"You have to dress up?"

"Yeah, and wear shoes. But it's worth it. They won't let you near the place if you don't act like you're there to pray and roll around. How about it?"

"I don't know." Terry sat back, listening to the radio, the adults commenting on news developments.

"Go ask," Ossie said.

"That's true about the snakes and all?"

"Cross my heart! Hurry up, they get started right after sundown."

Terry went into the living room and awaited Mama's attention.

"Mama, may I go to church with Ossie?"

"Church?"

"Yes, ma'am. Out the Pahokee road."

"With Ossie?" Mama said.

"Yes, ma'am. A revival."

"Oh yes," Deke commented, "I saw the tent."

Mama looked at Velma and the woman smiled, kept knitting.

"May I, Mama?"

"Mickey," Velma mused, "you look like somebody hit you with a dead fish."

"I must admit, I'm flabbergasted."

"May I, Mama? Ossie is waiting."

Mama eyed Terry suspiciously. "Ask Ossie to come inside."

Terry went to the door. "She wants to see you, Ossie."

"How come?"

"I don't know. Come in."

Ossie entered and Mama looked him up and down.

"Mysterious ways—" Velma muttered.

"All right," Mama consented, "I guess so."

Ossie sat on the commode while Terry washed those parts of his body that would be exposed after dressing. "No kidding about the snakes now, Ossie."

"I ain't kidding. You'll see."

They paused in the living room for final inspection and Velma said again, "Mysterious ways—"

"Put this in the collection plate." Mama gave Terry fifty cents. "I do mean put it in, don't spend it."

"Yes ma'am, but Mama—it's free!"

"For the Lord's work, Terry." Mama kind of laughed and lifted her eyebrows at Velma.

"You boys look nice," Velma remarked.

"Thank you." And they were gone, walking fast, now and then trotting a short way, the sun beginning to fade behind them.

Mickey turned to Deke and Velma, "Why do I smell something rotten?"

"Because you aren't stupid," Deke said.

"And you're a mother," Velma added

"Church," Mama stated. "that's a first."

Velma clicked the needles, repeating, "Mysterious ways—"

For a minute, Terry thought they'd be turned away by a tall, thin man standing at the entrance. But Ossie said, "Our mothers couldn't come."

"They sent you alone?" the thin man asked.

"Yessir."

He towered over them, eyes hidden in pools of darkness. "I don't know—"

Inspired, Terry extended the fifty cents. "For the Lord's work, Mama said."

"All right. Sit down, boys, and no running around during services."

"No sir."

Ossie selected a seat midway, but Terry insisted they go nearer the stage where several boxes sat with tantalizing promise. Ossie was hotly debating the best vantage for seeing the most women rolling when the tall man called, "No cutting up, boys."

"Listen," Ossie reasoned, "you can't turn around to look. If we sit in the middle we see up the most dresses!"

"Yeah, but the snakes—"

"Who wants to sit next to the snakes?" Ossie squeaked.

"I do."

"Hell no."

"Boys, I told you—" the tall man said.

"Yessir."

"Anyway, Ossie whispered, "If you want to go closer later, you can roll up there."

A woman sat at a small organ, eyes closed, playing music. The flaps of the tent ruffled with a faint breeze. The smell of kerosene testified to a recent spraying to hold down insects. Yellow light bulbs winked up close to the center pole, and on stage the pulpit stood stark, wood grain, with a peeling religious scene painted on the sides.

"Rock of Ages, cleft for me," a woman behind them sang, then hummed along for awhile before saying again, "Rock of Ages, cleft for me."

People came in dusty pickup trucks, fenders rattling, and afoot.

"Rock of Ages, cleft for me. . . ."

Terry heard a pan dropped, a subdued woman's voice chastising, then a baby began to cry. It came from a small house trailer on an edge of the clearing. On the sides of the trailer were painted the words: REVIVAL! MUSIC! BEWARE SATAN!

A man and woman walked down the straw covered center aisle handing out song books and paper fans which advertised, "McMurtry's Funeral Parlor."

"Rock of Ages, um-hm-hmmm. . . ."

Outside, a man tuned his violin, notes discordant, low; the lady at the organ didn't seem to hear, or care. She leaned forward, then backward, eyes closed, playing.

"Rock of Ages, um-hm-hmmm."

Terry took two song books, passing one to Ossie. Ossie held it with both hands, chin down, looking straight forward.

"Want a fan?" Terry inquired when the lady arrived to offer. Ossie shook his head. But Terry took one. Already he was beginning to perspire. The pews were nearly full.

Suddenly the organ rose, louder, stronger, and the tall thin man called, "All rise! Page two-twenty-two." Then, in a deep baritone, the thin man began, "I was sinking deep in sin, far from the peaceful shore—"

Terry stood beside Ossie, both in the shadows of adults fore and aft, and they stared at their books, moving their lips but making no sound.

Finally the minister strode onstage, shirt sleeves rolled

up, a bow tie cutting into the flesh of his neck. He shouted, banged the podium, Adam's apple bobbing and bumping his tie. He threw his fists into the air, arms quivering, and screamed about the devil and perdition and damnation.

Ossie nudged Terry with an elbow and Terry followed Ossie's gaze to a woman who had jumped up from her seat.

"Yes, sister!" the preacher hollered.

The woman wobbled and two men came to stand beside her. Her voice rose and fell, the words incoherent, and suddenly a lady collapsed into the aisle, twisting, contorting, and Ossie leaned over to better see as her skirt rose around her thighs. Their faces inches apart, Ossie looked at Terry and lifted his eyebrows twice.

Another. Then another. Screaming and clasping their hands, falling to roll around as others shouted, "Glory be! Glory to God! Glory, sister, glory!"

It was interesting. But it wasn't snakes.

They testified and sang some more. They passed a collection plate and Terry had to tell the thin man, "I gave you my money when we came in, remember?"

When the minister returned to the stage, he had changed shirts. The other was soaking with sweat. More singing, more preaching.

Then Terry saw a fluid, flowing skirt and beautiful raven hair which framed an almond face and haunting dark eyes. "The conjure woman—"

As if on wheels or silent skates, she floated onstage and across, going directly to a wooden box. Reaching in, and with infinite grace, she lifted the sensual form of a huge diamondback rattlesnake. Terry saw the reptile's forked black tongue lick lazily, testing the air for scent.

"As God gives us will—" the minister intoned.

The conjure woman caressed the serpent, letting it glide from hand to hand, the rings of her fingers glinting in the yellow light. She turned the snake so the reptile came straight for her face and she kissed its head. The rattler recoiled slightly, tensed. Terry clutched his trousers with both hands.

"For as the devil comes without warning. . . ."

A man went to the stage and the conjure woman handed him the rattlesnake and reached for another box. Then a woman and her child joined them. The rattlesnake slithered through the mother's hands, down to the floor, and the child reached to take it.

The conjure woman lifted the blunt, thick body of a cottonmouth moccasin and the serpent yawned, fangs extending, the alabaster roof of his mouth flashing white. Ossie nudged Terry again, indicating a pretty young girl rolling, exposed, but Terry saw only the hypnotizing eyes of the conjure woman, lifting the moccasin and slowly, slowly, taking the reptile's entire head into her mouth.

She held it, her lips blood red against the keeled scales, and Terry could not breathe, trembling from head to foot, imagining the forked tongue, fangs folded. . . .

The woman next to Terry slumped, froth rising between her lips, and Terry stepped back to avoid her twitching legs. He moved beside Ossie at the edge of the tent, watching the conjure woman lift the next snake and the next, to fondle, caress, and pass along the reptiles to the congregation. People were moaning, rocking in place, or prostrate on the straw-covered ground.

On the way home, walking mostly in silence, Ossie

said, "Didn't I tell you?"

"Sure did. That was something."

When they reached Camp Osceola, Ossie lit a cigarette, shared it with Terry, and carefully rolled his tie to put it in his pocket.

"Want to go tomorrow night?" Terry asked.

"Nah. They do the same thing every night."

"I wouldn't mind going again." Terry said.

"Really liked it?"

"Yeah! Boy. She put that moccasin's head right in her mouth. Did you see it?"

"No."

"No! You didn't *see*?"

"Jees-us," Ossie wheezed. "You are so dumb. Looking at snakes."

"She's something else, isn't she?" Terry marveled.

"Who?"

"The conjure woman."

"Oh. Yeah, I guess so."

"She doesn't look a hundred to me," Terry said.

"Maybe older."

"She doesn't look it," Terry countered.

Ossie blew smoke up in a thin wisp, rounded his lips and executed a perfect smoke ring in the still air.

"How about it, Ossie?" Terry insisted. "Go again tomorrow night?"

"I tell you, it's the same every night."

"That's okay with me."

"Not me. I got to go. See you."

When Terry reached the house, Deke sat on the couch and Mama in an easy chair. They were listening to Frank Sinatra singing on the radio.

Deke saw Terry first. "Hello, pilgrim."

"Hi."

"How was it?" Deke inquired.

"It was great!"

"Great?" Mama questioned.

"It was, Mama. You ought to go. You wouldn't believe it."

"Well. All right." Mama scrutinized his clothes for soil. "Tell me about it," she said.

"At first it was like any church," Terry related. "Then it got good. People started talking in other tongues—"

Mama grimaced. "I might have known." The comment made Terry pause and Mama had to say, "Go on."

"Then they began to fall down and roll around and—"

Deke put the back of a hand to his mouth.

"But, Deke, the best part was the conjure woman!"

"What?"

"She had a rattlesnake this long." Terry extended his arms. Deke shot a glance at Mama.

"She picked him up with her bare hands, Deke."

"I trust you did no such thing," Mama cried.

"No ma'am. I knew you wouldn't want me to. Anyway. Deke, she had a water moccasin this big around and when she picked him up he opened his mouth," Terry fingers opened to represent the fangs, "and you know what she did?"

"Terry—" Deke cleared his throat.

"Put his head in her *mouth!*"

"Dear God."

Mama threw herself backward, laughing. Eyes wild, Terry reported, "She held it, and held it, and held it until I thought it was going to suffocate."

Mama's shriek made Deke say, "Mickey, for heaven's sake—"

"May I go again tomorrow night, Mama?"

Mama wiped her eyes. "Once is enough, I think."

"I won't handle any snakes."

"It isn't that," Mama looked at Deke and laughed again.

"What then?"

"Terry, we aren't making fun of their religion. We aren't laughing at the people in the church."

"What then?"

"It's kind of a joke between adults," Deke offered.

In bed, wide awake, Terry lay listening to night sounds. Now and then, in the living room, Mama would laugh. When she did, Deke would say, "Mickey, honestly!"

Twenty-one

TERRY AND OSSIE sat on the railroad incline in the shade of Australian pines. Carefully, Ossie cut a section of sugar cane, peeling away the thick outer skin to reach the good part. Juice dribbled off his elbow and he swiped the arm against his shirt.

They saw Deke pull up in front of Terry's house. He honked his horn, *bee-beep-de-beep*! A moment later, Mama ran out to his truck. She stood with one foot and only her toe of the other foot touching the ground.

"Looks like they're getting kind of thick," Ossie said. "Nobody can resist the conjure woman."

"They're talking about supper," Terry guessed. "Deke always brings something when he's coming over."

Ossie peered through one eye squinty and the other eye closed to shut out the afternoon sun. "When a woman starts cooking for a man — watch out."

"Listen, Ossie," Terry reasoned, "if they like one another, I get to go to the swamps with Deke. That's what I wanted and it's working."

Ossie spit out a juiceless wad of cane pulp and cut another segment. He passed it on the blade of his knife and Terry took it.

"Next thing you know," Ossie spit, cut, chewed cane, "they'll be trying to get you out of the house — sending you for a left-handed monkey wrench — things like that."

Terry blinked. "What about a left-handed monkey wrench?"

"Boy, are you stupid," Ossie smirked. "You can use a monkey wrench with either hand."

Terry sucked pulp dry, spit it aside. "Anybody knows that," he said.

"You ever had you a woman?" Ossie asked.

A woman? Terry expelled pulp, thinking.

"You don't *know* what I mean?"

"Oh. Yeah. No."

"Yeah, no — which is it?"

"Yeah, I understand, and no, I haven't."

"Me either, really," Ossie said. "My grandfather says once you start you can't stop, so don't start until you don't want to do anything else because that's *all* you think about."

"I think about it," Terry said. But he hadn't, really.

"But not all the time. Once you start, it's all the time."

Terry watched Mama, standing on her other foot now. She hung on the window of Deke's truck.

"No skin off my nose." Ossie spit, cut cane. "I just know how men get to be when they start messing with women. They laugh real loud and drink a lot and they want her to sit in their laps no matter how hot it is

outside. They start wearing fancy clothes and ties and
slick back their hair with pomade even though it traps
gnats. They go out fishing or hunting and that's all they
talk about, this woman or that."

"Deke and Mama wouldn't do that."

Ossie finished his cane, folded his knife and stood up.
"I got to go," he said. "My advice is — watch out for the
left-handed monkey wrenches. Then you know for sure."

Mickey composed her letter with care:

". . . he lost his legs in the Pacific," she wrote, "and
Terry has become quite enamored with him. Hero wor-
ship, certainly. But also, Deke is a botanist and he's trying
to compile a book on local flora, which is something
Terry can appreciate. Honestly, Gerald, you should see it!
A legless veteran, a ten-year-old redhead, Lamar and the
Indian boy. Burrell Mason refers to them, including him-
self, as 'bits and pieces.' "

She tried to perceive the words through Gerald's eyes,
then continued.

"The other night we needed a fourth for bridge and the
poor fellow agreed —"

No.

Mickey threw away that page, began anew. "Deke came
over with Burrell and Velma to be my bridge partner (we
won) and I was relieved to find he is sensitive and intelligent. He seems to have a genuine regard for Terry, which
is most important. Do you remember Mayor Dekle at
Pahokee? Owned the grocery store there in the mid-
thirties? That's his father. I heard him tell Burrell and
Velma that he came to Belle Glade because his mother was
so distraught over his loss of legs. Evidently a daily scene

of pity and remorse which Deke is trying to escape. . . ."

She sipped hot tea, kneaded her forehead.

"Bless his heart —"

No.

She erased it. Erasures were maddening, making the reader wonder, "what?" With another page, she transcribed the acceptable part and now wrote:

"I think, Gerald, the thing those of us here miss the most is healthy, young, complete personalities. War depletes the nation of the cream of the crop, leaving the women with the elderly, the wounded, the men who feel they must explain why they did not go to war. I begin to ache for a receptive intelligence, which is one of the things I always admired about you. I treasure those long philosophical discussions after love, lying in the dark, your voice deep, your thoughts so well considered. But it won't be long now, will it?"

She rinsed her cup, standing at the kitchen sink. She saw Terry sitting on the cinders of the railroad incline, by himself, hands clasped, elbows on his knees. Ossie had been there earlier but was now gone.

She returned to reread her letter.

"I'm home, Mama." Ann trudged through with heavy steps. "Velma and Lamar came to get me."

"I know. How was school?"

"I can't read yet."

"That comes next year," Mickey said.

Terry came in the back door. "Want me to take Ann outside?"

"Please do."

At the door, holding Ann's hand, Terry asked, "Are you writing Daddy?"

"Trying to."

He chewed his lip, chin athwart. "Are you going to tell
Daddy about Deke?"

Mickey felt her face flush. "What is there to tell?"

"I don't know."

"I'll certainly mention it, Terry," she said irritably.

With the children outside on the steps, Mickey examined the words anew. She crumpled the page.

"Oh me," she said aloud, softly. "Oh me, oh me."

"Since Deke and I have no interest in *Jack Armstrong
the All-American Boy*," Mama suggested, "why don't you
take the radio into your bedroom?"

"Yeah!" Ann agreed.

"We can listen to *Inner Sanctum* and *Gangbusters*,"
Terry told Ann. He put the radio between their beds and
plugged it in.

"Not *Inner Sanctum*," Ann said. "It makes me sleep
scary because the door squeaks."

"All right. *The Shadow*, then."

He had no idea which came when, only that tonight
was a good night for drama. Terry got a program schedule
and crawled onto the bed beside Ann. Sitting by a window, he mapped the evening's entertainment. Then, coming slowly, he recognized a Packard driving along "C"
Street. He saw the driver look this way and that. The
packing house guard —

"Uh-oh."

"What?" Ann said.

From the living room, Mama's voice, angry, telling
Deke, "He charged me twenty-two dollars for an eighteen
dollar tire!"

Terry shivered with relief as the automobile passed. But

it halted, an arm beckoned several children playing up near Lamar's. With mounting dread, Terry saw Lamar now. The boy pointed — this way. The car drove on slowly and the children returned to jump rope: "Peas porridge hot; peas porridge cold; peas porridge in a pot, nine days old. . . ."

"Reporting it won't accomplish anything, Mickey," Deke was saying. "Proving black market is difficult and it's a serious charge."

"This war won't last forever," Mama fumed. "When it's over, Mr. Beaudry will find his black market customers will become his enemies. They won't forget."

The Packard circled the block, barely moving. Terry caught glimpses of it passing houses on a far street.

"Well?" Ann commanded, "turn it on." Terry flipped the switch and returned to the window. The big sedan stopped behind Mama's car. The unmistakable form of the portly packing house guard appeared. The man tossed his hat onto the front seat, looking at the house. *Going to get it now.*

"Ossie —" Terry said aloud.

Ann saw the guard approach the porch. "Who is he?"

"Ossie must have told again," Terry said. He heard Mama at the door, "Yes?"

"Mrs. Calder, I work over to the Blue Goose packing house. I came about your boy. May I come in?"

"Terry?" Mama said. "Yes, please, come in."

Mama introduced the man to Deke and the men mumbled to one another.

"What the problem is," the guard said, "is these kids coming over to play in dangerous places."

"Terry, you mean?"

"Him and the Indian boy," the guard stated. "This time

is enough to cause trouble with the law, and I don't want
to go to the law if I can help it."

"What is it?" Mama asked.

Ann shook Terry's arm. "Make it make some sound!"

"Shhh!" Terry stood at the bedroom door and immediately Mama yanked it open, looking down.

"Terry, come into the living room."

The guard sat in an easy chair, heavy legs spread, an
arm extended to the side, opening and closing his hand.
"That's him," he said, seeing Terry.

"Terry, would you explain what you were doing at the
packing house?"

Deke sat on the couch, eyes on Mama.

"Wasn't hard to find you, little buddy," the guard said.
"I asked the camp manager if he knew any redheaded
boys."

"Well, Terry?" Mama prompted.

"Just playing, Mama."

"Your idea of playing is turning on the electricity? That
could've killed him," the guard said, his eyes glinting in
fatty slits.

"Terry," Mama persisted, "we're waiting."

"I'm sorry, Mama."

"They're breaking the law, trespassing," the guard
added. "There were two. Covered with blood, looked
like. The other boy looked like his arm was cut off —" he
glanced at Deke's legs and coughed into a pudgy fist. "We
broke down some machinery, looking to be sure — it was
that real-life looking."

"Looking for his arm?" Deke queried.

"It looked chopped off, I ain't lying."

"I assure you," Mama told the man, "this will not
happen again."

Still he sat there breathing asthmatically, hand opening
and closing. "If it was my boy," the guard said, "I'd
thrash him good for his own sake. What if I'd had a
stroke? Damn near did, too."

Still he sat there, glaring at Terry. "I didn't want to go
to the law right off."

"We appreciate that," Deke said.

"I wanted to see how sensible the parents were."

"We thank you for that," Deke said. Like he was
Daddy. *Still*, he sat there, Terry burning under that mean-
as-a-snake-and-sneaky-as-a-weasel glare.

"Thank you for coming by." Mama took a step toward
the door.

"Didn't want to send him to jail without giving you
folks the chance to punish him yourselves."

"Thank you."

The man took a labored breath, put both hands on the
arms of the chair and grunted, rising. He bent his knees
and tugged at the seat of his pants. "I know you'll do
what's right."

"We'll skin him alive," Deke replied.

"We were all boys once," the guard said.

"We certainly were," Mama agreed. "But this —"

The guard looked at her, "Is serious," he concluded.

Mama walked him to his Packard and listened as he
added comment to condemnation.

"Terry," Deke said, "I didn't understand about the arm
cut off."

"It was Ossie."

"But how?"

Mama was in the door.

"Show me," Deke said.

Terry pulled an arm inside his shirt and inserted only

the elbow through a sleeve. "Like that."

Mama's mouth dropped open and she stared in horror.

"With catsup on it," Terry said.

Mama's expression of pain was so powerful, embarrassment so acute, Terry said, "Deke, I'm really sorry."

Deke laughed.

Mama opened and shut her eyes rapidly, laughed nervously.

Terry waited with one long and one short arm.

"With catsup, Mickey!"

Deke threw back his head, voice musical, pitched high, and Mama joined in. He reached for her and Mama collapsed beside Deke, his arm around her shoulder, patting. They laughed and laughed.

Terry slipped into the bedroom and closed the door.

"What is it?" Ann whispered.

"I don't know."

"Are you in trouble?"

"I don't know yet."

The radio made an ominous creaking sound of a rusting hinge swinging open and Ann seized Terry. "That's scary, Terry!"

He turned the dial without complaint. In the living room, Mama and Deke were still laughing.

Nobody could resist the conjure woman. . . .

Twenty-two

MAMA WORE A HAT with a net on it. She'd painted her legs like stockings and her fingernails were lacquered blood red. It was not her usual Okeelanta working clothes.

"Where are you going?" Terry asked.

"Palm Beach. I told you that."

"No, you didn't."

"I meant to," Mama said.

Deke and Ossie stopped out front and came toward the house.

"Where is Ann?" Terry questioned.

"Velma took her to the day-care center," Mama said. She stood at a mirror putting the net over her face down to the nose.

"Morning!" Deke said. He rolled onto the couch and propped himself up. "You look terrific, Mickey."

Mama waved a hand at him, dismissing the compliment.

"Heavy date?" Deke inquired.

"Anything but," Mama said. "The mill is changing accounting procedures. I have to catch a bus at 8:30, ride forty-five miles to Palm Beach, catch another bus to get where I'm going, attend a one and a half hour meeting, then sit there until 6:30 waiting for a bus to bring me home."

To Terry she said, "Velma will pick up Ann this afternoon. I'll be back about eight o'clock tonight. I'll get Ann from Velma's then."

"I could make it easier for you," Deke smiled. "Drive you to Palm Beach — we could use the same amount of time to have dinner. Maybe even catch a movie. We'd still be back by the appointed hour."

"I couldn't ask that of you."

Terry saw Ossie peer intently at one of his fingers, mashing the flesh as if trying to bring something to a head.

"Hey, no problem at all," Deke said. "Believe me, it'll be easier on you if I take you. I need a day off, anyway."

"I came to work," Ossie said sourly.

"We'll work tomorrow," Deke replied.

"You said come and I came. I lose two dollars."

"I'll pay you," Deke said. "How about it, Mickey? We can make this fun instead of a chore."

"May I go?" Terry asked.

"No. This is business."

"I'll stay out of the way."

"No, Terry. I can't drag a child to a business function."

"Nice hat," Deke said to Mama.

"Antebellum," Mama replied, and they both laughed. Then, "All right," Mama said, "if it's no imposition. They gave me money for the bus ticket and we'll spend that on dinner."

"A deal," Deke nodded. He took money from a shirt pocket, peeled off two dollars and handed it to Ossie. "A day's wages for your troubles, Ossie."

"What about my supper?" Terry asked peevishly.

"Velma will feed you."

"He can eat with me," Ossie said.

"Your mother might not agree, Ossie — but, thanks."

"No, it's all right," Ossie insisted. "We can eat free at the Glades Café where my mama works."

"See," Deke grinned. "It's all so easy."

"All right, Terry," Mama said. "Be here by eight o'clock tonight. I should be home before then."

"No later than that, certainly," Deke amended. "Well, fine — come on, let's go."

Terry watched them leave, through the window. Oh, boy, he had really messed up with this wish. . . .

"Want some toast?" Terry asked Ossie.

"No."

Terry washed breakfast dishes. Ossie sat by the table digging at a splinter in his thumb. "You got a needle?"

He went into Mama's bedroom, returned with a pin. Ossie worked at the sliver while Terry dried dishes, putting them away. He worried about Mama, Deke, what he'd done to Daddy.

"Want to go fishing?" Ossie asked.

"Not really."

"Me either. Ouch! This thing goes deeper and deeper. I can't get a hold on it."

Hunting Mama's tweezers, Terry looked first in a compartment of the treadle-driven Singer sewing machine. Not there. Then in Mama's top dresser drawer: Daddy's letters bound by a ribbon, cosmetics, but no tweezers.

Last time he needed tweezers, weren't they in Mama's jewelry box? But the box was forbidden. Locked. The key was in the dresser. Terry had seen it under Daddy's letters. He heard Ossie swear softly in the kitchen.

Mama called it her "jewelry" box always with a smile. The contents were familiar enough — a ring with a tiny diamond given to Mama by a man who'd wanted to marry her before she met Daddy in Birmingham. A delicate gold necklace with a broken clasp. "Costume" earrings with pendants, which Daddy didn't like.

He opened the box. A letter from Daddy. Not with the others? Terry lifted the airmail envelope, turned it. The postmark was this month. But, why —

"Did you find the tweezers?" Ossie called.

He took the implement to Ossie, returned to the bedroom, closed the door, and read:

"At last, good news! September embarkation . . . date not certain . . . ship not yet known . . . will try to call when these things settled . . . and Mickey, we're going to Colorado!"

Terry's stomach plummeted. He read on:

"I have a wonderful opportunity to buy part interest in a weekly newspaper, the Longmont *Ledger*. It was sheer luck — a friend introduced me to the owner, and he needs an editor — at last, me writing! I am so happy I —"

"Hey!" Ossie hollered. "Where are you?"

Terry folded the letter, placed it precisely as it had been. He replaced the tweezers and locked the box. Hands perspiring, he put the key where he'd found it.

"We could go down to the Glades Café and have a cold

drink," Ossie suggested.

Sickly, Terry sat on Mama's bed. "I don't have any money, Ossie."

Ossie put an arm around Terry's shoulder, sitting beside him. "Let's go by the café, Terry. If we can't get a cold drink free, I'll buy."

Walking the railroad ties toward town, they said very little. Every now and then, Ossie would put an arm around Terry and they walked in lock step for awhile.

When they reached the restaurant, passing through the sweltering kitchen, Ossie entered and flopped in his favorite booth.

"Hey, sweetie!" Mrs. Knight passed with a tray.

"We want two cold drinks, Mom."

"Help yourself, darling. I'm busy."

Ossie got two big orange drinks. "I heard that the niggers from the islands won't be coming back after the war," he said to Terry.

"Ossie, stop saying nigger. I hate that."

"The white men have used them and now to hell with them," Ossie noted. "Just like white people to do that."

Behind them, several men sat at the next booth. Ossie cut his eyes at Terry. "That's him," he whispered.

Terry twisted to see. "That's who?"

"The fruit that smokes the mentholated cigarettes."

Ossie glowered at his orange drink.

"Hey, m'darlin'," the man said to Mrs. Knight. "How's tricks these days?"

"Shut your mouth, Thevis."

The men laughed. Mrs. Knight bumped the swinging door going into the kitchen. Terry recognized him now — it was the man at Ossie's house the first time Terry went there.

"You ever want to cut a red one," the man said, "that is prime grade-A."

Mortified, Terry heard him say, "I shacked up with her for six months and boys, she kept on teaching me something new, everytime."

"How come you quit then?" somebody said.

"My mother took a dim view of it."

Laughter. Ossie was holding the drink bottle so tightly his knuckles were white.

"Ossie," Terry said, "let's go."

"I tell you, boys," the man continued, "she's got a dimple that only shows when she smiles and the dimple is right here." He touched his rear end.

More laughter. Mrs. Knight passed again, tray loaded. She studiously avoided looking at Ossie and Terry.

Voice lower, the man said, "Once in a lifetime a man finds one that can do this —"

"Ossie," Terry urged, "come on. Let's go."

Ossie lunged from the booth, through the swinging doors of the kitchen and out to the alley with Terry right behind.

"Sonofabitch," Ossie screamed. "Sonofabitch!"

Terry had to trot to keep up. "I'd like to kill him," Ossie said. "No. That's too quick. Torture him."

Terry listened to a series of grisly possibilities. They cut across by the theater but didn't stop to look at the photos of coming attractions. Past Mr. Beaudry's service station and into colored town.

"Bad enough the sonofabitch did it," Ossie said. "But now he has to talk about it. Men always talk about it."

Terry was appalled. "Deke wouldn't talk about Mama."

"Hell, yes, he would. With no legs — he'd talk just to prove he still does it."

"Ossie — I have to go see the conjure woman."

"Yeah," Ossie seethed. "Yeah! The conjure woman."

When they reached the sign of the hand, Ossie entered without invitation. With a candor that astonished Terry, Ossie told the conjure woman his problem.

"What would you have me do?" she asked.

"What can you do?"

She looked into Ossie's eyes. "Give him boils."

"Ain't enough."

"Give him warts."

"That ain't enough."

"Depends on where he gets them," she said softly.

Ossie considered this. "That's good," he conceded.

"Bring him pain where he needs to suffer," she purred. "Make his tongue swell so he cannot talk."

"That's good."

"We can make him suffer," she said.

"That's what I want."

"Ah, yes. But there are conditions. Prices."

"How much?"

"If I must do it all, very expensive."

"What do you mean?" Terry asked.

"If I do only the incantation, deliver the hex, you must do all else — it's cheaper that way."

"That's fine with me," Ossie said. "How much?"

"Fifty dollars."

"Fifty dollars," Ossie groaned, turning full circle on a heel. "How much can you do for ten dollars?"

She looked at Terry. "Perhaps you can help your friend."

"How?"

"Make his wish your own."

"I don't have any money."

"I told you before — we will trade."

"What for what?"

"For his wish — your hair."

"My hair!"

"Ten dollars, plus your hair."

"Give it to her, Terry."

"Wait a minute, Ossie. I have a wish, too."

"Ah," she said. "Two wishes."

"How much for two wishes?" Ossie bartered.

"What is the second wish?"

"I want to unwish a wish," Terry said.

She spread her ringed fingers on the table, looking at them. The bead curtain tinkled softly. Slivers of sunlight danced across the walls and sparkled on her hands.

"Every wish has a price," she said softly. "You should always be careful what you wish. But to unwish a wish is more expensive than the wish itself."

"We'll be right back," Ossie said. He dragged Terry into bright sunlight. "What are you going to wish?" he demanded.

"That Mama and Deke don't like one another too much."

"You're jacking up the price, don't you see that?"

"My wish is important, Ossie. My daddy is coming home. When he finds out what I did — there's no telling what he'll do."

Ossie rubbed his mouth with a hand, gazing away. Down the street, Bahamians were making music with tambourines, clickety sticks and metal drums.

"I can't get my wish without your hair," Ossie said.

"If I wish Mama to stop liking Deke," Terry said, "I

won't ever get to the swamps. If you promise to help me get to the swamps, I'll give her enough hair for both of us."

"Okay."

"Indian's honor?" Terry asked.

Ossie made a fist and touched his chest. "Indian honor."

They entered again and Ossie slouched against a wall squishing spit between his teeth. "We'll make you a deal," he said. "Ten dollars plus all the hair you want for two wishes."

"That would be a lot of hair."

"You can have it, though," Terry said.

"What will your mother say?"

"She likes me to get my hair cut."

"Ten dollars and Terry's hair," Ossie confirmed. "For that, we both get our wishes."

"Um-m." She touched Terry's hair, feeling the texture of it. "What is your unwish?"

"That my mama and Deke won't like one another too much."

"It will take a lot of hair," she warned.

"You can have what's left," Terry said. "Is it a deal?"

"You must follow my instructions precisely," she told Ossie. "Otherwise it will fail and the price is the same. You understand this?"

"I understand."

She slipped her hands into the sleeves of her dress. "Then bring me the money and we shall begin."

They jogged back to the Glades Café. Thevis was still there.

Stunned, Terry watched Ossie approach the man unannounced. "I need ten dollars," Ossie said.

"Ten dollars!"

"It is little enough to pay," Ossie said. "I heard you talking. Give me ten dollars or I'll tell my grandfather and he will roast you on an open fire."

"Jeeze, will you listen to this!"

The men shifted uneasily.

"Ten dollars and we forget it," Ossie said.

"What're you going to do with ten dollars, boy?"

"Get me a woman."

They laughed and one man punched Thevis on his shoulder. "Better pay up, white man."

His face crimson, Thevis counted out the money. "That's the end of it, boy. You got me?"

"Yes," Ossie said. "I got you."

As they walked out the kitchen door, Ossie said, "I've got him, all right. And he's paying for it."

They ran all the way back to the conjure woman's booth. She was waiting.

Without counting it, she folded the money and reached under the table. Her skirt rustled, elastic snapped. Then, "This you must do," she said, and pushed a penciled list at Ossie.

Terry read over Ossie's shoulder. "His hair?"

"A snip of his hair."

"Why is hair so important?"

"It is where the body stores memories of things we eat and drink."

"How are we going to get his hair?" Terry questioned.

"Does he not get his hair cut?"

"Oh, yeah. The barbershop."

Ossie had his finger on the next item. "Dust where he's walked."

"It must come from the very place where his foot has stepped," she cautioned. "Be sure it is the dust from only there, and not off to either side. I will not inflict someone who deserves nothing."

"I can do that," Ossie said.

"Fingernail clippings!" Terry cried. "How can we get that?"

"If necessary, we can do without it. But if we have them, the hex will be much more powerful."

"Some personal apparel," Ossie studied the list. "What?"

"Shirt, trousers, socks, a handkerchief will do."

Ossie groaned. "Something he will carry with him?"

"A pocketknife, a comb, his belt —"

"He wears suspenders," Ossie said.

"Something you are sure he will carry. The hex will ride that item — very important. Be sure."

"How long does he have to carry this thing, whatever it is?" Ossie asked.

"The longer and more often, the better. Does he wear a hat?"

"Sometimes. Not always the same one."

"The more often, the better," she said. Terry leaned on the table, reading her note.

"A wallet is ideal," she suggested.

"I don't know about that," Ossie said. "How could I get it?"

"As I have said, if I must do these things it is very expensive."

"We'll do it," Ossie declared. "Somehow."

But outside, walking down the street, Ossie stared at the list and shook his head. "You going to help me?" he asked.

"We made a deal. You're going to help me, aren't you?"

"Yeah." Ossie folded the list. "Ten dollars. It would've been cheaper to burn his house down."

"But if she can do all those things —" Terry marveled. "Can you imagine him with his tongue so swollen he can't talk!"

The image was satisfying. Ossie hung an arm around Terry's shoulder. "I owe you one big favor. That's my promise."

"Your promise is to help me get to the swamps, Ossie."

"Okay. Anything," Ossie asserted. "Anything you want."

They strolled along railroad tracks, across the trestle and back toward Camp Osceola. Now and then, as an idea struck one or the other, they spoke. Otherwise, they walked quietly, thinking.

"We might sit outside the barbershop six weeks before the creep gets his hair cut," Ossie said.

"Yeah, we could."

"We sure can't cut his fingernails."

"How many do we need?" Terry asked.

Ossie consulted the list. "It doesn't say."

They walked a shiny rail, Terry trying to do it with arms down like Ossie on the next rail over.

"Mr. Cantrell won't let anybody hang around the barbershop, Ossie. Kids go in to read comic books, and he makes them get a haircut or get out."

"I know it."

"How're we going to get in at the right time, then?"

"I don't know. Be ready to get a haircut, I guess."

Ossie put an ear to the rail, peering along the track toward infinity. "Nothing coming," he surmised. Back to walking the ribbon of steel.

"Hardest part," Ossie said, "is getting something away that he'll carry with him, and getting it back to him without him knowing it. And what? Nobody wears the same things all the time."

They sat on the rail at the back of the packing house, smoking one of Ossie's cigarettes.

"If he was still coming to see Mom," Ossie said, "this would be easier."

"Think he will?"

"No. She got mad at him about something and he quit coming. Just as well. I never liked the menthol-smoking fruit in the first place. Anyway, the theater manager brings me leftover popcorn sometimes."

Ossie spit in the cinders. "If I go asking my mom for money for a haircut, she's going to smell a dead skunk in the sunshine."

"I'll do that. My mama likes me to get my hair cut."

"We need all the hair you've got," Ossie said.

Terry puffed the cigarette, returned it.

"The part I like best is the warts," Ossie laughed.

"Depends on where he gets them," Terry said.

"That's what I mean."

"Oh." Then, comprehending, "Oh! Hey, that's really good — you think she can do that?"

"You know Mr. Bemis at the bank?"

"The baldheaded man?"

"She made every hair fall out because he cheated a nig — a colored woman — on a loan she'd made. It happened a few years ago."

Terry puffed. The smoke scorched his tongue.

"She can fix Thevis, all right," Ossie said. "If we do what she says, she'll fix him good."

He grinned, hugged Terry, his breath smelling of

tobacco. "Think we can do our part?"

"We can try."

Ossie flicked away the cigarette and stood up. "She must use red hair for something special. It got us forty dollars off the price."

"Yeah." Terry stood up, too.

"I couldn't trust nobody but you with this," Ossie said.

"Don't forget our deal, Ossie."

"I won't."

They parted at the main entrance. So far, Terry had seen wishes come true, so he had no doubt his unwish would happen also. That was a relief. No telling what Daddy would say if he came home and found Mama in love with Deke.

It would've been his fault, too.

But now — his dream of going deep into the Everglades was ruined.

The house was empty. Ann at Velma's. Mama and Deke — who knew where?

Terry wished he hadn't come home so soon.

He went into Mama's room, unlocked the jewelry box and read Daddy's letter again.

Colorado.

Wherever it was, he bet they didn't have swamps.

Twenty-three

"IF YOU HAVE TO write a message," Ossie directed, "use code. B is for *A*, C is for *B* and D is for *C* — like that. Now, see if you can read this."

Terry took Ossie's note and read: *nffu nf upojhiu.* Laboriously, he translated, "Meet me tonight."

"Right!"

"It would be easier to use invisible ink," Terry suggested.

"Yeah, but I don't have any."

Terry got his supply from a hiding place beneath his bed. He wrote a note, carefully dried it, handed it to Ossie.

"I don't see anything."

Triumphantly, Terry took the blank paper, placed it in the oven and turned it on. A few moments later, the ink magically appeared in brown letters.

"Wow," Ossie said. "Where'd you get that?"

"Captain Midnight spy kit," Terry said. "It cost a dime plus three boxtops from cereal. I found out how they made it when Ann drank some."

"How?"

"It's nothing but lemon juice."

"It works," Ossie approved. "Okay, we'll use invisible ink."

"I'm going to wear my cape, okay?"

"It's awful hot."

"Yeah, but you can hide your face like this." Terry swooped the cloth to cover mouth and nose, peering over a draped forearm.

"That's all right at night," Ossie said, "but it's kind of noticeable in the daytime."

"I meant at night."

Ossie helped Terry make his bed and put away the morning dishes. Well before eight o'clock, they were in position.

"Thevis owns this place," Ossie explained. "He lives in back."

A sign on the window read: CASH LOANS: chattel-home-auto-signature.

In a crouch, Ossie led Terry down a narrow walkway between the buildings. He pointed at a barred window, an upturned bean hamper below, and put his finger to his lips commanding silence.

Terry climbed up, looked in. A light bulb hung on a cord from the ceiling. He saw a filthy lavatory and a metal shower stall with mildewed curtain. Beyond, in the bedroom, the victim was dressing, his back to Terry.

Ossie took him further down the alley to a door secured by a looped chain. Ossie pushed and the barrier yielded enough for him to squeeze through. Terry did it easily.

The place was full of old furniture. On tiptoe, Ossie led Terry to a door between the man's bedroom and the storage area. He pointed first to a knothole — Thevis was still dressing — then to the latch — unlocked!

They retraced their steps, crossed the street and hid behind garbage cans facing the loan office.

"Watch now."

Thevis stepped out, secured his office door and hooked a thumb in his suspenders. He strolled half a block to Cantrell's barbershop.

Ossie and Terry ambled past.

Thevis was laid back in a chair, feet up, his face swathed in a steaming towel. He was alone.

"Mr. Cantrell is in the back making coffee," Ossie reported. "He stays gone a couple or three minutes. Same thing every blessed day!"

Freshly shaved, Thevis went to the Glades Café for breakfast. Ossie and Terry entered by the kitchen, took their regular booth, watching. Without asking, Mrs. Knight gave them breakfast.

"Wish I could be invisible like the *Shadow*," Terry whispered. Ossie sopped egg yolk with a wedge of toast. "Who knows the evil that lurks in the minds of men? The *Shadow* knows — ah-hah-hah-haaa."

After a second cup of coffee, Thevis waved away the waitress, paid his bill, walked out with a toothpick in his mouth and returned to start his business day. Three days in a row, the same thing.

Thursday, he deviated, going to the Sawgrass Hotel for breakfast.

"See, this is what messes up most criminals," Terry

warned Ossie. "The unexpected."

Grimly, Ossie sat on a couch in the hotel lobby, peering through a tropical fish aquarium, watching Thevis flirt with a waitress. They went into the rest room to be less conspicuous. A sign over the urinal said, "We aim to please; you aim too, please." On a wall somebody had written "Flush the commode, Pahokee needs the water." Beside it, a drawing of a pregnant girl and a notation: KILROY WAS HERE.

"Who's Kilroy?" Terry questioned.

"Nobody."

"He's somebody," Terry insisted. "He's been nearly everywhere I've been."

"It's a joke."

Terry buttoned his pants, trying to think what could possibly be funny about being everywhere.

Back to the aquarium, goldfish swimming in their line of vision as they watched Thevis pat his mouth with a linen napkin.

"You suppose fish ever get thirsty?" Terry asked.

"I don't know. Watch him, here he comes."

"They breathe water," Terry deduced, "but do they drink any?"

Toothpick rolling between thick lips, a thumb in his suspenders, Thevis left the hotel.

"Going to the post office," Ossie observed. "Follow him inside."

"Why me?"

"He knows me. Go on!"

Terry entered, loitering under a poster of a dying soldier which pleaded, "He gives his life — you only loan your money. Buy War Bonds."

"Gimme a penny postcard, Ace," Thevis was saying.

Rejoining Ossie, Terry said, "He didn't see me." They followed at a discreet distance, back to the loan company. Later that day, Thevis returned to the hotel for a Lion's Club meeting. Terry and Ossie stood outside the cloistered room listening to men sing *God Bless America*. A porter told them they couldn't stay there.

"Okay," Ossie said, walking toward Camp Osceola, "same thing everyday except Thursday. You ready to make the hit?"

"I don't know if we're ready."

"Why not? We can sneak in his room when he goes to breakfast. We can sneak in at lunch. We need something he wears and we need something he carries all the time. Those are the hard things to get."

"If he leaves it when he goes out to eat," Terry said, "he isn't carrying it *all* the time. I think we need to get in there when he's undressed."

Ossie stared into space. "That means at night."

"Most likely. We'd better start with the easy stuff."

Which was the dust where Thevis had walked. They sprinkled it outside the office and Thevis walked right through it, his alligator shoes powdered by silt, but unnoticed. Ossie carefully retrieved only that which had been trod upon. They put it in one of Deke's botanical envelopes which they'd borrowed.

That night, with Deke, Velma and Burrell Mason at the house, Terry asked Mama, "May I get a haircut?"

"A haircut!"

"Yes ma'am."

"You *want* a haircut?"

"Yes ma'am. It's too short, Mama."

"Cutting it won't make it longer," Mama said. "You can wait. School will be starting in a month or so."

His blood chilled. Think about that later.

"I need to get Lamar's hair cut, too," Velma shifted cards in her hand.

"I'll take him," Terry said. "How about Monday?"

"That'd be fine." Velma selected a card, put it on the table. "But I was thinking of tomorrow."

Did Thevis go on Saturday? That's when all the kids went. "All right," Terry said. "I'll take Lamar tomorrow."

"Not this Saturday," Mama countered. "Deke is driving us to Palm Beach."

"Do I have to go?"

"Are you ill?" Mama said incredulously. "We're going to the beach, to a movie, and we're eating at Morrison's Cafeteria!"

"I have to help Ossie, Mama."

Mama waved a hand in front of his eyes. "Beach-movie-Morrison's," she said.

"I promised I'd help him. He needs a favor and I said I would."

"I'll keep an eye on him, Mickey," Velma volunteered.

"No complaining because you couldn't go, Terry," Mama warned.

"No ma'am."

Deke spread his cards and Burrell groaned. "That's twice tonight, damn it."

"What Ossie is doing can't wait?" Deke asked.

"No sir."

Mama and Deke looked at one another. "All right," Mama said.

The next morning, Ossie glared at Lamar and questioned, "What's he doing here?"

"He wanted to come. I thought he was going to get a haircut, but his mama changed her mind."

Wouldn't do any good to get his hair cut today anyway. Thevis holed up last night and he's drunk as a pickled owl. Lamar'll get in our way, Terry."

"I won't," Lamar said.

"Terry," Ossie slapped his leg in exasperation, "damn it!"

"He's got to come, Ossie. His mama said so. You'll do what I say, won't you, Lamar?"

"Yeah!"

"If you don't," Ossie shook a finger in Lamar's face, "I'm going to hang you out to dry."

"I will," Lamar wailed.

"Sure you will. Ease up, Ossie."

"Ain't this some shit?" Ossie wheezed. "I was going to get the most important thing — something he carries."

"What?" Terry asked.

"His teeth."

"Teeth!"

"He's got false teeth. Puts them in a glass beside the bed and hasn't touched them since he went on the binge. We could sneak in and get them easy, right now!"

"Lamar, you wait here," Terry commanded.

"I want to go."

"Do what you're told!" Ossie snapped.

"We'll be back in a few minutes, Lamar."

"I want to go, Terry." Lamar's lips colored, the first sign of tears to come.

Terry pushed Lamar backward gently, pointing at the ground. "Sit here and wait. You have to do what I tell you."

"I want to go, though."

"We'll be back in a minute. Come on, Ossie."

They took a circuitous route to be sure Lamar didn't

follow. But when they looked again, Lamar sat across the street from the loan office, obediently waiting.

They sneaked in the rear door, into the storage area, and peeped through the knothole. The bed was empty. So was the glass beside the bed.

Outside again, Terry railed, "If it hadn't been for Lamar, we'd have walked in and he would've caught us, Ossie!"

"He's been asleep all morning."

"He isn't asleep now. And I didn't see any teeth."

"Lamar," Ossie questioned, "did somebody come out of that place?"

"Yeah."

"Where'd he go?" Terry asked.

"Uh, to the café."

Sure enough, there sat Thevis, bleary-eyed and eating.

"We'll get the teeth last," Terry said. "We need a lot of other things first."

"No telling when he'll finish and where he'll go," Ossie seethed.

"Tell you what," Terry said. "You watch him. If he starts back, come running and tell me. I'll go get the clothing stuff and see what else I can find."

"Go."

Terry raced down the alley, through the storage room and into the bedroom. Trembling, he checked the bathroom. Under the sink was a pair of undershorts, BVD's. He took them. The room smelled like mold. He looked under the bed — toenails! Shivering so violently he had difficulty grasping the tiny arcs, Terry gathered several and put them in his pocket. What else?

"Terry!" Ossie at the door. "Run!"

It took tremendous willpower not to bolt. Terry

stepped outside, closed the door as it had been, and walked deliberately to the exit.

"BVD's," he gave them to Ossie. "And these."

"Toenails — wow!" Ossie whacked Terry on the back.

"All we need now," Terry said, "is something he carries with him."

"Yessiree," Ossie gloated. "And you know what he just did?"

"What?"

"Bought another fifth."

They sat in a booth of the Glades Café for so long, Mrs. Knight offered to treat them to a movie.

"By the time we get out," Terry reasoned, "he's bound to be asleep again, Ossie. We'll get his teeth and take them to the conjure woman."

"One thing is missing," Ossie stated. "We need his hair."

"Before she can hex his teeth?"

Ossie dashed from the theater line, up the street, into the conjure woman's booth. He returned, shoved some boys who'd shoved him for "breaking line" and told Terry, "She said the teeth are perfect! We can get the hair later."

They watched one Gene Autry film, which was good for booing when cowboys sang their songs. Then they saw a war movie, *Guadalcanal*. They'd seen one of the Bugs Bunny cartoons before, but it was still good.

It was dark when they emerged.

"I have to go home," Lamar said.

"In a minute, Lamar. Wait right here."

"No," Lamar said. "I'm going home."

"Let him go!" Ossie insisted.

"His mama thinks he's with me, Ossie."

"We have to do this now," Ossie declared.

Lamar had disappeared beyond a streetlight, too far away to catch easily. Terry followed Ossie to the loan company.

Through the knothole they saw the snoring man lying naked. In a glass, immersed in liquid, the teeth.

"If he wakes up and sees me," Ossie whispered, "he'll go straight to my mom and I'll be dead. You have to do it."

Quivering, Terry pushed the door. It creaked. He lifted it slightly, pushing again. He groped through the warehouse of used furniture, pushing his feet along the floor testing for obstacles. When he reached the man's bedroom, Terry peeked inside. Thevis lay, mouth open, arms outstretched, the mattress sagging beneath him. Terry tiptoed to the bedside table, reached into the water, but the teeth clicked against the glass. He was shaking too much to trust himself, so he took the whole thing. Back through the dark warehouse to Ossie and they shut the door. When they stepped into the alley, Terry was sopping with perspiration from tension.

The conjure woman accepted the dust and underwear, toenail clippings — and the teeth grinning through glass. Terry had never seen her smile before. She was beautiful.

"With this," her voice was susurrous, "we could curve his spine. If only we had the hair —"

"We'll get it Monday," Terry stated.

"Good. Good. This is very good."

She put the glass before her, fingers weaving, hands undulating over the teeth. She muttered words Terry could not understand, her dark eyes reflecting the flicker of a candle flame. Then she brought out a steamy jar and Terry recognized pieces of elephant's ear plant. She squeezed juice from the leaves into the glass with teeth. The substance turned milky.

"His tongue shall swell," she intoned. "He will suffer for the evil things he has said."

"How about the warts?" Ossie asked.

"That will come. First we need his hair."

She looked into the envelope. "You are positive this is only that which was beneath his foot?"

"Yes ma'am. Positive."

"Return his teeth," she said. "Tomorrow he begins to pay."

Monday morning, with Lamar tagging along, they watched Thevis leave his office, stride purposefully to the barbershop and take his place beneath a hot towel. It was really easy. Terry stepped in as Mr. Cantrell stepped out, and with one deft snip he had hair. Thevis mumbled something under his towel, but he didn't sit up.

The conjure woman accepted their final offering, and they had to leave because she had another customer.

Terry, Ossie and Lamar ate breakfast at the Glades Café and watched Thevis devour his food.

It was a couple of days before Ossie reported that, true to her word, the conjure woman had made his tongue swell, and Thevis, the mentholated fruit, couldn't talk.

Terry turned on his side, staring into the dark. In the living room, the adults laughed at something Rochester said to Jack Benny. He heard Ann sigh, stir.

He'd tried to find Colorado on a puzzle map of the United States, but it must have been one of the missing pieces. It was either near Canada or Mexico, or possibly Pennsylvania. No place near here.

He scratched his sunburned nose with the back of a wrist. The radio was loud enough to hear audience responses, but little else. Mama asked if anybody wanted coffee.

Terry swallowed dread, his stomach knotted. He could ask Mama, but she'd know he'd been in her jewelry box. Trouble.

Daddy coming home and Mama hadn't told him. He turned; turned again; he wasn't sleepy at all.

What about school? Would Colorado be cold like Birmingham? Did it have factories?

He had asked Ossie. Ossie's reply was, "Must be north of Lake Okeechobee."

He nearly asked Velma, but some inner warning told him he'd better not. Who would know? And then — where was "Longmont?"

The melodic three tone chime of the National Broadcasting Company came to his ears. He heard an announcer give the time.

Ann had said they had fun in Palm Beach. They saw a full-length cartoon film, she'd said. They ate at Morrison's Cafeteria, then went *back* to the beach again. She didn't remember any more, because she'd fallen asleep on a pallet Deke had put in the rear of his truck.

He shut his eyes, trying to remember what Daddy looked like with blue eyes. He couldn't remember anything but the way his voice sounded when Daddy sang. The song came to mind, "*Kemo, kimo, darrywhere, hi-me-oh, hi-me-oh, in come kitty sing sometime nip cat — singsong kitty catch-a-ki-me-oooh.*"

Daddy had a deep voice when he sang.

Deke's laughter, musical, high —

Terry turned, exhaled, eyes opened again.

Maybe when Daddy called from overseas, Mama was going to tell him how much they liked it here. Maybe Daddy could buy part interest in the Belle Glade newspaper instead. Burrell Mason didn't own it anymore, so maybe it was for sale.

Despite the heat, his hands felt cold.

What would Daddy say? If Mama said, "No, Gerald, we're staying in Florida with the swamps and Lake Okeechobee and —"

He heard Deke laugh again.

Would Daddy be angry? His feelings hurt? Would he go alone and leave them? What then?

Mama would work at Okeelanta Sugar. Terry could gig frogs with Ossie.

He kept swallowing, mouth bitter.

If only he had somebody to talk to.

Somebody who knew where Colorado was.

Twenty-four

DEKE PULLED OFF the pavement under pines border-
ing a canal. He peered along the water's edge.

"See any, Terry?"

"Not yet, Deke." They were seeking one elusive plant.

"It will have blue blossoms."

"I don't see any," Terry said.

Slowly they bumped along the shoulder of the road.
"Gumbo limbo," Deke murmured, "marbleberry, button-
bush, icaco —"

"Deke, when are we going to the swamps?"

"These are the swamps, redhead."

"I mean, where there's no highway — really deep in the
swamps?" Terry was thinking of the conjure woman, even
now working her magic to dampen the relationship
between Deke and Mama. If they didn't go before it
ended, he'd never go. Besides, they would be leav-

ing for Colorado.

"Poinciana, dumb cane," Deke recited. "Showy rattlebox, *Crotolaria*. We sure do need rain."

The morning sun cast long shadows across the road. In the distance, a smoky pall hung over the glades. Muck fires.

"Deke, what do you say?"

"About what?"

"Going camping deep in the swamps?"

"Are you watching for the flowers?"

"I am. Deke — please — could we go soon?"

"Go where?"

Exasperated, Terry sighed, looking across endless fields of grass, watching the curl of distant smoke.

"Why don't you ask me something I can answer," Deke said amiably.

"Okay." Terry sighed again.

"So ask me."

"Does a fish get thirsty?"

Deke laughed.

"A fish breathes in water, but does he swallow it? Water in a goldfish bowl goes down, but that's evaporation, isn't it?"

Deke shook his head, smiling.

"A fish is cold-blooded," Terry debated himself, "so he's the same temperature as the water. He can't perspire. So he probably gets enough water with the food he swallows. Don't you think?"

"Probably. What's that one — is that one?"

"No sir, that's the tip of a hyacinth."

"Better give me another question, redhead."

Terry ran through his mental list of mysteries. "One thing I never could figure," he said, "was how an electric eel shocks things without killing himself."

"Um-hm."

"Baby eels can see when they're born, but they go blind from being shocked when they get older, so electricity does affect them."

Deke looked at Terry, then back at the canal bank.

"If a horse walks into shallow water with a bunch of electric eels, they can make enough electricity to knock the horse down," Terry continued. "So why doesn't it kill the eels, I wonder?"

"Where do you get questions like that?"

"I don't know. Just wondering. Deke, how can nobody win a war?"

"Even the winner pays a price for victory," Deke said. "So both sides are losers."

"But *somebody* wins."

"One outlasts the other, but maybe both sides are broken."

Terry saw alligators lolling like rough-bark logs on the banks of the canals.

"If Lamar hadn't gotten hurt, do you think he'd be smart?" Terry questioned.

"Judging by his parents, I would assume so."

A minute later, Deke said, "If things had been different, Lamar might have made a football player for the University of Florida."

"They don't let Lamar play football."

"I would think he'd make a great tackle."

"Everytime he catches a pass, he runs home with the football."

Deke laughed softly.

"Ossie is a good player," Terry commented. "But he won't play because he doesn't like white people."

"Is that one?" Deke pointed.

"No sir. Jimsonweed. Or morning glory."

"It has blue blossoms shaped like that," Deke said. Then he patted Terry's leg. "You know flowers pretty good."

"Yes sir." Terry heaved a sigh. "I wonder what kind of flowers they have in Colorado?"

"Colorado?" Deke squeezed Terry's leg, playfully. "Why Colorado?"

Terry shrugged his shoulders. "I don't even know where Colorado is."

Deke laughed again. "I think your brain is suffering for lack of nourishment. We'd better stop for lunch."

Lunch was sandwiches Deke had made at home and iced tea from a Thermos bottle. They stopped at a road-side picnic area. A Seminole family in a pickup truck occupied an adjacent table. The Indian woman wore the traditional long skirt and full blouse, beads sewn into the fabric.

"Ya-ho-la," Terry said, and they nodded, smiling.

In the canal, fish flicked water, taking insects unlucky enough to have flagged and fallen. The pines murmured, hushed.

"When you look where Ossie walked," Terry was saying, "his feet go straight. My toes turn in if I forget to keep them pointed out."

"You take after your mother," Deke said. "Her toes turn in slightly."

"Did your toes turn in?"

"I never thought about it."

"You could look at your mama's toes and tell."

The Indians were talking in low tones, speaking their language. A girl younger than Terry stared at him and he smiled. She ducked her chin, turned away.

"Ann looks like Mama," Terry said. "I look like Daddy."

"You look like Mickey. Little dimples next to your mouth. The way you bite your tongue when you're concentrating. I wouldn't worry about your toes turning in."

"It looks all right when it's a girl," Terry said. "But pigeon-toed boys look like eggbeaters when they run."

Deke threw back his head, laughing.

"But Mama says, 'There's always personality.' "

Deke gathered food remnants and threw them in the canal. A needle gar examined a morsel, took it.

"Mama says character will straighten your teeth," Terry related. "She means, nobody notices your teeth if you have a good personality."

"Come along," Deke said. "Let's see if we can get a few more specimens."

"If I rode on the front fender, I could see more," Terry offered.

"Better ride inside."

Deke was right. Going down a dirt road a deer leaped up from the grass and he had to snatch on his brakes. It threw Terry against the dashboard.

"Are you all right?" Deke examined Terry's forehead.

"It's okay."

Deke brushed back hair, looking. Then, unexpectedly, he kissed it.

"You're sure you're all right?" Deke asked.

"Sure I'm sure."

Turning the truck around, they took the other side of the road, following the shoulder again.

"Deke, where is Colorado?"

"Out west."

"West? Are there cowboys and Indians?"

"I've never been there."

The truck lurched over a stone. Terry saw slider turtles slip off a log into the canal. A heron stood in blue relief against the brown of scorched saw grass and water sedge.

"Are there any swamps in Colorado?" Terry questioned.

"Plenty of mountains," Deke said.

"Larger than Red Mountain in Birmingham?"

"Much larger. So high the snow never melts on the top. Why this interest in Colorado?"

"Just wondering."

"You wonder a lot."

"I never saw a mountain in a swamp," Terry said, glumly.

"Are you watching the canal bank?"

"I don't see anything but regular plants. Deke, would you take me to the swamps even if my daddy came home?"

"If he would allow it, yes."

"Would you take me if you didn't like my mama as much? If she didn't like you as much?"

"But I do like her. I think she likes me."

"But if you *didn't* and she *didn't* — would you take me?"

Deke glanced at Terry, then back at the road again. "I tell you, redhead," he said, "I've been thinking. The reason your mama doesn't want you to go into the swamps is because she's afraid for your safety."

"I know it."

"She doesn't see the beauty of it like you and me," Deke said. "So, I've been thinking — maybe we could get her to go camping with us."

"Hey, that's a great idea!"

"That way she can see there's nothing really fearsome."

"Yeah. Great, Deke!"

"Maybe we could go this weekend."

"Tomorrow is the weekend."

"Maybe even tomorrow," Deke said.

"Wow, yeah, wow!"

"We'll talk to Mickey when we get back," Deke said. "For now, though, let's find what we're looking for."

"Yes sir!" Terry leaned out the window. He could feel freckles popping out on his ears, the air warm and dry. But they still didn't find what Deke wanted. Picking up speed, Deke pulled out onto the highway, a stretch called "Alligator Alley."

"Better come back in and sit down, redhead."

Grinning, Terry did so. "I sure am glad we're going, Deke. If I don't go before the war is over, I won't ever go."

"Why not?"

"They don't have any swamps in —" Terry halted.

"In Colorado," Deke said.

"Not if they have mountains," Terry said cautiously.

"You think you're going there, don't you?"

Terry had said too much.

"What makes you think that?" Deke asked.

"Daddy wrote Mama a letter."

"When was this?"

"I don't know. I found the letter in Mama's jewelry box. She didn't show it to me."

"What did the letter say?" Deke's voice sounded funny.

"He said he was coming home soon. He said he was going to buy part interest in a newspaper in a place called Longmont. It's in Colorado."

"I didn't know your father was interested in writing."

"Neither did I."

Deke pulled off the highway and stopped the engine. "Mickey hasn't mentioned this to me," he said. He stared across the glades, blinking his eyes.

"Want to do me a favor, Deke?"

"What?"

"Don't tell Mama about Colorado."

"Doesn't she know?"

"She doesn't know I know. I was looking for tweezers to get a splinter out of Ossie's finger. I'm not supposed to go into her jewelry box."

Deke started the truck again. The tires sang on hot asphalt as they drove toward Belle Glade.

"Will you promise not to tell, Deke?"

"I can't promise that, Terry."

Deke's Adam's apple kept bobbing, swallowing. Sensing something deeper than he knew, Terry fell silent. A few minutes later, Deke hit the steering wheel with the flat of his hand. There were tears in his eyes.

Mama's car was parked at the house when Deke and Terry arrived. Deke turned off the motor and sat without moving. Ossie and Ann were sitting on the front steps.

"Home early?" Mama called from the porch.

Terry got out as Mama came to the truck. "How was your day, fellows?"

Seeing their faces, Mama said, "What is it?"

"Can you take a drive with me, Mickey?"

"I have supper on the stove, Deke. What is it?"

Ossie joined them. "I left a message in invisible ink, but Ann drew pictures on it because she thought it was blank paper."

"Deke," Mama asked softly, "something wrong? Something Terry has done?"

"Thevis is getting warts," Ossie whispered.

"Deke?" Mama insisted.

"Have you heard from your husband, Mickey?"

"Gerald? Well, yes — the last I heard he's in Rome, Italy."

"Any news?"

Mama stood with her apron bunched in both hands. "Same news as before."

"Is he coming home?"

"Home," Mama said flatly.

"Yes, damn it, is he coming home or not?"

Don't tell. Please. Don't tell.

"Deke," Mama said, "come join us for dinner."

"I have other plans. Answer my question."

"Yes," Mama said. "He's coming home."

"Are you going to Colorado?"

Mama's face flushed and she turned to look at Terry. "You've been in my jewelry box, haven't you?"

"I didn't mean to, Mama. I was looking for tweezers. Ossie had a sticker in his finger and —"

"Go to the house, Terry."

"Mama, I didn't mean to."

"I said, Go to the house. All of you."

"Deke, we're still going to the swamps, aren't we?"

"Terry! Go to the house. Take Ossie and Ann with you."

"Deke — please — we are going, aren't we?"

Deke started the motor and Mama said earnestly, "Come for supper. We'll talk after supper."

"Deke," Terry implored, "please —"

"Terry," Mama screamed. "Go to the house this minute!"

Terry took Ann's hand, her eyes wide and a little frightened. "What is it, Terry?"

"I don't know."

"Hell you don't," Ossie said. "The conjure woman, that's what."

Twenty-five

"YESTERDAY," TERRY TOLD Ossie, "Deke said he'd ask Mama to go camping. I think that's what they're talking about."

Ossie threw a pillowcase with clothes into Deke's truck. "He came by my house after dark last night," Ossie confided. "He told my mom we'd be gone a week, maybe."

"A week? I don't think Mama will go for a week."

She was in the kitchen with Deke right then. This morning she'd said she wasn't going to work today.

"He said be here at the break of dawn and here I sit, waiting," Ossie grumped.

"Lamar!" Velma yelled. "You forgot your toothbrush."

"Uh — oh, yeah." Lamar ran toward home.

Ossie lit a cigarette, blew smoke down on his chest. He looked up at the sun. "What's the hold up?"

Mama. She'd sent Terry out of the house the moment Deke arrived.

Listening to their indistinguishable voices, Ossie said, "This could take all day. Why don't you go see what's going on, Terry?"

"I'm ready!" Lamar announced. His toothbrush was in his hip pocket.

"Go see," Ossie urged Terry.

He paused on the front steps. The tone of voices inside suggested he should knock. "Mama?"

"What is it?"

"May I come in?"

"Of course you can come in," Mama said sharply. But when Terry entered, Mama snapped, "What is it?"

"Deke, Ossie said he's ready."

Deke was on the floor beside Mama and she was standing at the kitchen counter. Without turning, Deke said, "I'll be out in a few minutes, Terry."

"Mama — are we going with them?"

"Go outside, Terry."

Instead of leaving the way he'd entered, Terry walked past them, taking the back door. On the rear steps, he sat down. Deke was saying something he couldn't hear. Mama replied in kind.

"Mama?"

"What, Terry?" She sounded angry.

"May I come in?"

"What is it now?"

"May I come in?"

"Terry, I'm talking with Deke. Go with the other boys and wait."

Terry edged toward the kitchen door, looking. "Mama, may I have a drink of water?"

Deke whirled, crossed the kitchen in three bounds. "Didn't you hear your mother?"

"Yessir."

"She said, get out! Go wait with Ossie and Lamar."

Stung, Terry started to walk through and Deke grabbed his arm, turning Terry about-face. "Out!" he said.

"Yessir, Deke."

On the back steps again, Terry felt a shiver of dread. Deke was in the door and he shouted, "Go with Lamar and Ossie!"

"Yessir."

When Terry returned, Ossie lifted his eyebrows. "Well?"

"He's not ready."

"Got me here at daylight and here I sit."

"I got dibbies on the window," Lamar said.

"Yeah, we know," Ossie flipped away his cigarette.

When Deke came out of the house, he got into his chair with Mama standing in the doorway. "About time," Ossie murmured.

Even before Deke got to them, Terry knew he wasn't going.

"Deke, what did she say?" Terry whispered.

"You aren't going, Terry. Get in, Ossie," Deke commanded. Ossie did so.

"Wait a minute, Deke," Terry said. "Let me talk to her."

Terry ran to the house, but the truck started before he reached the door. Inside, Mama was sitting with her arms on the table, hands clasped.

"Mama, Deke is leaving."

Mama closed her eyes.

"Mama, did you make him angry?"

"He's hurt, Terry."

"But what happened?"

"I'm not sure."

"Mama — Mama, listen — they're leaving right now. Ossie and Lamar — Mama, please let me go."

"Terry," Mama stood abruptly, "let's not start *that*!"

"Mama," Terry fought tears, "please, this once, please."

"Nothing has changed, Terry."

"Not once have I gone to the swamps — please!"

"You went with Deke most of this past week. You spend a night at Kramer's Island."

"Those aren't swamps, though. You can see town lights and hear people talking. The swamps are different. It isn't the same at all."

"Well, you cannot go."

"Mama!" Terry cried, "this might be the last time! We'll be in Colorado and —"

"That's another thing," Mama said. "You not only went into my jewelry box, you revealed the contents of a letter that was confidential. Confidential means *private*, Terry."

"I was looking for the tweezers," Terry said. "Mama, they're going. This once. You know it's all right. You know Deke now. Please."

He saw Mama's chin quiver and she turned away.

"Mama, please. There aren't any swamps in Colorado, are there? *Please*."

"All right," Mama said, voice odd, "you may go."

"I may?"

She had tears in her eyes.

Terry sought confirmation. "It is all right? He plans to be gone longer than two nights."

"Go."

He went out so fast the screen didn't bang shut until

Terry had reached the street. The truck was gone. He had no extra clothes, barefooted — but there wasn't time to worry about that. Terry only hoped it didn't occur to Mama before he was out of earshot.

Twice, automobiles passed, but they ignored his frantic signal of an extended thumb — and on he ran. His ribs hurt, lungs burning, heart bursting. He topped the dike, crossed the bridge, and — they were getting into Deke's airboat.

"Wait! Deke! Wait!"

Ossie said something to Deke and the man twisted to look. Terry gathered his remaining strength and ran again.

"I can go, Deke," Terry gasped.

"Can you," Deke said. A statement.

"Yessir. Mama said so."

Deke pushed the starter button and the motor roared, the propellor slowly turning in sympathy to the vibrations.

"Where can I sit?" Terry hollered.

"Terry," Deke said, "you know your mother did not say you could go."

"But she did. Really."

"No."

"Deke, I swear it. You could come and ask her. Really!"

Deke stared at Ossie and Terry said, "Indian honor, Ossie, I swear it."

"No," Deke said. He motioned Ossie into a jump seat.

"But she did!" Terry insisted.

"Very well," Deke replied, "and I'm telling you that you cannot go."

"We're going camping," Lamar yelled.

Deke engaged the gears and the prop whirled. Wind blew Terry's hair and Mr. Owen pulled him back a step, pushing the airboat away with one foot.

"We're going to cook on a fire!" Lamar waved.

Mr. Owen put his hands in his hip pockets, watching the boat turn into the canal. Even from here, they could feel the backwash from the propellor as Deke gave the motor gas.

"How about a free soft drink?" Mr. Owen asked Terry.

"No, thank you."

He stopped on the bridge, listening to a distant thumping, watching birds settle after rising before the uproar. Disappointment became anger, then tears. He walked and wept. He thought about catching a ride on a boxcar. Stay at hobo jungles, drink poor-man's tea and eat sardines out of tin cans. He could do that. But he went to the packing house instead and climbed the hot metal ladder in the rear. With the furnace of the loft at his back, he sat in a window, his legs dangling, looking across miles of glades under a blue bowl of cloudless sky.

He blamed Mama. But she had yielded. She had finally, at last, yielded.

Terry felt sick in his stomach. It was Deke. Deke had used him for no pay. Maybe he never wanted Terry to go. He wasn't as strong as Lamar. He wasn't as old as Ossie.

He climbed down the ladder and went home. Mama was still at the kitchen table. When she saw Terry, she took him in her arms and held him.

"He didn't believe me, Mama."

"I'm sorry."

"I told him 'Indian honor' and he didn't believe me."

Mama held him tightly and after a few minutes, Terry realized she was crying, too.

Mr. Rollins, the camp manager, banged on their door. "Mickey! Gerald is calling from Rome. Come to the administration building."

"He's on the phone?"

"He will be in a minute. The overseas operator is calling to be sure you're here."

Mama ran, legs flinging outward from the knees in the funny way of girls, and Terry was right beside her. In the camp office, everyone sat, not working, waiting, smiling. Mama accepted a Coca-Cola which she didn't drink.

When the call came, Mama clutched the phone in one hand, the receiver in her other, "Gerald! In Rome? Yes, yes, I can hear you."

A woman at a desk wiped tears and smiled at the same time.

"No, Ann isn't here, Gerald. Terry is. What? She stays at the day-care center when I'm working. Didn't you get my letter? It isn't hard on her at all. Or me, in fact — what?"

Mama listened a moment. "Gerald, you know I haven't minded working. Of course we'll get back to normal, but I haven't minded at all — what? Yes, he's here."

The receiver was wet from perspiration when Terry pressed it to his ear. "Talk in there," Mama instructed, "talk loud."

"Hey, Daddy!"

"Hey, boy! You sound grown up."

"You too."

Daddy laughed. It had a ring of familiarity. "When're you coming home, Daddy?"

"September fifth. Have you been taking care of Mama and Ann?"

"We take care of one another."

"That's fine. Well, we'll be back to normal soon. Your mother can stop working and be home to look after you. We'll make up for all these lost months."

"Are we going to Colorado?"

"We sure are! What do you think about that?"

"When are we going?"

"As soon as I get home."

"They don't have swamps," Terry said.

"How about that! You can learn to ski on snow — they have high mountains. We'll be over a mile high above the ocean, did you know that?"

"No sir."

Mama took the telephone, laughing. Daddy talked and Mama repeated, making notes, "Naples to England to New York. Which ship?"

Then, softly, "I love you too, Gerald."

Mama laughed, eyes darting around, "Another child? We can't discuss that on long distance, sweetheart."

Then when she hung up, everybody hugged Mama and laughed and cried.

"He has blue eyes?" Ann stared at Daddy's picture.

"Blue," Terry affirmed.

"Mama," Ann asked, "do we get to see the ship he comes on?"

"No, we'll meet Daddy in Birmingham at the railroad station."

"I'd like to see the ship," Ann said.

"That's in New York. Too far to go with two children and so many servicemen trying to get home themselves."

On the radio a woman sang, "I'm always chasing rainbows — pretty rainbows in the sky. . . ."

"I have to see about packing, moving," Mama murmured.

"When are we going?" Terry asked.

"In a week or two. We'll visit Grandmama until Daddy comes."

"A week."

"Won't this be a great adventure?" Mama said, eyes wide, but it was a put-on expression.

"Are you going to have a baby?" Ann asked.

"Goodness!" Mama said.

"Terry said you were."

"Terry won't be the father. Or mother."

Ann laughed in a shrill note, "That's silly, Mama."

Another "soft" song came from the radio, *Till the End of Time*. Mama liked that kind of music.

"He has big teeth, Mama." Ann touched Daddy's photo.

"The better to bite you with, my dear."

Ann shrilled again, "Mama, you're so silly!"

When Ann was in bed, Mama went to the calendar and looked at the number of days Daddy had been gone. On today's date, she wrote boldly, "30." That many days until Daddy would arrive.

"Ladies and gentlemen, we interrupt this program to bring you a special news bulletin. The War Department announced the development of a new super bomb which was dropped on the Japanese city of Hiroshima. The destructive force was said to be the equivalent of twenty thousand tons of TNT. Reports released by the military say the bomb was delivered by a single B-29 bomber. The blast reportedly lighted the sky and created a mushroom-shaped cloud that rose miles into the atmosphere. The War Department would only say that the destruction was utter and complete. Estimates of deaths range as high as a hundred thousand. We repeat. . . ."

Mama stared, mouth open.

"Mama?"

"Dear God," she said.

"Mama?"

She lifted a hand to silence Terry and listened to the bulletin repeated word-for-word.

"Is the war over, Mama?"

Another man on the radio was now saying, "destructive force of twenty thousand tons of TNT, the shock wave alone would —"

"Mama, is the war over?"

Somewhere, a horn was blowing, people shouting.

"Mama, is it over?"

"A hundred thousand," Mama said dumbly, "men, women, children — God help us."

"Is it over, Mama?"

"I don't know," she said.

Velma snatched on the latched screen door with such force the lock broke. She ran into the living room. "Mickey, did you hear? We dropped a super bomb on the Japs! It killed over sixty thousand, maybe as many as a hundred thousand!"

Another voice on the radio, more excited, ". . . nuclear . . . revolutionary concept . . . atomic. . . ."

"Get dressed!" Velma yelled, "we'll go celebrate!"

"No. Ann is asleep, Velma."

"Wake her, then! This is the end of the war."

But when Velma left, the radio did not say it was over. The mixture of voices, near and far, kept saying how "awesome" was the bomb, how brilliant the blast, how "utter and complete" the destruction.

But Mama sat, as if struck, repeating, "God help us. . . ."

In bed, Terry could not sleep, thinking about children who had, perhaps, that day been sitting on their back steps reading. Maybe one was reading about birds, as Terry had been doing. The women, like Mama, who knew only what their governments did, and not why or how. That was how Mama explained her reaction to Terry. "People like us," she had said.

Now, for sure, Daddy would not have to go fight the Japanese, Mama acknowledged.

The following day, Terry went to Chosen, waiting. Mr. Owen said Deke had forgotten to say when he would return.

"Aren't you worried?" Terry asked.

"Not with that Indian kid along," Mr. Owen said.

On Thursday, the ninth, another bomb was dropped. Again, people danced in the street, horns blared, sirens wailed and Mama sat listening to the radio as if it were America, not Japan, that suffered the blows.

The next morning, Mama took Terry with her to the Okeelanta Sugar Mill to collect her pay.

"Hate to see you go, Mickey," her boss said.

"Thank you, Harvey. But everything is about to change in our lives."

Beyond the glassed-in office, huge rollers droned, mashing stalks of cane to get juice.

"You've done a fine job here," he said. "I'll be happy to recommend you to anybody."

"I think my husband intends for me to remain at home to be a mother and wife."

"Don't blame him one bit."

A workman entered, talking to another man. "Looks like we'll get twenty-seven tons to an acre despite the drought. The yield is running 156 pounds of sugar to a ton so far."

Mama shook hands with her boss, "Thanks for everything." He nodded, then turned and walked away.

When the whumping of the airboat could be heard, Terry and Mr. Owen were on the dock, waiting. Finally the boat came up the canal toward them.

"The war's over!" Charlie Owen shouted.

"Over?"

"We hit the Japs with two super bombs. Wiped out two cities with two bombs, Deke!"

Ossie stepped onto the dock, taking a line to secure the boat. Lamar was pocked with insect bites, his cheeks and forehead dappled with red blotches.

"A secret weapon," Mr. Owen was telling Deke. "President Truman called it the Manhattan Project or some such."

"We went down there all those days," Ossie whispered to Terry, "and didn't do nothing."

"Did they surrender?" Mr. Owen and Lamar helped Deke onto the dock.

"Not yet, Deke, not officially, but they've said they're ready."

"Two bombs?" Deke said. "Only two?"

"Two! A-*tomick* bomb, they call it."

Ossie took Terry's arm and they walked away from the men. "It was awful," Ossie said. "I had to feed Lamar every meal. He whimpered and cried like a baby. I ain't going again. It ain't worth no amount of money. I'm through."

"Lamar! Ossie! Stow this gear, will you?"

"Ran out of cigarettes, ate lousy food and just sat there, I tell you," Ossie reported. "We didn't collect one plant."

Terry picked up the microscope and Deke called, "Careful, redhead, don't drop it."

Lamar loaded equipment without a word. Ossie got a cigarette from a passing fisherman and lit it.

"I tell you, Terry. He didn't come out of the tent except to eat and pass gas. Sat there like a zombie. Lamar crying and Deke didn't even seem to hear half the time."

Mr. Owen was relating the news, Deke now in his wheelchair, both sipping beer.

"You owe me a favor, Ossie," Terry said.

"I know it."

"I mean to collect."

"Okay. What is it?"

"You said anything, right?"

"Sure. What is it?"

"I'll see you tomorrow."

"Hey! Wait and Deke will give you a ride home."

"No. See you tomorrow."

Twenty-six

THE GLADES CAFÉ was crowded with Saturday morning customers. Ossie watched Lamar guzzle a soda. "I once seen a wrestling bear drink the same way," Ossie said. "Can't you learn not to stick the whole bottle in your mouth, Lamar?"

In the next booth, Terry heard a man croon loudly, "*And when I die, please bury me, under a ton of sugar, by a rubber tree —*"

Others joined in, "*Lay me to rest, in an auto machine, and water my grave, with gasoline. . . .*"

Everybody laughed.

"The conjure woman needs your hair," Ossie told Terry. "She said come this morning."

"I want to go to the swamps, Ossie."

"So, go."

"In Deke's airboat."

"Shit."

"I want to go, too," Lamar brightened.

"You know how to run it. You have to go with me, Ossie."

Ossie shook his Pepsi-Cola gently, let it fizz past a thumb into his mouth.

"Will you do it?"

"I want to go," Lamar said.

"That's the favor?" Ossie questioned.

"Yes."

A man behind them reported, "The new Ford Super de Luxe will be rolling off the lines in Detroit this month, according to the news."

"Personally," somebody responded, "I like the looks of the Nash. Did you see pictures of those?"

"Studebaker . . . Hudson. . . ."

"Will you, Ossie?" Terry persisted.

"No."

"Why not?"

"You know why not."

"Can I go?" Lamar asked.

"Ossie, you owe me a favor."

"I ain't stealing."

"This isn't stealing. We'll bring it back. You said you'd do me a favor. You said anything."

"Not this. This is trouble."

"You got me in trouble, telling the man from the theater about me with the bats."

"He never came to see your mom."

"No thanks to you though. You snitched and I was your friend anyway."

Ossie shook his drink, Pepsi foaming.

"You needed help with Thevis. I helped."

Mrs. Knight passed their table, "Doing okay?" but she didn't wait for a reply.

"It was me who got toenails and hair and BVD's."

"I want to go," Lamar said loudly.

"Shut up, Lamar," Ossie snapped.

". . . the test bomb in New Mexico vaporized a steel tower . . . imagine what it did to those Jap cities. . . ."

"I stayed your friend no matter what," Terry said evenly.

". . . they accepted terms of unconditional surrender. . . ."

"When you asked for a favor, I did it. You wanted to scare the packing house guard and I helped you. *He* came to the house."

"Nothing happened, though."

"Okay," Terry said. "Don't help me. I'm not paying the conjure woman with my hair."

Mrs. Knight wiped a nearby table. Ossie looked at the bottom of his bottle to see where it was made.

"See Thevis over there scratching?" Ossie said. "He won't be the only one if you don't give her your hair."

"You gave your word to me, Ossie!"

"Deke would kill you and me both," Ossie countered.

"My daddy will be home September fifth. My mama says we're leaving in a week or so."

"Leaving?"

Terry fought tears. "Going to Colorado."

Ossie stared at Thevis, clawing himself under cover of a tablecloth.

"They don't have swamps in Colorado. If I don't go now, I won't get to go at all. Maybe forever."

"No way we can do it and get away with it."

"I don't care."

"I guess not, if you're leaving. It'll be me has to pay for it."

"You going to drink your pop?" Lamar queried. Terry gave him the remainder of his soda.

". . . going to the poorhouse, maybe, but I'll get there in my Packard. . . ."

"Okay," Terry said angrily, "I'll do it by myself."

"Can I go?" Lamar asked.

"Yes. You can go."

"Get yourselves killed," Ossie warned.

"Not if you helped."

"Ain't this some shit?" Ossie said.

". . . but how can the bomb be that small and so powerful?"

Another man replied, "A new kind of explosion called fission or fusion or some such."

Ossie made moist interlocking rings on the table with his bottle.

"You never had anybody but me for a friend," Terry's lip curled. "Best friend you ever will have, too. A friend is supposed to help."

Ossie dipped his bottle in another wet spot to make more rings.

". . . trouble yet to be . . . all our men coming home needing jobs. . . ."

Face red, Terry said, "Even now, if you needed a special favor, I'd do it for you. If you asked me to do this and you were going to Colorado, I'd do it for you."

"Then pay the conjure woman your hair like you promised."

Mrs. Knight came over, nudged Ossie to give her room and sat with them. She wiped her forehead with the back of a hand. Lighting a cigarette, she blew smoke toward the ceiling.

"Can I go camping, Mom?" Ossie questioned without looking at her.

"Sure, sweetie. When?"

"Right now."

"When will you be back, so Mom won't have to worry?"

"Tomorrow," Ossie said.

"Maybe day after tomorrow," Terry interjected.

"Tomorrow is long enough," Mrs. Knight said. She put her cigarette in an ashtray and went to a customer. Ossie puffed on the cigarette.

"We have to take food and stuff," Ossie said.

"We'll eat what's out there," Terry directed. "There's plenty to eat all around us."

"No."

"Why not? That's how the Indians do it."

"Yeah," Ossie said, "and they spend all day everyday doing nothing but getting food, too. You want to spend your time hunting things to eat? Trapping rabbit or fishing?"

"I suppose not."

"Can I go?" Lamar whispered.

"No," Ossie said.

"I want to go."

"No. You cry and carry on — no."

"I won't cry," Lamar said to Terry. "Can I go?"

"He has to go," Terry asserted. "He might tell Deke, if he doesn't. Besides, he can help build a chickee."

Ossie shook his head. "Ain't this some shit?"

"We'll each get a few cans of food from our houses," Terry planned. "Then we can go get the boat."

"Walk right up, get in and take off," Ossie ridiculed.

"I thought about it. When Mr. Owen is inside the store, we'll get in and paddle down the canal. Once we get away from the dock, there's nothing he could do anyway."

"Except shoot us."

"He won't. We're too young to be shot."

Mrs. Knight paused at their table, puffed her cigarette, disappeared into the kitchen. Ossie retrieved the butt, smoking.

"This makes us even," he said.

"Okay. Even."

"You'll be gone to Colorado and I'll lose my job."

"You said you wouldn't go again, anyway."

"I might change my mind."

"So will Deke. He can't do it without you."

Ossie crushed the cigarette, oblivious to his mother who passed with a tray. "Okay, but I do all the driving. I drive the boat, understand?"

"That's what we need you for, to run the boat."

Ossie went to his mother, said something, and returned. "Okay," he said, "let's go see the conjure woman."

While Lamar and Ossie waited outside, the conjure woman snipped Terry's hair. She took each red shock and placed it in a bowl.

"Your mother will be angry," she predicted.

"I know."

"What do I say when she comes to me?"

"Say I paid you to do it."

"Why would she believe that?"

"Because I pay Mr. Cantrell at the barbershop."

He heard the gristly crunch of blades, watched the pile

of hair grow larger.

"Did you get your wish?" she asked.

"I got it. But you're right. From now on I'm going to be careful what I wish."

"That is wise."

Terry heard somebody teasing Lamar and without rising, he shouted, "Stop that!"

He heard Lamar say, "He was teasing me, wasn't he, Ossie?"

The shears snipped, slowly, hair falling into the conjure woman's hand.

"What will you do with the hair?" Terry asked.

"It has magic for colored people."

"I wish it had magic for me."

"It does. People do not forget you. That is magic."

Thinking of the packing house guard, Terry said, "That's not always good."

"It is better than being forgotten."

"Will you look after Deke when we move to Colorado?"

"If it is his wish, he will come and ask." She picked strands from his shoulders, placing them in the bowl. Terry's head felt cool.

"I don't care whether you look after him or not," Terry said suddenly. "Maybe look after him a little," he amended.

She removed the bowl and scissors. "You are going to Colorado?"

"Yes."

"Would you like to wish for happiness there?"

"No. I'll try hard to do it by myself."

She flicked hair from his shoulder with a jeweled finger. "I would like to kiss you," she said.

And she did. Gently. When she drew back, she looked at him a long moment.

"*Somebody* is going to be happy," she said.

"We need a paddle," Ossie whispered. "Get one out of another boat."

"Steal it?" Terry asked.

"You're stealing a boat," Ossie said sharply. "Why not steal a paddle?"

Terry ran to a rowboat and got an oar. He ran back to Lamar and Ossie who were kneeling, out of sight.

"Now listen to me, Lamar," Ossie warned, "do just what I tell you."

"I will."

"Don't say a word. Don't holler at anybody. Get in the boat and sit in a jump seat and don't say one word."

"I will."

"You'd better," Ossie said, "or so help me, I'll knock you overboard and leave you."

"I will, Ossie."

Ossie peered over a retaining wall toward Mr. Owen. "Terry, cast off the lines, get in and push us away from the dock. If we're lucky, we'll sneak by. But if he sees us, you got to sit down in the other jump seat and don't stand up because that throws the thing off balance. We might turn over. Understand?"

"I understand."

"I'll go first," Ossie said. "You bring Lamar and the food."

Terry watched Ossie go to Deke's boat and uncap the gas tank. Ossie stuck in a finger. He'd already explained that Deke "topped off" the tanks after each trip to hold down condensation. Now, Ossie waved them on.

The boat hull slapped water when Lamar got in. They waited, watching, but nobody came to see. Terry untied the mooring lines and gently pushed the craft backward out of the slip. Lamar sat dutifully, saying nothing.

Ossie dipped the oar and black water swirled. The boat inched toward the canal. He dipped again, rowing.

"Hey!" Mr. Owen yelled. His shout came back from across the glades, "hey . . . hey . . . hey. . . ."

"Hey!" Mr. Owen came onto the dock and Ossie paddled furiously. "Hey, boys! Come back here."

"He's going to get in a motorboat, Ossie," Terry warned. They heard the yank of a starter cord, the sputter of an engine. Terry gripped the gunwale as Ossie abandoned all caution, climbing into the high seat of the pilot. He turned a switch, pulled out the throttle, pushed the starter button. Behind them, Mr. Owen's outboard motor coughed, fired, died.

The airboat reverberated beneath them as the powerful engine started and the propeller began a slow turning movement inside its wire mesh covering. Now, Mr. Owen had his motor going and was casting off to give chase.

Ossie held the steering handle, put the motor in gear and the craft shuddered. He overreacted, throwing air too sharply aside and they made a complete circle. Drifting sideways into the canal, Ossie gave it gas and the boat picked up speed.

Terry moved to go forward, but Ossie screamed, "Sit down!" Terry sat where he was, his trousers soaked by water shifting in the bottom of the boat. Mr. Owen was returning to the dock. He would call Deke first. Then what?

"He's gone!" Terry yelled, but Ossie couldn't hear over

the deafening roar. "He's gone!" Terry hollered, but Ossie was concentrating on the ribbon of water stretching away south, hair flying, cattails and sedge a brown blur on both banks, birds rising by the hundreds as they approached.

Lamar sat as he had been taught by Deke, arms inside, hands in his lap, eyes squinted against wind and sun. Ossie eased the rudder one way and the boat skittered, turning to follow a curve, then straight again, the bow up, a foamy mist blown from the stern by a tornadic thrust of the propeller.

They flew past a man fishing; two boys on a dike waved and Terry waved in reply. Like a hurtling flat stone, they skipped and settled, skipped and flew, at times the hull rising above water only to fall and skip again.

In rhythmic riots, herons, egrets, cranes and ducks beat upward from the marsh, their cries muted by the thunder of this intruder. From an apparently flat terrain, flame trees seemed to rise in alarm, stark and vivid as they passed, then settling again as distance separated the boat from what lay behind.

Like an airplane they flew — flew! Swish! Saw grass came and they crossed it. Swish! The brittle rat-tat-tat of insects striking the propeller screen.

Past navigational aides of the intracoastal waterway, past the last remnants of houses and irrigation stations, past an oncoming boat making slow progress homeward, past thickets bounding Lake Okeechobee to the north, past all that was sullied and reshaped by man — into the open endless glade that was, to Terry, "the swamp."

Grinning, Ossie pointed at flecks of pink and white fowl stretched across a wide pond and so fast did they come, the tongues of the screaming creatures could be seen in open beaks as they veered away, climbing as a moving cloud. Sunlight flashed as Ossie turned, spray skewing, and thousands of diamond reflections broke into tens of thousands of particles as water met air and the afternoon rays of the sun.

Alligators were caught, heads high, bodies lifted, alarmed but unsure which way to flee, dashing to water only when the boat had passed them by. Out of the grass came a leaping, white-tailed herd of deer bounding this way and that, crossing and crisscrossing, hind feet kicking at the noise.

Tatatatatat, insects accumulating on the screened propeller housing. *Tatatatatat*, like sleet on a sheet metal roof. Buzzards moved in majestic sweeps, blundering, laboring, barely head high when the boat passed between and beneath them. They followed water, their only need at this moment, the medium that transported them, and on they flew.

Banana trees, floating hammocks, rafts of hyacinths so thick a man could walk upon them. Ossie, in the high seat, was first to see it all and he pointed, facial flesh flattened — a bear! The creature stood on its hind legs, watching, then turned to dash a short distance before wheeling to look again.

They entered another river, or perhaps it was the same all along, now more confined by the terrain, and sunlight glittered between branches of cypress bearded by Spanish moss, the dwelling of perching birds that darkened the sky in their masses. Into the open again, as far as the eye could see, perfectly flat and infinite space dominated by a sea of grass that rippled as would water beneath the slightest breeze.

Ossie pointed — another bear. Another. Then, in a daring turn, the boat reversed so abruptly, the craft faced away from the direction it was traveling. Ossie jabbed a finger — yes! A tawny puma bounded away with heart-stopping grace, long tail flowing behind.

Trouble at home. Trouble at home.

But this was worth it.

Tears stinging his eyes, it was not fear of punishment that made Terry cry — he felt muscles in fibrillation, lungs filled with air so sweet no one could imagine it without having drawn a breath under this azure sky, surrounded by places perhaps no man had ever trod.

The sun peeped over trees of a distant horizon when, finally, Ossie eased the throttle and the *rum-rum-rum* of the propeller shifted to a whacking sound. Lamar looked up at Ossie, hands folded even now.

"Some baby, ain't it, Terry?" Ossie grinned.

"Some ride!"

"Better look for a place to camp, before dark," Ossie said.

The panorama, once featureless, at this slow speed took focus: sandy hammocks, low dunes, high ground. Terry scanned the fan-like leaves of palmetto scrub. Mud turtles on sunken logs plopped into water, reappearing with heads lifted like periscopes.

"How about there?" Ossie suggested.

"Looks good."

Ossie squinted overhead, to the horizons. Checking for rain clouds. It didn't do to get caught in your sleep by a thunderstorm that could raise water level in minutes.

Ossie cut the motor and the craft lapped toward shore. Lamar stood and his weight grounded them. Terry got out and pushed from behind until the boat beached. The engine smelled like burnt oil and Ossie checked it with a dip stick. He closed gas cocks, took a mooring line ashore to secure it. More than one camper had been stranded by a boat that mysteriously responded to still waters which flowed smoothly but steadily toward the sea.

"You and Lamar build a chickee," Ossie commanded. "I'll get firewood and set up camp." He stood a moment, expectantly. "No gnats or mosquitos yet. Let's hope the wind doesn't change to bring us any."

Lamar handled a machete like a professional, cutting fronds at the spiny base, laying them aside to be carried to camp. He hacked saplings for framework, and inside an hour, a fire was blazing, the chickee constructed with a platform to get them off the ground.

From the food they'd brought, Ossie prepared their meal — stew from a can, boiled potatoes, hot coffee brewed in a saucepan. To the stew, he added onion sprouts Terry had found, and the cloves of a plant much like garlic, but milder.

"I can cut cattails or bamboo shoots," Terry offered.

"We have more than enough as it is."

The sun was slipping away, red and blue blending to make purple that glimmered on water like liquid flame.

"Get some moss to bank the fire," Ossie directed, and Lamar did so.

The smoke rose in a perfect column, reaching cooler air where it turned at a right angle and floated away undissipated.

Lamar spooned his dish. "This is good. Can I have some more, Ossie?"

Ossie ladled stew, dividing the balance between them. He sipped coffee from Deke's tin cup. Somewhere a bull gator grunted.

"Calling a mate," Ossie observed.

"They have an odor the female smells," Terry said.

"Did you know that? It comes from under the male's jaw when he grunts like that."

"No shit," Ossie said without interest.

They heard a fish break water, leaping. Swallows darted for insects in a vermilion sky.

"Wash out your pans with sand, then water," Ossie stated.

Then, with cigarettes in hand and the last of the coffee, they leaned against backrests they'd made by sticking poles into the soil.

With the final illumination of day, the first evening star winked feebly, tree frogs began a tentative chorus, crickets and cicadas followed suit.

"This is what I like," Terry whispered.

"Not bad," Ossie acknowledged. He jabbed a thumb at Lamar dozing.

"Lamar, better get in the chickee," Terry said.

"Okay — uh, okay, Terry."

Ossie lit one cigarette with another and repositioned himself. "Wish I had me a frog gig right now," he said.

"Yeah."

They said nothing for long periods, listening to the symphony of insect fiddles, the contrapuntal harmony of amphibians. They watched the Big and Little Dippers appear, and Ossie added fuel to the fire.

"I sure wish Colorado had swamps," Terry said.

In the chickee, Lamar heaved a final sigh before slumber.

"I wish I could come out here everyday," Terry added.

"Not me. I like good water and a roof that don't leak."

"That chickee won't leak," Terry said.

Ossie sighed, gazing up at the stars. "No moon," he observed. "Or maybe a late one. Have you noticed the last few days?"

"No, why?"

"Lamar wakes up and gets spooked when it's dark."

"He'll be all right," Terry breathed, contentedly. "I'll sleep with him."

They dozed, awoke and smoked another cigarette. In the black of total night, Terry stood and asked, "What're those lights?"

"Muck fire, maybe."

"No, I see that. This is a town, I think."

"Belle Glade," Ossie said.

"Belle Glade! We must've come fifty miles."

"No, we didn't."

"But we did."

"No," Ossie said firmly. "I doubled back. Owen's fish camp is about ten miles up that river."

"But why?"

"What difference does it make?"

"I wanted to be all the way into the swamps, Ossie."

"Until you stood up and looked hard, you thought you were. It's all the same as this."

"Tomorrow I want to go deeper."

"No."

"Ossie!"

"No, and that's that. If we had to, as it is, we could walk out without the boat in the morning. I did what you wanted. But I'm not going to be stupid about it."

Fuming, Terry sat again, accepted another cigarette which they shared.

"We're still even," Ossie concluded.

"Okay. Even."

They listened to night sounds, the rustle of creatures in the grass, a splash of water somewhere afar. Lighterknots spewed gasses in the fire, sap vaporizing.

His eyes black in the dark, reflecting the campfire, Ossie stared at Terry's head.

"What is it?" Terry asked.

"The conjure woman knows about warts and stuff," Ossie said soberly. "But she don't know nothing about cutting hair."

Twenty-seven

ASLEEP, LAMAR GROUND his teeth and turned. Terry awoke, fingers tingling from lack of circulation. Lamar was on his arm. He pulled free and crawled out of the chickee. To the east, cypress trees were etched in silhouette against a coming dawn.

Near the airboat, Ossie sat on a log, smoking. When he saw Terry, he pointed without a word — an alligator stalking coots unaware.

Here the river left its banks and the glades began: grass spread southward broken only by clumps of stiff-bristled palmetto, thatch palm and water oak. After a night of migratory flight, thousands of waterfowl fell in circling spirals to the endless lake that was the swamp. Like the tongue of a cat on fur, a breeze licked marsh grass. A deer stood with legs spraddled and touched the lips of its own image, slaking thirst.

Terry inhaled deeply. Night blooming cereus, musky deciduous growth, the Christmas scent of conifers. Here as nowhere else, the world was in concert, a purring contentment: a myriad of fins, quills, beaks and bills, the sigh of rustling foliage, bubbles wobbling up from watery dens; it was peaceful and exciting.

"Bobcat," Terry whispered, and Ossie nodded. Yellow eyes wary, tufted ears perked, the cat placed each deliberate paw with care lest it snap a twig as it came into the open.

Lamar stumbled out of the chickee, yawning. He rubbed his eyes with both fists. "I'm hungry, Terry!" The bobcat whirled and, with a bound, disappeared.

"Want me to build a fire, Ossie?" Terry questioned.

"No. We're going home."

"Going home? Ossie, I want to stay here all day."

"I told my mom I'd be home."

"You said today. It's still today tonight."

"We're going home," Ossie said, standing.

"I'm hungry, Ossie," Lamar whimpered.

"You can eat at home. Get your things together."

"Ossie," Terry said, "this is my last time maybe forever. Let's stay all day, okay? We can cook things we find right here — really good food — okay?"

"No."

"Why?" Terry demanded.

"I was dumb to let you talk me into this."

"You owed me a favor."

"And we're even." Ossie threw the oar out of the boat, putting things in order.

"Terry," Lamar complained, "I'm hungry."

"I told you to get your stuff together," Ossie snapped. "The sooner you do, the sooner we get home and you can eat."

"I'm hungry now!"

"Dumb ox," Ossie muttered.

Terry grabbed Ossie's arm. "There's no reason to go back early."

"Well, we ain't staying. That's that."

"Why?" Terry yelled.

"By now, Deke has gone to my mom and there'll be hell to pay, that's why."

"It won't make it any better or worse to stay all day."

Ossie checked the fuel, opened gas cocks.

"You aren't being fair, Ossie. You're going back on your word."

"I said I'd bring you and I did."

Terry watched him stow utensils. Lamar kneaded his eyes, saying, "I'm hungry."

"You can push off the boat," Ossie placated, giving Lamar the oar. "Now, let's go."

"When you needed help with the guard at the packing house," Terry accused, "I helped you. I helped you catch bats and I took your tattling to the theater manager. Now you're going back on your word."

"If we stay out here, they'll be sending people to look for us."

"We can go farther out, then."

"Listen," Ossie said, "you wanted to come and we came. A long time after you're gone I'll still be here. Now get in the boat and let's go."

"I'm not going."

"You ain't staying," Ossie warned.

"You — Indian!"

Ossie looked at him dispassionately. "Get in the boat, Lamar," Ossie ordered.

"I get to row?"

"Get in," Ossie said.

"Indian giver, that's what you are, Ossie."

"That's funny," Ossie said without humor. "A white man saying Indian giver. They're the ones who give and take back. Get in the damned boat."

Terry shoved him. Ossie turned, arms at his sides. "Everything you asked," Terry said, "I did it. I did *everything*."

"I ain't going to fight about it," Ossie grumbled. "Get in and let's go."

"You know what you are, Ossie? You know what you are? You're as bad as any white man. Your word isn't worth any more than a white man's word. You're just what the Indians said you are — American!"

Ossie struck out and Terry dodged.

"American!" Terry yelled. "You're so ashamed of what you are, you take a name like 'Knight.' Suppose somebody explained it to Mr. Night Song just that way?"

"Shut your mouth, Terry."

"Beloved old man," Terry taunted. "I wonder what he'd say if he knew what you really think?"

"I'm going to knock your block off," Ossie threatened.

"What if I told him you said he's crazy?"

Ossie picked up sand and threw it.

"I kept your most secret secrets —"

Ossie pointed at the boat and shouted, "Lamar, get in the boat!"

"Never once said a word about your mama —"

Ossie turned slowly and stared.

"I did what a friend is supposed to," Terry said. "I kept my word, kept your secrets —"

Ossie advanced. "You're asking for it."

"Quit it, Ossie," Lamar shrilled.

Terry circled the chickee, putting it between them.

Ossie lunged, Lamar yelling, "Stop it, stop it!"

Terry tore free, running, and Lamar screamed, "Quit it, Ossie!"

Ossie grabbed Terry, cuffing his head, shaking him, and they fell to the ground, rolling.

"I ought to kill you."

"Indian giver!"

Ossie seized Terry's shoulders, shaking him violently, Terry's head bumping sand.

Suddenly Ossie pitched forward, his chest on Terry's face.

"Get off, Ossie."

He felt Ossie quiver.

"Ossie, get off." Terry rolled him over, spitting sand. Ossie's legs twitched.

"Ossie?"

"Run, Terry!" Lamar hollered.

Terry looked at Lamar, still holding the oar.

"Ossie?"

"Run, Terry!" Lamar yelled.

Terry shook Ossie gently and the boy's head lolled. Blood rose in an ear. "Ossie!"

Ossie's legs quivered, jerked, quivered.

"Lamar, come quick!"

"No."

"Hurry, Lamar. Ossie is hurt."

"No. He's fooling."

"He's not fooling!" Terry screamed. "Come help me."

"He'll grab me," Lamar said.

Ossie convulsed, a movement that drove fear through Terry's chest. "Ossie." He lifted Ossie's head and the skull shifted between his hands.

"I — what — I —" Terry sat on his knees, looking, seeking. "Lamar, come help me!"

"He'll hurt me."

"He won't hurt you, I promise. Come help me."

"No."

One of Ossie's arms moved as if to rise, then grew rigid. Terry saw specks of sand on Ossie's half-closed eyes. "Lamar!" he shrieked.

"He'll hurt me, Terry."

Terry tried to lift Ossie, and the boy was stiff and limber at the same instant. He held Ossie under the arms, dragging him. Too heavy.

With control that summoned all his will, Terry went to Lamar and took the oar. Voice lowered but still quavering, he said, "Lamar, you have to help me."

"Ossie will hurt me."

"He won't hurt you. He's knocked out."

"He's fooling."

"He's not fooling. Help me put him in the boat so we can go home."

"I hit him."

"I know it. Now you have to help me. Come on."

"I don't want him to hurt me."

"He won't. Come on."

Together, they lifted him into the boat, an odd sound trickling from Ossie's throat. Water sloshed and a rusty sediment spread around Ossie's head.

"Sit like you're supposed to, Lamar."

"Can you drive the boat?" Lamar brightened.

"I'm going to. Sit down. Don't stand up."

"I won't."

In the pilot's seat, Terry was higher than he had anticipated. Shivering, he tried to remember Ossie's moves. He

buckled the safety harness, turned a switch, adjusted the choke. He pushed a button and the motor rumbled, started.

"Terry!" Lamar pointed at things they were leaving.

"Sit down!" Terry yelled.

But the boat was directed the wrong way. He had to get out, feet mired in mud, to push the boat away from ashore. He thought he saw Ossie breathe. It was Ossie's eyes, the pupils strangely different, that told him otherwise.

The gears grated, propeller engaged, and the sudden gust threatened to capsize them, the craft turning in circles. Terry tried again, easing the throttle; Lamar sat below, hands clasped.

By pushing the fins one way, it deflected the wind and gave them direction. Slowly, they picked up speed, but the boat shuddered and every ripple was a bump under the hull. Birds swarmed, the boat wavered, drifting, and Terry sobbed.

"Up that river about ten miles," Ossie had said last night. Terry gave the motor more gas.

"Don't stand up, Lamar!"

"I won't."

They passed a man fishing in a rowboat, and he clutched his hat to keep it from being blown away. Against an imperceptible current they moved upriver, the roar drumming Terry's ears. In the distance, he could see the dike.

He glanced back at Ossie but accidentally pulled the steering bar, turning them around. Lamar waved at a black man and woman fishing with cane poles, their corks bobbing as the airboat passed too close. Wind from the propeller blew up their lines, fouling them in limbs of an Australian pine.

Hours it took. Forever, it seemed. Ossie lying beneath him, water shifting back and forth wetting one side of his body. Then Terry saw Mr. Owen standing on the dock and he cut the motor, an echo pealing away like diminishing thunder.

"I called Mr. Dekle!" Mr. Owen yelled. He went to his motorboat, yanked a starter cord. "What you boys did was wrong. It was stealing. Like stealing a car."

Water lapping the hull, the high seat swaying, airboat drifting. Lamar sat motionless, waiting. Mr. Owen's outboard started and he steered standing up. "This was a bad thing you did, boys!"

Mr. Owen idled his motor, lifting it to approach in a drift. "Mr. Dekle is very angry —"

He saw Ossie.

"God in heaven," he said.

He took a line, pulling them slowly toward the dock. Terry heard a vehicle and looked up to see Deke's truck cross the bridge, coming fast. Deke slammed on brakes and stopped in a cloud of dust. He got out of one door, Mama the other.

"Deke!" Mr. Owen called. Deke vaulted toward the dock on his arms.

Terry made no move to come down as Mr. Owen tied the airboat to a cleat. Deke bumped out the dock and again Mr. Owen called, "Deke!"

Terry saw color drain from Deke's face and the man steadied himself with arms in front.

"Dead, Deke," Mr. Owen said.

"I hit him, Deke," Lamar reported.

"Are you sure, Charlie?"

"You see he is," Mr. Owen replied softly.

Mama was coming toward them on high heeled shoes, stepping carefully between the cracks.

"Better — better call the sheriff, Charlie."

As Mr. Owen hurried off, Deke said, without looking away from Ossie, "Tell him to bring the boy's mother, Charlie. She's at the Glades Café."

"What is it?" Mama questioned as Mr. Owen ran past. She came nearer, looking. Terry saw her hands go to her face.

"He was going to kill Terry," Lamar said amiably. "So I hit him with a paddle."

"No!" Mama screamed. Deke glanced at Terry, still strapped in the high pilot's seat. He went to Mama and she screamed again, "No, no!"

When Mr. Owen returned, he said something to Deke. Then he came to help Lamar and Terry out of the boat.

The sheriff's car arrived, light flashing but siren mute, and Mrs. Knight fought off restraining hands to throw herself on Ossie. She cradled his body, holding his head, then withdrew trembling fingers to stare at them. Some men lifted her away.

Deke had pulled Mama to her knees and was rocking her in his arms when the camp manager drove up with Velma and Burrell Mason. People in an ambulance had Ossie on a stretcher, a strap around him in two places, a sheet over all his body except bare feet.

"I hit him, Ma," Lamar explained.

Velma reached out with both hands, lips purple, and touched Lamar's face. "He was going to hurt Terry, so I hit him."

Terry turned as the sheriff put a huge hand on his shoulder. "Terry is that right?" he asked gently.

"Yessir."

"What happened?"

"We had a fight. Lamar hit him."

"Then what?"

"We came home."

"I did," Lamar confirmed to the sheriff.

Terry slipped sideways between the cars and trucks, watching the ambulance doors close. The attendants, wearing white smocks like doctors, got in and drove toward town.

Terry began to run.

Like a machine, without sensation, he ran, through dust thrown up by vehicles rushing to Chosen, took a shortcut through a cane field, down railroad tracks and crossed a trestle into colored town. Now with the sign of a hand in sight, Terry halted, his breath a rale.

The beads rippled musically.

"Ma'am, are you there?"

"Yes, I am here."

"May I come in?"

A ringed hand parted the curtain and Terry entered. A candle flickered, the beads tinkled.

"Sit down."

Mouth parched, gasping for breath, Terry sat across from her. He tried to speak and she put a finger to his lips. "Catch your breath," she said. She held his hand.

"Please take back all my wishes," Terry said. "Give me a new one."

"What is this wish?"

"I want Ossie to be alive."

The light played in her eyes. She peered at him without movement, without blinking, until Terry said, "He's dead."

"Osceola?"

"Yes ma'am."

Moisture on her lips caught the light and she was still as stone.

"Can you make him live again?"

"How did this happen?" she whispered.

"Lamar hit him with an oar. Ossie and I were fighting. Ossie is —" he swallowed air. "Ossie is my best friend, ma'am. Please."

"Dead," she said.

"Can you do it?"

"Does his mother know?"

"Yes ma'am. Ma'am? Can you?"

She squeezed his hand and pulled him to his feet. She brought him to her and her arms encompassed him, holding him close.

"It was my fault," Terry sobbed. "I wanted to go to the swamps. I made Ossie take me."

"It is no one's fault. Not yours. Not Lamar."

"I told him I had helped him and I kept his secrets. I knew things about his mama and I — I want to tell Ossie I'm sorry."

"He knows."

"Lamar didn't mean to —"

"Shhh."

"I didn't know Lamar was going to do it."

"Shhh, child, shhh."

"Can you, ma'am? Can you make him live again?"

"He lives now where all men wish to go."

"No! I want him back."

"Perhaps if you could see, you would not wish this for him."

"Please — *please!*"

She rubbed his back with tender strokes. "The Indians believe when a person dies he is everywhere. If you wish to bring Ossie to you, all you do is think about him and he'll be there. Like Mr. McCree . . . ."

Terry pulled away. "That's not enough," he cried. "I want him here, alive!"

He saw tears. "I'm sorry," she said.

"You can't do it?"

"No," she said. "I can't do it."

When Terry entered the house, Velma and Burrell Mason were sitting on the couch with Deke. Terry stood at the door, everybody looking at him. Mama held out her hands and he went into her arms, eyes dry.

"I've been worried about you," Mama said quietly.

"I'm sorry. Are you angry, Mama?"

"No."

Finally, Mama said, "If you take a bath, you'll feel better."

He left the room without daring to glance at Deke, or Velma or Burrell.

In the bathroom, feeling cold, he watched blue-green water fill the tub. He heard Velma, her voice harsh from crying. "I don't know what to do," she said.

Terry peeled away dirty clothes.

Deke opened the door; he was on the floor. "Are you going to be okay, redhead?"

"Yessir."

"Mind if I come in?"

"No sir." Terry eased aching legs into hot water. Deke pushed the door closed.

"I want you to know, everything is all right between

you and me," Deke said.

Terry began to cry silently.

"This is nobody's fault, Terry. Not yours, not Lamar's."

It was what the conjure woman had said.

"Where did you go after you left Chosen, Terry?"

"To colored town."

"What for?"

"To ask the conjure woman to make Ossie live again."

Deke came over to the tub, hooked an elbow on it to hold himself upright.

"She can't do it," Terry reported.

"No," Deke said softly, "she can't."

"Deke, I wish I hadn't made Ossie take me."

"Don't think about that, Terry. I feel like I should have figured out how to handle this better. Anyway, you and I are still pals — understood?"

"She said Ossie is where all men wish to go," Terry said.

"The conjure woman?"

"Yessir. Deke? I don't think Ossie wanted to go there."

Deke nodded, face pained.

"She said that Indians believe heaven is everywhere," Terry related. "She said Ossie is everywhere people think about him."

"That's what the Indians believe," Deke confirmed. "Personally, I happen to think that's how it is, too."

"If I could hear him," Terry said, "I'll bet he's cussing."

"Terry —"

"I'll bet he is," Terry said. "Cussing me good."

He lifted his eyes toward the ceiling. "I'm sorry, Ossie —"

Twenty-eight

MAMA WRAPPED DISHES in newspaper, putting them into packing crates. Day after tomorrow, the moving people would be here, she had said.

"Mickey?" Velma and Lamar stood in the front door. Lamar wore a suit, his trousers too short. It was the first time Terry had ever seen Velma wearing high heel shoes. "Do you have time for us, Mickey?" Velma asked.

"Of course, Velma. Come in."

Eyes wide, Lamar looked at Terry and Ann without greeting.

"Sit down, Velma. I'll pour coffee. Lamar, move those boxes off the couch for me."

"I will. I'm strong!" Lamar halted. "I have to be careful."

"That's right," Velma said.

"I might hurt things."

Mama stood over two empty cups.

"Easy does it," Lamar said, as if by rote.

Mama carried coffee to the couch and sat with Velma.

"I did a bad thing, Miss Mickey," Lamar reported. "I killed Ossie."

"You didn't mean to, Lamar, and —"

"No," Velma interrupted, "it was bad, Mickey."

"Yes," Mama said softly. "It was bad."

"I must never hit anybody again."

"No," Mama said.

"They might lock me up. Forever and ever."

Mama put a hand on Velma's wrist. Lamar joined Ann and Terry at the breakfast table. Ann gave him her cold toast.

"We're going to see Ossie," Lamar said.

"You can't," Ann shrilled. "Ossie's dead."

"We're going anyway."

"Can I go, Mama?" Ann asked.

"May I," Mama corrected.

"May I?"

"No. You're going to the day-care center."

"Want to go outside, Lamar?" Terry suggested.

"I can't."

"We'll sit on the back steps."

Lamar looked to his mother and she nodded, ashen.

"Me too!" Ann cried.

"No," Mama said sharply.

On the rear steps, Lamar sat, eyebrows bobbing. "Pa is real mad. He said *don't go!* Ma said, *yes we are!*"

"Where is Ossie?"

"I don't know."

Terry tried to listen to the conversation inside. He heard Deke and Mr. Mason now.

"Are they going to lock you up, Terry?"

"Nobody said so."

"They might lock me up. Forever and ever."

Burrell Mason's voice rose in the living room. "For God's sake, Velma!"

"It's the thing to do," Velma insisted.

Deke and Mama spoke, moderating.

"It isn't Ossie's mother you're thinking about," Velma accused. "It's yourself, Burrell."

"If that boy had killed Lamar," Burrell countered, "we wouldn't want him and his mother showing up to say they were *sorry*."

"If they didn't," Velma snapped, "I'd resent that!"

"Like hell you would."

"You stay home and hide, Burrell. Lamar and I are going."

"Pa is — uh, Pa is real mad, Terry."

Terry put an arm around Lamar.

"You think anybody is going to appreciate it?" Burrell said. "You think that boy's mama is going to say, 'Thank you for coming, Mrs. Mason'?"

"We're going," Velma declared. "That's that."

In the heavy silence that followed, Terry sat comforting Lamar, patting his back.

"Why take Lamar, Velma?" Mama questioned gently.

"He needs to know — to understand."

"It won't make any difference," Burrell argued.

"He's got to understand what he did," Velma said.

"Perhaps we should go together," Mama suggested.

"That might be a good way to do it," Deke agreed.

"Not me," Burrell stated.

"Of course, not you," Velma cried.

The front door slammed. "Oh God, Mickey," Velma moaned.

After awhile, Mama came on the back porch. "Terry, we're going to the funeral home."

"May I go?"

"You don't have to."

"I want to."

"All right. Get dressed."

In the bedroom, Ann was trying to pack her toys. She had more toys than space. She dumped the box to begin again.

"Where're you going?" she asked Terry.

"To see Ossie."

"Ossie's dead."

"Comb your hair," Mama called, "brush your teeth."

"Can I go?" Ann hollered.

"No. Are you dressed, Ann?"

"Yes ma'am."

"I'll tell Ossie you said hello," Terry offered.

"He can't hear you. He's dead!"

"I'll tell him anyway." Terry laced his shoes. He'd grown. His toes were crowded.

On the way to the day-care center, Ann made a final plea, but Mama refused. Then, driving toward the funeral home, following Deke, Velma and Lamar who were riding in Deke's truck, Terry said, "Mama, are they going to put Lamar in jail?"

"No."

"He thinks they are."

"He needs to understand that could happen, Terry."

"But they won't do it?"

"No."

The parking lot at the funeral home was full of cars. They had to park down the street.

"Deke can't write his book without Lamar and

Ossie," Terry remarked.

"Lock the doors, Terry."

"If we didn't have to go to Colorado, I could help him."

"Terry. Not now." Then Mama turned and seized him, hugging Terry too tightly.

"Ready?" Deke came in his wheelchair.

Mama took a deep breath, smoothed Terry's hair. Velma was across the street with Lamar, waiting.

Walking beside Deke, Terry said, "What are we supposed to do?"

"What do you want to do?"

"I don't know. Say good-bye, I guess."

"Do that."

"Deke? Where will they bury Ossie?"

"They're taking him to Big Cypress."

"The reservation? He wouldn't want to go to the reservation."

"It's home."

"But Ossie wouldn't like it."

"That's where his people are, Terry."

"He doesn't like Indians."

"I doubt that was true."

"I've been thinking — he probably loved Mr. Night Song. When nobody else was around, Ossie called him 'beloved old man.' So he probably loved him."

When they entered the building, Terry smelled a peculiar, almost sweet odor. A man intoned, "Sign the guest register, please."

Lamar waited with Terry as the adults complied. When people stared, Lamar met their gaze with eyes wide. Somewhere, an organ played.

Deke reached out to touch people who blocked their

352 *Judith Richards*

way, Mama and Velma following down a long hall. Terry
recognized a cook from the Glades Café and the man who
owned the restaurant. The guard from the packing house
stood with the theater manager. And Thevis!

In a large room, at the far end, an open coffin was
surrounded by flowers. Sitting next to it, Mr. Night Song
held his cane wrapped with crepe paper. Indians Terry had
never met sat along a wall. Mrs. Knight was with them, a
black veil covering her face. Beside her was the conjure
woman.

At the coffin, Terry whispered, "A suit and a tie!"

"Hush," Deke said firmly.

Ossie laid with his hands at his sides. Was he supposed
to be peaceful? Going to the reservation forever, wearing
white men's clothes?

"Is — uh, is he dead?" Lamar asked.

"Yes."

"I — uh, I didn't mean to, Ossie."

Velma and Mrs. Knight began to cry.

"Mr. Night Song," Terry said, "I'm sorry."

The old man peered from deeply set eyes.

"I'm sorry, Mr. Night Song."

Deke nudged Terry and they moved to Mrs. Knight.

"Mrs. Knight," Deke said, "is there anything we can
do?"

She shook her head.

"Ossie was my best friend, Mrs. Knight."

"I know."

"I'm sorry."

"I know, Sweetie."

Terry turned to the conjure woman and she reached for
his hands. "Ossie hears," she murmured. "Ossie knows."

As they started to leave, Terry returned to the coffin

and bent near, speaking to Ossie alone. "I'm going to think and call you everywhere I go. When I get to Colorado, we can see the same places. You come like a bird, or on the wind. Okay?"

"Terry —"

"I'm not going to say good-bye," Terry told Deke.

When the moving van arrived, Velma hugged Mama gruffly. "I'll miss you, Mickey."

"I'll miss you, Velma."

"Write."

"I will."

Then Lamar hugged Mama. "I'm going to special school, Miss Mickey."

"That's wonderful, Lamar."

Deke and Mama kissed quickly, awkwardly. "You have all enriched my life," Deke said. "For which I am thankful."

"I wish you could meet Gerald. If ever you come our way —"

Deke laughed and waved a hand.

Mama watched him rolling toward home and Deke did not turn to look at them again. "All right, redheads," Mama said, "let's go to Birmingham."

"Are we ever coming back, Mama?"

"I don't know, Terry."

"It's up to Daddy," Ann mimed from the rear seat. "Daddy is the boss now."

They drove north, through Pahokee, and on a canal bank, Terry saw an alligator and thought of Ossie.

Mama put a hand on his leg and shook gently. "How are you doing?"

"All right."

When they reached the rolling hills around Tallahassee, Terry thought of Ossie again — and again in the clay area of Alabama where cotton fields spread in all directions.

It took two days before they climbed the highway winding up Red Mountain. At the top, an arm lifted to immortalize steel and iron, a statue of Vulcan overlooked Birmingham in the valley below. An acrid aroma made Terry wince.

"Ummm," Mama smiled, "it smells like home."

Terry considered thinking of Ossie, to show him what it was like. Haze that turned air acid to the nostrils, industrial fumes spreading ochre ash across the city. Railroad tracks choked by cars laden with ore and smokestacks stabbing at a sun grown dim. But Ossie probably had better things to do: swooping on the wings of a hawk, the wind shrill in his ears as he dived for prey; or gliding across the glades with a breeze. Or, maybe rising as a cloud, higher and higher before darkening to fall as rain. Ossie could be anything! The nod of a blossom, a cougar stalking deer, a fish leaping into sunshine before darting away among the hyacinths. He could be a rock unmoved in a thousand years, with water flowing around him. Ossie would be having fun, surely — anyplace. Or everyplace.

Mama said, "What're you smiling about?"

Terry laughed through tears. "Ossie," he said.